THINGS WE COULDN'T SAY

THINGS

WE

COULDN'T

SAY

JAY

COLES

Scholastic Inc.

Copyright © 2021 by Jay Coles

This book was originally published in hardcover by Scholastic Press in 2021.

All rights reserved. Published by Scholastic Inc., *Publishers since 1920*.

SCHOLASTIC and associated logos are trademarks and/or registered trademarks of Scholastic Inc.

The publisher does not have any control over and does not assume any responsibility for author or third-party websites or their content.

No part of this publication may be reproduced, stored in a retrieval system, or transmitted in any form or by any means, electronic, mechanical, photocopying, recording, or otherwise, without written permission of the publisher. For information regarding permission, write to Scholastic Inc., Attention: Permissions Department, 557 Broadway, New York, NY 10012.

This book is a work of fiction. Names, characters, places, and incidents are either the product of the author's imagination or are used fictitiously, and any resemblance to actual persons, living or dead, business establishments, events, or locales is entirely coincidental.

ISBN 978-1-338-73419-5

10 9 8 7 6 5 4 3 2 1   22 23 24 25 26

Printed in the U.S.A.   40

This edition first printing 2022

Book design by Baily Crawford

TO DANIEL TRONE, MY GUY FOR LIFE. THANK YOU FOR ALWAYS BEING THERE FOR ME, ESPECIALLY WHEN I NEED YOU MOST. WE'LL ALWAYS HAVE COLORADO.

ONE

I'M SO BORED DURING Mrs. Oberst's lesson on Harper Lee's *To Kill a Mockingbird*, I could literally kill an actual mockingbird right now.

And I mean, it's not just that her voice sounds like a quail that has a rubber duck stuck in its throat. To tell the truth, I'm not into the whole notion that Harper Lee wrote this book to talk about how bad racism in America is. It's not a book about racism. It's a book about white people's feelings on racism.

I try my best to tune out Mrs. Oberst's lesson, like I do with most other lessons of hers. The problem is, when I do that, I get trapped in my thoughts. And sometimes my thoughts transport me to dark places.

Like now. My thoughts transport me back to when my birth mom walked out on the family.

My mom opens the front door wide, so I can see the rain splashing in the street. She waves at me with tears in the corners of her eyes and says, "Bye, bye, G-Bug!"

Some of her hair is in her face as she takes a step out the door, the rain getting her all wet, the thunder roaring in the distance. I want to reach out and grab her, maybe protect her.

But it doesn't work. My hands don't work.

I want to call after her, but my voice fails me. I want to take a step forward, but I can't.

Something tugs at me on the inside, but I don't know what it is. She gets farther and farther away from me. Darkness creeps from all around and swallows her.

Thick tears roll down my cheeks, working fine.

Something touches my back. I can tell it's Pops by the way the hand feels. Hard and calloused. But I stay focused on the darkness as it completely consumes her and sneaks over to me. The thunder and sirens get louder and closer—loud enough for me to realize this might just be how I'm going to feel forever.

Mrs. Oberst slams a book on my desk to bring me back. I jolt in my seat, nearly falling out, causing some of my classmates to crack up.

"What does the character Atticus represent?" Mrs. Oberst, in her polka-dotted dress and glasses on the bridge of her white, pointed nose, asks the class. She walks around the aisles of the classroom with kind of a strut, like she's not one to play with. And with the amount of detention slips she's written, I'd say she isn't actually one to mess with.

Ayesha Chamberlain, one of my best friends since elementary school, raises her hand. She's my Black best friend. Olly is my other bestie, and he's white, but if you ask him, he'll try to say he's beige because he's not like other white people. Olly's dope and I wouldn't trade his white—I mean *beige*—ass for a million dollars, but if you flipped open the dictionary to white privilege, you'd see a picture of Olly and his family. He even dresses like he comes from money. Ayesha and I became friends with him around the same time when we first got to high school and saw this lonely-looking kid sitting in the corner by himself at lunch.

Mrs. Oberst calls on her. "Yes, Miss Chamberlain?"

"Um, never mind," she says hesitantly. "I forgot my answer."

"Are you sure?"

"Yeah," she goes, but then she locks eyes with me. "I think Gio has an answer, though."

Shit. What the hell is she doing? I was definitely not raising my hand. I was drawing some random music notes on a piece of paper as an escape from this hellhole, but now Mrs. Oberst is staring at me.

"Giovanni," she says. Mrs. Oberst calls me by my full government name because my name comes from a book by James Baldwin that she loves. This isn't a coincidence. My birth mom loved the book, too, according to Pops. "What do you think?"

Honestly, if I'm being real, I'd straight-up just tell her off about my feelings on this book, but I don't. There's a place and time for hood me to come out. Right now is not the time, I'm telling myself.

"I'm not reading the book," I say, and swallow hot spit.

"And why is that, Giovanni? Do you think you're better than everyone else in this room?"

"No," I say, looking around. "I just don't relate to it." I'm probably sounding like a real dick.

"You sound ridiculous, Giovanni" is her response. And what

I really wanna do is let her know that her class is almost as ridiculous as her Party City wig. But I don't.

She continues her silent strut, waiting for someone else to volunteer. I try to avoid all eye contact, because, like I said, Mrs. Oberst doesn't play—and she will call us out, if she wants.

I see a white hand go up out the corner of my eye. I look back and it's Penelope Roe. She's the head cheerleader and is known to be a real Blue Lives Matter supporter. Her and her boujee parents who bought her a hot pink Mercedes to drive to school.

"Yes, Miss Roe?"

"He's the lawyer and therefore he's the hero. He shows the judge that racism is wrong."

I look back at Ayesha and we both roll our eyes. I know Ayesha wants to fight her. She wants to fight everybody.

Without raising her hand first, Ayesha interjects, "Actually, that white man isn't the hero. The man is complicit in the oppression of Black people."

Problematic-Ass Penelope Roe goes all the way quiet. Ayesha and I high-five with our minds.

Ben Davis High School is *pretty* diverse, like more than half the school is Black or brown, but white folks 'round here still act a fool.

The bell rings, so I don't have to roll my eyes at another white kid who's suddenly realizing racism is a thing. I've got basketball practice tonight, and I'm looking more forward to it than ever since we've got a string of big games coming up.

That's the kind of distraction I don't mind: a clear one.

The other thoughts are way too messy.

I make my way to my locker, where Ayesha and Olly meet me, the air smelling like recently lit weed and gym socks. I trade out the books from my backpack and put in the ones I need for my homework tonight. The Paramore poster in my locker makes me smile for a second.

"Can you believe that bitch talking 'bout how that white man was a hero?" Ayesha goes, smacking away at her gum.

"Yeah, I know, right," I say. "She's trash."

"Can't believe I almost dated her," Olly says.

"Yeah, I'm glad you didn't, dude," I say.

"I would've probably stopped being your friend. For real," Ayesha says.

"Dramatic," Olly says. And I laugh. He's kind of right, though. Ayesha is pretty dramatic, but it's one of my favorite things about her. I wouldn't change her for the world. We dated when we were freshmen and now we're all juniors. We broke up because it was weird going from childhood best friends to awkward hand-holding and terrible kisses.

"Screw you," Ayesha says to Olly. Then she play-punches my arm.

"I'm sorry," Olly says, still laughing.

Ayesha clears her throat. "Whatever. Are we hanging out tonight or what?"

"We can," I say.

"Our usual? Kreamy Kones?" Olly asks.

"I'm in," I say.

"I'll text you guys after my date."

"Your date?!" Olly and I practically shout in unison, over all the chatter of the noisy hallway as everyone leaves for whatever they do after school.

"I met someone," Ayesha says, averting her eyes, like she's full of all the dirty little secrets and we're about to get an earful if we pry her enough.

"Who?" I ask, slamming my locker shut and staring at her.

Her curly hair's so long it's in her face, but I can still see her look around as if she wants to make sure no one else hears her. She pulls me and Olly to the side a little bit.

"I didn't tell you all because I knew you'd both make it a big deal." She pulls out her phone. "I've been using MatchUp."

"MatchUp is for hookups, Ayesha." I sound like an overprotective brother. I would know because I went through this phase last year where I met up with some random girls every now and then for a quick hookup and even some guys, too, as an experiment to see if I was really into guys the way I started to think I was. Somehow making out with a random guy helped me figure things out, like icing on the cake. But now that I know, MatchUp is over for me. What started as a kind-of experiment cemented my for-sure truth. Dudes are hot and I think I can also see myself being with one.

"That's what you think, but it's different with Trevor. He wants more than just sex."

She flashes us both a picture of him. He doesn't look bad. His profile photo is of him wearing a suit at somebody's wedding and he's got dreads. I've always imagined Ayesha ending up with somebody with dreads, so it's kind of funny.

"He go here, Yesh?" I ask. I call her Yesh sometimes. It's one of the many nicknames I have for her. She has even more for me.

"He goes to Pike."

"Oh." It sounds like I'm sad, but I'm not. Pike's our rival school. And maybe this slips out because I'm pissed she didn't tell me. We tell each other everything. She was the first person I told that I was bisexual, in the middle of a McDonald's parking lot two months ago. The least she could've done was tell me about this Trevor guy, right? Or maybe I'm being childish about this.

"He better not be a fuckboy," Olly goes.

"Says King Fuckboy himself," Ayesha snaps back. She's queen of the clapback. And I can never contain my laughter, even in serious moments.

"How long has this been going on? Is it official?" I ask.

She grabs for my hands as I put on my backpack again. "He asked me out last night." She's grinning so big I know she's happy. I haven't seen her this happy in a minute. If she's good with him, I'm good with him.

"I'm still gonna have to meet him first, though," I say.

"Yeah, of course."

It goes quiet and it's like we're the last ones left in the school. Olly puts on his Nike snapback and says, "All right, I guess I'll see at least one of you tonight. Have fun at practice, Gio." Something about this last part is sarcastic. He'll never let go of the fact that he didn't get to be on the basketball team after he tried out last year. On the bright side, he's on the school's intramural flag football team, which I personally think is awesome.

Olly walks away and now it's just Ayesha and me. The two of us live in the same neighborhood and usually ride home from school together, but not on the days I have practice. She kisses me nice and soft on the cheek and says, "I'll see ya."

"See ya," I say back.

I turn to walk in the other direction, toward the gym. I need to get to the locker room before practice to change into my jersey and basketball shorts. Usually, I'd wear them under my school clothes, but for some reason I forgot today.

I hear a familiar clicking of heels and look up to see Mrs. Oberst approaching me, clipboard in hand, glasses still on the bridge of her nose like they're glued there or something.

"Giovanni." She says my name in a single breath and inhales deeply.

I blink. "Yes, Mrs. Oberst?" I'm sounding all proper and shit because my stepmom and my Pops taught me how to act around white people.

"What's going on with you?" she asks.

I look around like I'm searching for an answer. "What do you mean?"

"You were very out of it during my class today. You also said that you weren't reading the book I assigned."

I don't say anything. I stare at her forehead, so it gives off the appearance that I'm looking her in the eyes.

"You realize your grades depend on successful completion of the book, no?"

"Yeah," I murmur shyly. "I mean yes, ma'am."

"I've noticed that you haven't been focused a whole lot lately—you might want to ask yourself why that is before it's too late. You have a C in my class, but those can quickly turn into Ds and Fs."

Damn. I got a C? I mean, it's only February, so I've got time to get it up before the semester is over and summer arrives, but damn. The thought of getting my first D or even F has my heart in my throat.

Mrs. Oberst clears whatever is caught in her esophagus and asks something else. "Everything okay at home? I know students who are sometimes out of it around here have some difficult home lives."

I swallow thickly. Shit. She's being so nosy.

I think for a moment, not really knowing how to answer her question. I mean, things are *okay*. Karina is still holding the family together, doing what she does best even though she's a part-time nurse.

"Things are good," I say, even though when I say it, it doesn't feel entirely accurate.

"Any gun fights or shootings in your neighborhood?" Mrs. Oberst asks. She sounds a lot like Mr. Dickey, the school guidance counselor, who's always checking up on me because he grew up in the hood, too, way back in the day. But, look, just because I live in the "ghetto" doesn't mean I'm out here holding a Captain America shield everywhere I go. I'm gonna give her the benefit of the doubt and not let the ghetto jump out of me to cuss her out. I've done that before. Not to her specifically, but to another teacher I had—Mrs. Winkler, last year in sophomore geometry, for asking if my Pops was in jail. I let her have it.

Mrs. Oberst's question comes back around. "Nah," I answer, "I'm good. Everything is good in the Haven."

"Are you sure? I'm here to help." She sounds like a character in a book she'd teach us.

"I'm sure, thanks." I fake a smile.

Between her and Mr. Dickey I get probably every question from the *How to Save a Black Kid from the Hood* and *How to Be the Savior to a Black Kid with Anxiety and Trauma* manuals. I mean, they know all I've been through, which is part of the problem. They know Desiree, one of my friends from elementary school, died when we were kids. They know my birth mom walked out on the family when I was nine and never came back. And they know that I've been going to counseling off and on when I need to. Because it was so hard after she left—and it's still hard. That anxiety and the nightmares sometimes come back in these huge tidal waves I can't escape, so consuming I think I'll drown. But still. I shouldn't have to talk about any of this when I don't want to. Besides, today's been mostly a good day. I want to keep it that way for as long as I possibly can.

"Do you think basketball is a distraction?" she asks out of nowhere.

"Basketball isn't a distraction. It's my escape," I say. 'Cause it's the truth. Basketball and music are my things.

"Very well."

"Basketball helps me clear my head when I need to. When

my thoughts are so loud, basketball turns them down." This is so much more than a distraction.

"Okay. If you ever need anything, Giovanni, don't hesitate to reach out," Mrs. Oberst says in such a sincere voice that I almost fall for it.

I nod at her and say, "Thanks again."

"Not a problem." She smiles widely, showing her teeth, and continues walking past me down the hallway, heels clicking and clacking in the distance, fading into nothing.

TWO

LATER AT PRACTICE, COACH Campbell has us working on our jump shots, so everyone's doing a shootaround.

I head into the locker room and get changed into my practice gear and then head back out to the main floor. Our gymnasium is big, like one you'd see in a midsized college. It's pretty decked out. We're the home of the Giants, so there's a large purple BD Giants symbol in the middle of the floor and purple and white stripes on the walls. Even the basketball backboards are purple. Usually, the gym would smell like sweat and must, but it smells like fresh paint for some reason, and I'm hoping not to get high off it. Especially since I've recently stopped doing weed.

Malik is shooting around at the three-point line. I go over to join him. Malik is our team's starting small forward. I'm the point guard. He's in the 7th Street Disciples, a gang in the neighborhood I live in. He's also a notorious drug dealer (the one who got me my weed when I wanted it). But people don't talk about that here on the court because it's irrelevant. He's here to shoot and play, because maybe that's his escape. I'm not going to question that, and I'm not gonna say anything to get him kicked off the team, either. The way I look at it, nobody is perfect, so why should he have to be in order to play ball?

"Sup, Malik," I say.

I watch him retrieve the ball and brush the sweat from his hairline. "Sup, bro."

"Nothing much. Just ready for our big game on Saturday."

"Same, bro. Same." He's got kind of a faded, nappy Mohawk that I'm honestly jealous of. Truth is, I used to have a crush on him, before I had to force myself to get rid of it because he's 100 percent straight. And even if he wasn't, making an approach would have been tough because I'm still figuring how to be out (beyond Olly and Ayesha) and comfortable with it. There's no way in hell I could've told Malik about my crush on him.

I find a ball lying around, throw up a mid-range shot, and bank it in. The feeling of a ball making it in the hoop is one of my favorite feelings in the world, and it's even better in a real game, when there's a crowd there to cheer for me.

Malik retrieves both of our balls and comes back.

"How's Ms. Diane?" I ask. That's his mom. She was recently diagnosed with ALS.

He sighs and gets in a shooting motion. Without any eye contact at all, he says, "She's good. Wants me to stop being out there in the streets and all, but oh well."

"Yeah, but health-wise, she's okay?" I'm super protective of Ms. Diane. She's known me since I was a baby. And she was really close with my birth mom before she left.

"Yeah, she's taking it one day at a time. You know ALS can be real tricky, bro."

"I bet." I don't know much about ALS, but I did my research on it when Malik first told me she had it. Apparently, it makes all your muscles stop working and there's no cure for it. Some people diagnosed with it only live for a few years.

Some of the other guys on the team are shooting and dunking and practicing their dribbling when Coach Campbell comes in and blares his earsplitting whistle. We all walk over to the stands. Along the way, we high-five each other and slap each other's butts. It's our tradition.

Coach Campbell, a man with pale skin, a big round extended belly, and a big poufy mustache, has his arms around some white kid with really curly, really red hair—like, a type of red I didn't even think was possible for human beings.

Everyone chatters quietly.

"Listen up, listen up," Coach Campbell demands. His voice is loud and booming.

Everybody shuts up at once.

Coach Campbell continues. "I want to introduce all of you to your newest team member. This is David York. He's our new transfer from some school in the middle of Kansas. But we're excited to have him. He'll be starting, so Erick, we'll be dialing back some of your minutes."

Erick Blakely looks away and sighs. He's been our starting shooting guard for the last couple years, but he's been so injury-prone lately that he knows it makes sense for his minutes to be scaled back so he doesn't get severely injured before he even has a chance to play in college.

Savtaj hisses like Coach just dissed Erick.

"Anyway, let's give David a big, warm Giants welcome!"

We all roar and cheer and clap for him. It's a thing we do that's kind of annoying.

David's caught off guard and his eyes are wide. "Thanks, everyone."

Some people greet David with high fives and handshakes. Some greet him with actual full-on hugs. I just wave at him. Not because I'm being shy or anything, but he makes a face like even all of this attention is a bit much for him. And honestly, I get it.

Coach blows his whistle again and practice begins.

Soon enough not only is my jersey sticking to my back like scotch tape, but my boxers are sticking to my junk in the same way. I'll need a shower before I hang out with my friends.

Luckily, Ayesha can meet up with us before her date with Trevor. I meet up with her and Olly at Kreamy Kones in our neighborhood, West Haven. The Haven is home and where my heart is.

Auntie Nisha, my Pops' sister, owns Kreamy Kones, so we get free ice cream whenever we come. This place would put any DQ to shame. There's a surprisingly hipster vibe inside with random minimalistic paintings scattered on the walls, wood-paneled flooring, Polaroid pictures of local politicians and up-and-coming B-list celebrities who've eaten here extending from strings from the ceiling. There are even dairy-free options.

A girl that I remember from the last time I was here works the cash register. I squint to read her name tag: Janae. She's got box braids and a nose piercing. I remember auntie Nisha telling me that this girl came to her looking for a job when she got put out of her house.

"My auntie Nisha around?" I ask her.

"Nah. She just left," this Janae girl lets me know. "I can take a message for her, though."

"No, that's okay. I was just gonna tell her hello."

"Oh. She only comes in here once a week to check up on the shop and restock."

"Oh, dope," I say. "I should know that from how much I come here."

"I guess. So, what kind of ice cream can I get for y'all?"

I order my usual mint chocolate chip ice cream with cookie dough and sprinkles. Yes, I'm an eight-year-old inside apparently. Ayesha gets plain chocolate ice cream with extra chocolate syrup. Olly gets a couple scoops of vanilla and adds gummy bears on top. He's a plain ass for real.

We find an open seat in the back. For as much as we come here, we should have our own reserved table every damn time.

Some light music plays in the background from some unseen speaker. It's Ariana Grande, which makes Ayesha really happy because that's one of her favorite singers. Mine, too, but I'll never admit that out loud. She even starts lip-syncing "Dangerous Woman," and it's hilarious when she pretends to hit the high notes.

Ayesha brings up Trevor, and I listen for a moment but end up tuning her out. Not intentionally, but I notice Malik outside the window, standing next to a busted fire hydrant. He's talking to some guy who might be buying weed from him. There's a quick pang of sadness that snakes through my chest for a moment. I debate running out there to stop whatever he's about to do, but that would most likely be a bad idea. He'd be pissed at me.

It's not until Ayesha calls my name that I zoom back to the present. She's asking, "What about you, Gio?"

"Huh?"

She stares at me. Olly does, too. It's like I've missed an hour's worth of conversation and I'm trying to play catch-up.

"Have you found someone?"

Someone? "Huh? If you're asking me if I'm on MatchUp, the answer is nah."

Ayesha laughs. "MatchUp isn't the only way you can meet someone."

I kind of roll my eyes at her. She's one to talk. "Says the one who just met someone on MatchUp."

"Oooooh, are you jealous?" She bites her lip. "Sounds like you're jealous."

Olly's eyes get wide. "Yeah. It does kind of sound like you're jealous, man."

"No. I'm not jealous." Ayesha and I are way over. Like over, over with a capital *O*. Nothing left in that tank, but maybe I'm being weird. I don't know.

Ayesha settles into her seat a little bit more. "Hmm."

"So?" Olly runs a hand through his mop-like blond hair and leans in. "Anyone catch your eye at school?"

My face gets warm, and it gets hard to speak all of a sudden.

I look out the window to search for Malik, but he's gone. Then I look back at Olly and Ayesha. "Uh . . . I don't know." Am I supposed to know? I'm not really big on love or relationships. And honestly, I haven't been searching. I'm one of those people who firmly believe the universe is in charge of love. The universe landed me Ayesha and so we dated and got things wrong. I don't know if I can go through that again. And no, I don't necessarily *believe* in love, like I don't think that's something that's meant for me, but I know it's out there and it works out for other people. I say, "The universe just hasn't been on my side lately and, shit, I think I'm okay with that."

Ayesha groans and makes an innocent face. "Ah, come on, Gio!"

I look at her and then at Olly, who's waiting for me to say something good. I can tell I'm about to get really defensive. I hate being put in the spotlight. "I don't need to find anybody right now. I'm perfectly okay being single. I'm confident enough in who I am. I don't need somebody else."

"What you trynna say?" Ayesha goes, craning her neck to give me a look.

Olly makes a sizzling sound, like that's a burn or something. He diverts his eyes.

"I didn't mean it like that. Sorry," I say. "I'm not trynna imply anything."

"Well, what did you mean?" she presses.

"I mean, it just feels kind of wrong thinking about dating someone because I need to. I don't need to. In fact, some people in the world choose singleness for life. Maybe that'll be me."

"Monks, right?" Olly says. "Wait . . . or are those eunuchs? Shit."

"Olly," Ayesha stops him.

It gets quiet. "So you'd die a virgin?" Olly whispers.

"I wouldn't die a virgin." I mix around my ice cream. "Besides, why do you assume I'm a virgin?"

His eyes are big again. "You had sex already?"

Ayesha and I make eye contact for some reason. "No," I answer him with a bite of cookie dough.

She puts her arms up. We didn't go all the way. We did stuff, but not stuff like that. That's when we knew we were more comfortable around each other as friends.

"Then?" Olly's so persistent and it's annoying.

"I mean, being a virgin isn't a bad thing," I say. "And maybe someday I'll go all the way and won't be one."

"But right now is the time to lose your virginity," he goes.

"Have you lost yours yet, Olly?" Ayesha asks, defending me in some sense.

"Yep. All the girls want a piece of me. I'm like a deep-fried candy bar: really bad for you yet irresistible."

"No girl wants to lay you, Olly," Ayesha fires back.

"Well, except Grace," Olly says. Grace is his *girlfriend*. Allegedly. We've never met her since she doesn't go to Ben Davis or live in Indiana at all. But weirdly we all follow her Instagram account, which only has like three photos and a handful of friends. Olly says it's a Finsta.

"She's. A. Bot," I say, punctuating my words with my fists as they strike the table.

"She's not a bot," Olly fires back.

"Have you and Grace talked on the phone yet?" I ask him.

"Not yet, but we will soon."

"Olly, you've been dating for how long now? Three months? And you haven't even heard her voice? That's not a good sign that she's real."

Olly rolls his eyes and sighs. "She's a real person, okay? We've traded . . . pictures."

"You sent dick pics to a bot?" Ayesha goes, her mouth falling open wide.

"No, I sent them to Grace," he says, and looks away before adding, "I hope."

Ayesha's laughing into her pink jacket sleeve, ice cream spilling down her face.

"It's not funny," he says.

"It's a little funny," I say.

"No, it isn't."

Ayesha and I can't stop laughing. I finish up my ice cream, scraping the bottom of the cup for all the leftover sprinkles.

"Ready to hit it?" Olly goes after a while. He's sensitive and doesn't like getting picked on sometimes.

"Yeah, I should probably get back," I say. "I promised Theo I would help him with his homework. Though I'm not sure how much help I can be. Middle school math feels scarier than trig." My phone conveniently pings, but it's just a text from Pops about today's Bible verse of the day. I usually ignore them because they're about how being me means being against God.

"If you can't figure it out, let me know, and I can ask my dad."

Ayesha's dad, Mr. Chamberlain, was a math teacher at Ben Davis before he dedicated all his time to the grocery store in our hood.

My phone buzzes in my pocket. I take it out and notice an email notification. I click on it because it's from an email address that I don't initially recognize.

To: GioTheGr8@gmail.com
From: missjackie01@global.net
Subject: It's Me!

G-Bug,
It's me. I have been thinking about you more than usual lately and wanted to reach out to you. I found your email online.
I'll be in town this weekend and would love to see you and Theo. You can email me back here or text me at the number below. Hoping to hear from you, my sweet G-Bug.

Love, Mom

I gasp and my heart pounds in my chest. I feel like I've been blasted by Sub-Zero and I'm frozen in place. Curious eyes wait in front of me, but I don't know what to say to Olly and Ayesha— or do, besides point to the email and show them my phone. They know about my mom. They know I haven't seen or heard from her since she left. When they see the email, I can tell they feel my astonished confusion—at least, their faces seem that way.

Olly goes, "That can't be real."

Ayesha just puts a hand over her mouth. "Gio." She puts her other hand on mine. "What are you gonna do?"

I'm still frozen and can't even think, let alone respond. I let out a breath that I had forgotten I was holding.

Ayesha takes my phone, locks it for me, and puts it in my pocket. She and Olly stand up from the table and I follow like the walking dead, zombie-ing my way outside, getting lost in my thoughts.

Staring at the ground once we're outside, I step off of the sidewalk and onto the street to cross to the other side. A horn blares to life. My head twists fast, and I see a motorcycle speeding toward me. My stomach drops instantly. *Shit.*

"Gio!" Ayesha screams.

I jump back to the sidewalk and trip on the curb, falling onto the pavement. I hear the screeching of brakes and then Ayesha and Olly screaming some more.

"Fuck" is all that comes from my gut. I feel blood trickle from my arm, my thoughts frenzying, my chest tight as shit. I'm gasping for air. It feels like the whole world is spinning into a blur.

Blinking my eyes back to focus—a pair of long eyelashes appear in front of my face. Ayesha.

She yelps and kneels down next to me. "Gio," she says. "Gio, are you okay?"

"Can you hear us?" Olly goes like I've just blacked out or something. They're both being dramatic about what just went down.

I nod at them, then grab Ayesha's hand after she stands and offers it. "I'm okay. Just a little scraped up." I feel like I've been hit by a bus, even though I wasn't even run over. And it's all my fault. I was too distracted to look where I was walking. That damn email.

"Holy shit, holy shit, holy shit," a low voice says, coming closer and closer. It's the guy who hit me. He's got on some Converse that match his black leather jacket and his face is as red as his hair. It's the new guy on the basketball team—somehow I remember his name's David.

I breathe in and out, hoping my chest goes back to normal.

"Shit," he says. "Are you okay? I didn't see . . . I'm sorry!"

Ayesha helps me get up on my feet. It feels like someone's pouring acid on my spine and everything inside my chest is on fire, but I manage to stand upright, only letting out a slight moan.

I clench all the muscles in my body. "I'm okay," I respond to him.

"We've gotta get you to a hospital," Ayesha insists, her words moving quick and sharp and determined.

"No," I moan.

"I'll take you guys," David rasps, his eyes wide.

"Come on!" She tries to pull me up. I flinch.

"No, Yesh," I repeat. "I'm a'ight, okay?" I hurt all over, but I don't want to go to the hospital. I'm not trying to make this a big deal.

I exhale and flinch, putting my arm around Ayesha, her entire body shaking, tears cascading down her face. She looks up at me with her big brown eyes, silently telling me both how much of a dick I'm being while simultaneously reminding me of how much she cares for me. I put my other arm around Olly's neck as they help me up.

"Are you, like, sure you're okay?" David says. "I'm so sorry. I tried to swerve to avoid hitting you, but I would've flown off and the bike would've run you over completely. And I just . . . I'm sorry, man. I'm sorry."

"It's not your fault," I say. "I should've been more careful." Looking both ways was one of the simplest things my birth mom taught me in the short time I knew her, and I can't even do that right. I shake my head hard to get the thoughts of her out of me. Thinking about her made this happen in the first place.

I stretch out my arms and legs, taking my arm from around Ayesha's neck.

"See, look, I'm fine. No broken bones if I can move like this," I say.

I notice scratches on my arm, blood trickling down from colliding with the street.

Olly sees it and goes, "Ewwwwwwww!" He's like that around blood.

"OMG! You're bleeding," Ayesha says, noticing also. She opens up her purse and pulls out a purple square package. She rips it open, peels off one side, and wraps it around my arm. It takes me way too long to realize what it is.

"Oh. My. God. Is that a—"

"It's a pad," she says, balling up the package in her hand. "Just hold it in place for a bit."

"What the hell, Ayesha?" I stare at my arm, the pad covering most of the scratches, the blood slowly getting all soaked up. This is the weirdest thing ever, but it's also working.

"Sorry, I don't have any Band-Aids."

I roll my eyes playfully. "Whatever."

Olly's suddenly laughing at my misery. This must be his payback for what happened at Kreamy Kones. He's a troll.

Motorcycle Boy decides now's the time to introduce himself. "I'm David."

"Ayesha," she says. They shake hands.

When he turns to me, I say, "I know who you are. I'm on the basketball team, too. Gio."

"Oh man. I'm so, so sorry. This is even worse. I didn't recognize my own teammate."

We both shake his hands. "It's fine. We didn't officially meet anyway."

"This is a pretty crazy way for us to meet, right?" He sort of laughs.

"I'm gonna get him to a hospital or a clinic," Ayesha says, leading us all in the direction of where the city bus stops.

"That's a good idea," David says. "I better go get my bike. But I'll see you tomorrow."

"Yeah," I say, Ayesha rushing me along. "See ya."

Once we're a good distance away, I say to Ayesha firmly, "We're not going to a hospital."

There's a silence that's shattered by sirens coming in all directions. I have no idea if it's the cops, an ambulance, a fire truck, or all three. Either way, I don't want to be around when they get here. No one ever taught me to be afraid of the sirens or anything—it's just that there are a lot of bad things I associate with sirens like this, like cops coming to arrest some of the boys in West Haven. Or just being a kid in bed, hearing them outside, wondering if something bad had happened to my mother and they were making their way to her.

I squeeze my eyes shut.

No, no, no.

My throat gets thick.

Mom.

I shake my head hard and cover my ears until the sirens pass.

We get to the bus stop and wait for the bus to come. I lean against the sign.

"You okay, Gio?" Olly asks.

Ayesha takes this as her cue. "There are a bunch of clinics in the area. You sure you're okay? We can get off on the way back to the Haven."

I nod at them. "I'm straight." *stares into camera*

Ayesha sighs. "Y'know, I've never known anyone as stubborn as you." She looks at me and then straight ahead. "I'm glad you're alive, though. I don't know what I would've done if . . ." She stops there and then hops onto the bus once it pulls up.

I look away and my legs don't hurt as much, so I can walk onto the bus on my own. "I can't believe I have a damn pad on my arm," I say as I get on.

The three of us all laugh boomingly even though it kind of stings to do that, like I injured something inside me, too, in all this. Olly and Ayesha sit in front of me on the bus. I sit next to some lady who looks so old she probably doesn't even notice someone is sitting next to her or that her bottle of orange juice is spilling all over her dress.

I pull out my phone despite the pangs in my arms from hitting the pavement. I find the email from my birth mom. I read and reread it and reread it. Part of me wants to reply, but I wouldn't know what to say. Part of me wants to toss my phone out the bus window and pray that God wipes my memory in my sleep.

THREE

⬥⬥⬥⬥⬥⬥

ONCE THE BUS DROPS us off, the sky begins to get dark. It's that time of day when the sky starts to look more like melted sherbet. Mosquitoes fly annoyingly around my arm like they smell blood.

Ayesha and I are practically neighbors, and Olly walks with us through the Haven. He lives a mile or so away in a gated community, but any time he rides the bus with us he gets off early and walks the rest of the way to feel like he's from here, too. It's kind of funny . . . and kind of sad. I know he's scared to walk through our hood deep down. I can tell by all the faces he makes, some like he's constipated and others like he's being held at gunpoint. I know he just tries to pretend like he's a hard-ass.

Sure, West Haven is the hood, but it's more than just that. There's something special about this neighborhood that I'll never quite know how to put into words. It's like it knows me through and through, like it knew me when I was in my birth mother's womb.

I pass the park, where no kids are playing but addicts and homeless people sleep on the benches and slides, even in this forty-degree weather. I walk across the street onto Seventh and King with Ayesha.

"Whaddup, Li'l Charles? Whaddup, Ye-Ye?" some random guy shouts from a passing car with spinners on the tires and hydraulics, bumping some loud Kanye West. We both wave at him as he passes.

"You know him?" I ask her.

"I ain't ever seen that bald-headed fool in my life," Ayesha says.

"Me either," I say, and laugh. But I'm the neighborhood pastor's son and Ayesha's family owns the only grocery store in the Haven, so we're practically celebrities here.

That's a downside. But some of my favorite things in the Haven are the series of Black- and brown-owned businesses in the shopping district. We've got Sweet Things, a candy shop that's owned by Ms. Diane (Malik's mom); July's Barbershop—he's Ms. Diane's oldest son. We've got the Chamberlain Grocery Store, owned by Ayesha's folks—Arvin and Anita Chamberlain. And this isn't a business, but we even got Pops' church just down the block. It's called Union Temple and sits just on the corner of Seventh Street where the gang hangs out. Pops moved the church there intentionally to *save* the "lost youth."

Eventually, after saying bye to Ayesha and Olly, I make it back home, where I can smell my stepmom Karina's famous taco pie. I walk into the kitchen area where the wooden dining room table is and Karina's playing Monopoly with my little brother, Theo. Too bad I've already had dessert before dinner and am people'd out. I probably won't hang out with them.

Besides, I'm trying to sneak upstairs to the bathroom so I can get this damn pad off my arm.

I don't celebrate how successful I am at this until I get to the top of the stairs. The first thing I do is take something to ease the pain: a bath. I make sure to bury the pad at the bottom of the bathroom's trash can. I don't want to have to explain how I was basically hit by some kid from school on a motorcycle because of an email I got.

There's a knock on the bathroom door.

"Giovanni, you in there?" It's Karina. She uses my full name and that motherly concerned voice. She may not be my birth mom, but this is the concerned voice I imagine my birth mom might've had, if she'd stayed long enough to actually be a mom to me.

I pause, splashing some water on my face before answering her. "Yeah," I say, my voice cracking.

"You okay, honeybunches?" I hate it when she calls me *honeybunches*. Isn't that a cereal?

"I'm fine," I kinda lie, holding my phone and staring at the email again.

"Theo said you were helping him with his homework tonight, right?"

"Yes, ma'am."

There's a short pause. "Well . . . okay. I'll let him know. Dinner will be ready soon. We're having your favorite." Once upon a time my drool might've already started mixing in with the bathwater at the thought of Karina's taco pie, but there's something else taking up space in my brain.

She goes quiet again, and this time I know she's walked away. I sit in the tub, scrubbing everywhere, getting rid of every spot of blood, washing the cuts on my arms.

When I finish, I drain the dirty, bloody water, dry off, and squeeze into some gray joggers and a plain white T-shirt. I double-check to make sure the dirty pad is as far at the bottom of the trash can as it can be before going downstairs. Our cute little black-and-silver Yorkshire terrier, Biscuit, waits for me when I get out and jumps on me excitedly. She's so excited that she pees a little near my foot.

"Bad girl," I say to her. She whimpers a little bit because she knows what she did, but her tail is still wagging because she's so happy to see me.

Once I get downstairs, I sit at the dinner table. It's quiet as hell as Karina serves the four of us family style. She really did throw down. Taco pie with guacamole and cilantro *and* lime rice.

Pops clears his throat lightly, sticking his fork into his slice of taco pie. "How was your day, Gio? Did you get my verse?" He takes a swig of a beer in front of him. I can tell that it's not even his first. He has that glossy look in his eyes that he gets when he's had too much to drink. Yeah, Pops is a pastor, but it seems as though he loves drinking just as much as he loves Jesus. Nobody at the church knows about this side of him, though. They don't see this when he's giving sermons and telling folks how they should live their lives.

"The day was good. And yeah, I got it." A half lie. It *was* good hanging with Ayesha and Olly, of course. But I hated

Mrs. Oberst's class. And the whole motorcycle thing.

"Memorize that verse?" Pops asks.

Shit. I should've known that was coming.

"No," I say shyly after a moment of silence. My shoulders slump as I watch his eyes narrow on me like he's some kind of bird and I'm prey. "But I'll memorize all the verses you sent me this week over the weekend. I promise." I shouldn't promise this because unkept promises are the worst, but it's the least I could do to escape his hawk eyes.

Karina slices me a piece of taco pie and makes sure to give me two scoops of guacamole instead of one. She knows how much I love it. She gives Theo his without guacamole, since he's allergic to onions and hates avocados because he thinks they look like "alien fruit."

"My own dad would make this for me and my siblings," Karina says. "He was an elementary school janitor, but he loved to cook. This was one dish that I loved when he was able to cook. Before he died, I told him that I would make it for my future family." She's told me this story so many times, but each time it feels sadder.

It's quiet again.

Biscuit growls softly at my feet.

"Biscuit, get!" Pops shouts, shooing her away. She darts upstairs. One time, when we left her here with him, he hit her with a broomstick because she chewed up a pillowcase. We try not to leave her alone with him.

Out the corner of my eye, I notice Karina watching Theo and me as we eat.

She clears her throat. "Earlier today at Target, Gio, I was remembering when you and Theo were little and would come home from school. The two of you would watch all those Disney Channel reruns for hours and hours. I remember one time, I saw y'all in there dancing and singing along to the Jonas Brothers and Hannah Alabama."

"Hannah Montana," I correct her, laughing and trying not to be embarrassed. Theo laughs, too. "Yeah, that used to be our stuff, wasn't it, Theo?"

He swallows and starts singing so off-key about slipping into lava.

"Noooooooooo, Theo!" I shout, covering my ears, laughing even harder now.

He continues, getting louder. All the *baby*s and *oh*s super off-pitch.

"You both used to want Jonas Brothers everything—T-shirts, posters, even Jonas Brothers–themed birthday parties with their faces on the cake. We got you two the full-series set with all the albums for Christmas one year. Where are they at?"

"In the trash," I say, suppressing another laugh. "Where they belong."

"Liar!" Theo murmurs. He knows I still have all of them in my room somewhere.

Around our house, storytelling is what keeps us going. It's what brings us closer together. Karina started it when she started dating Pops, even though Pops never says much, only eats and drinks and leaves the table to get lost and numb with more beer and his game shows. The storytelling helps me forget all the shitty things that come and go in my head for a little while.

"It's about time to start thinking about colleges, right, Gio?" Karina asks.

This is one thing I don't want to talk about tonight. I have a whole 'nother year before I have to think about colleges. Duke and IU are on my list, but for now, that's about it.

"I haven't gotten any emails or anything yet," I tell her.

It goes quiet—so quiet I can almost hear her thoughts. "You've got time" is all she says back. "But make sure when the time comes, you think about Harvard." She has this fantasy of Theo and me getting into an Ivy League school for some reason.

"What you need to be doing is taking away all that time you spend on that damn basketball and helping out more at the church," Pops says out of nowhere, pieces of guacamole in his beard. "You're the pastor's kid. You've got to accept your calling, boy."

It's quiet. *My calling? Working up at the church isn't my calling,* I think to myself.

But these are words I can never say out loud.

"Anyway," Karina says so I don't have to say anything else, "I didn't mean to cause any trouble. I'm so, so proud of ya, honeybunches. You and Theo make me brag to the people who come into my office."

I nod at her and then Pops, my eyes falling back onto my plate, where there's a pile of taco meat and diced tomatoes left untouched.

Karina is a nurse at an urgent care clinic but wanted to go

to Harvard when she was my age. Despite all this, though, she's always told me that I never have to stick with one thing forever—that our passions are always changing. And unlike Pops, she always reminds me that I've got all the time in the world to figure life out. I'm seventeen, and I shouldn't need to have everything planned yet.

Instinctively, though, my eyes go back over to Pops.

"You keep sticking with tossing balls back and forth, you ain't gon' get anywhere," he says. Negativity that stings, but I push through it. Whispering under his breath, he adds, "People up at the church already talking about you being one of those . . . uh . . . homosexuals."

This one more than stings, but I try not to react. I told him about me being bi when I first figured it out—I told him and Karina and they had opposite reactions. Pops didn't believe me. He said I was confused and made me pray with him. When we went up to the church, he had me kneel down at the altar and ask forgiveness and let the good Lord work in my heart to free me from my sin. Through tears, I did what I was told to do. Once I got back home, I buried myself beneath blankets, plugged in my headphones, and didn't leave my room for hours.

From his pulpit, Pops lectures us about what he thinks the Bible says about people like me. Every time, it stings—no, more than stings. It hurts worse than being hit by a motorcycle. It sucks that even family (people who are supposed to love you no matter what) can make you feel like the ugliest, most terrible thing at the bottom of an ocean.

"Gio is bisexual, Charles. Whether you like it or not, he's bisexual," Karina says.

"No, he's not!" Pops fires back.

"Yes, I am!" I yell, my jaw twitching.

"No, you ain't," Pops yells, slamming his fists against the table. "That ain't how God made you."

"Charles, enough!" Karina shrieks abruptly. He doesn't respond, just settles onto his seat.

It goes quiet again.

My legs shake from anxiety. Fork clicking against the side of my plate. Words rumbling in the back of my throat, making it hard to find the right ones. Eventually, I do.

"I—I g-got an email from our mom today," I say, nearly choking on the syllables.

Pops freezes. "What?"

I flash him my phone and let him read it. "I got it earlier and I . . . I don't know what to do."

"Delete it," he says plainly. "She left. She doesn't need to hurt this family any more than she already has."

I can't just delete it. Can I?

I exhale loudly.

Karina's taken the phone from him and is reading the email herself. "Let him respond, Charles," she says when she's done. "It's his mother."

Pops slams his fists against the table once more, and we all jump back. "I said delete it. Delete. It. Now."

Out of fear, I do exactly as I'm told. I click the delete button and watch it disappear in front of my eyes. That's the end of that, I guess . . . but something doesn't feel right with me about deleting it.

Dinner seems to be drawing to an awkward end, but Karina surprises us with a peanut butter cheesecake. A needed bright spot. This time, she's even cut up little Reese's Cups and put them on top with whipped cream. Theo nearly eats half of it before she takes it off the table.

"One more piece," Theo begs, poking his lips out and everything.

She denies him, sliding the cheesecake in the fridge. "Tomorrow," she says.

He pouts as if he's six again, but he just turned eleven a week ago. I rush over to him and rub the top of his head.

"I'm gonna help you with your homework, bro. I'll meet you in your room?"

Theo grins and nods. He likes when I make time to spend with him. He has severe social anxiety, like he gets super nervous when he goes outside, and can even conjure up hundreds of worst-case scenarios, like fearing a large asteroid will fall from the sky to crush him. I have to walk him to school every morning because of that.

Theo scrapes his plate in the trash, sits his dishes in the sink, and then dashes upstairs. Pops grabs another beer from the fridge and heads for the living room to turn on whatever game show he's been watching lately. I don't know what number this is for him, but I'm sure he'll try to beat yesterday's seven-beer count.

I help Karina clean off the table and wash the dishes—something I haven't done in a while. She grabs my bicep and I flinch, my eyes squinting from the pain shooting through me, but I manage.

"How's Olly and Ayesha?"

"They're doing a'ight," I answer, scrubbing the remains of a plate with a yellow sponge. "We were at Kreamy Kones earlier. Gave Olly a hard time about his imaginary girlfriend."

"Oh yeah?" Karina laughs. "How imaginary are we talking?"

"The girl apparently lives in middle-of-nowhere Utah and only has three Instagram photos. She also refuses to video chat with him."

"Sounds pretty suspicious, if you ask me. How'd they meet?"

"Some app."

"These days, all kids are meeting on apps. Back in my day, we didn't even have a phone to text."

"Yeah," I say, drying a couple plates with a rag.

Karina lifts up my hand, pushing it closer to the light. Up close, I can see the bags under her dark brown eyes from not getting a lot of sleep lately. I'm sure she's had more late nights dealing with Pops.

"You got a cut right here," she says, thumbing it.

I pull away. "Yeah, I scraped it earlier."

She furrows her eyebrows and places a hand on her hip like the most concerned parent. "You clean it out? That's how you get blood diseases. Open wounds." She would know.

I nod. "Yeah, I did."

"Good," she says, and goes back to focusing on drying the dishes. "Be careful."

"Will do," I say. "I'm gonna go help Theo with his homework like I promised."

"Okay, honeybunches." A quick breath. "Hey, would you mind stopping by the Chamberlains' store and grabbing some things for me at some point?"

"Sure thing," I say with a tight-lipped smile before turning away and heading up to put on my big-brother cap and save Theo from whatever math problems he's having trouble with.

"Oh . . . and, Gio?" Karina says.

I turn around and raise an eyebrow. "Yes?"

She opens up a drawer that I've never had a reason to open and pulls out something. "Don't listen to your dad. He doesn't know what he's saying when he's drinking. But . . . I thought I would give you this."

I look at what she hands me. It's a photo of my birth mom. I don't know how she got it or how long it's been in the drawer, and I don't know why she's choosing right now to give it to me.

I look up at her with confused eyes.

"I think you should try to get in contact with her, if you want. If you don't, that's totally okay, too. I support you no matter what, honeybunches." She smiles and I can see the gap in between her teeth.

"Thanks, Karina," I say.

"Of course," she says back. "It's been so long. If I were in your shoes, I would want to know. Now's your chance. You only get so many."

FOUR

THEO'S BEDROOM DOOR IS cracked when I get to the top of the stairs. I can see him with his headphones on, blasting Kidz Bop loud enough for me to hear it. He's casually dancing, carefree and unbothered. I haven't seen him like this in a while. I almost don't want to interrupt him.

I knock twice, and he doesn't even look back. He can't hear shit with the headphones that loud.

I knock again, louder this time, and then he falls back on his bed, one of his headphones popping out. He motions for me to walk in. Biscuit rushes in and jumps up on the bed. We've had her since I was in sixth grade. She's getting old, but her energy hasn't aged a day.

"Hey, li'l bro," I say.

Theo nods and says "Hey," then reaches for his backpack. It's an old one of mine that he asked for because it makes him feel cool.

He pulls out a thick blue algebra textbook. He's in sixth grade and is already two years ahead of other kids his age. I admire that about him. He's weird, like most little brothers in the world, but he's smart and geeky as hell, and I think *that's* kind of cool. It's clear Theo got the brains and I got the brawn.

"What are you guys learning? What do you need help with?" I ask, sitting down on his *Adventure Time* bedspread.

"Polynomial functions, I think," he says. "Descartes's rule of signs."

"Oh, fun," I say sarcastically, not really having a clue what he's talking about.

There's a beat as I flip through his textbook to the right page.

"Well, are we gonna get started?" he asks.

"A'ight, lemme look and see if I can figure it out," I go.

One look at the stuff and I instantly know I won't be useful. I'm in trig right now, but I don't remember much about polynomials or some old, probably white dude named Descartes. I try my best to pull some knowledge from deep within my memory, not really knowing if the answers or formulas I'm giving him are even accurate.

Eventually, Theo solves all the assigned problems and checks his answers in the back.

He doesn't even need my help. I'm not mad, though. I wanted to hang out with him, too. Watching him get it himself is awesome and reminds me that I really need to spend more time with him. I've just been so caught up with basketball. I rub the top of his head, my fingers grazing his curls.

"I think that's how Mr. Walters taught us to do it," he goes.

"I remember Mr. Walters. He's good at math, so I'm gonna trust that the way he's teaching you guys is the right way."

"Yeah," he goes, showing me his homework for review.

"Good work," I say, giving him dap, then lifting up to walk to his door, covered in all things Marvel Universe.

"Wait. Gio. One last thing," Theo says.

"Yes, li'l bro?"

"You ever think about Mom?"

I pause probably for the longest minute of our lives. The day she left gets stuck in my head, and I catch my breath.

"All the time, man. All the time." Sometimes even when I don't want to. Sometimes I wonder if things would be different if she were still here with us. I wonder if Pops would drink like he does. I wonder if Theo would still need me to walk him to school every morning. I wonder a lot of things and I might not ever know the answers. And I tell myself that it's . . . okay.

"What was she like? Was she nice?" Theo asks.

"I don't remember a lot, but I do remember she gave us a lot of toys for Christmas. And I know she always took us to the park to play when we were younger."

I almost forget, but I show him the photo Karina gave me, unsure of how he'll react.

Once he grabs it, his eyes light up. "Is this her?"

I nod.

"Whoa. She looks like me!"

Theo's smile makes me smile. I say, "I know, li'l bro. You want to meet her?"

"I don't know," Theo says, looking away. I wish I knew what exactly is running through his head.

"That's okay. You don't have to know right now."

"Can you make sure she's safe for me first?"

"Yeah, I'll do that for you, Theo." I want to add *if I ever see her again.*

I never really have the right words to say when she comes up with Theo or with Pops.

"Wanna play Xbox later tonight?"

"Sure." He nods and grins.

"*Call of Duty, Halo, NBA 2K*, or X-Men?"

"*Call of Duty.* Definitely." He smiles bigger, showing his chipped front tooth.

"Okay. Deal!" I say, even though I was kind of hoping he'd say X-Men or 2K since I'm better at those. Maybe another time.

There's a pause as I step outside of his door.

"Mom loved us. You know that, right?" I say, catching myself by surprise.

He doesn't say anything, doesn't move a single muscle. Just stares at me.

"She loved us. She had to." I don't know what else to say, really. How do you even explain to a child that their parent isn't around because they just didn't want to be? And maybe I don't have to have the right words, but trying to keep Theo from falling apart always keeps me from falling apart, too. The doctors have diagnosed my brother with PTSD, which, in some way, led to his not being able to walk outside by himself, without me or Karina at his side.

Theo nods like he believes me.

I turn back and head down the hall to my room. Sometimes when I think about my mom, I get this really weird feeling in my gut like something's off, like something's not right. Before

I started taking anxiety meds, I used to get these weird dreams where she'd save me from a burning building over and over again. I never knew where we were or why the building was even burning. None of that really mattered. Just the fact that I was in her arms and I could actually touch her was everything to me.

Back in my room, I get changed into the Paramore T-shirt I always sleep in. After, I lie across my bed, tending to all of my social media notifications. I put in my headphones and listen to Paramore on repeat, starting with their first album. I listen to them to mellow out. And I don't really need to mellow out right now, but they're perfect to fall asleep to, also. They're my first favorite band of all time.

"Emergency" plays through my headphones. It's one of those songs that you feel in your soul and carry in your bones. As soon as my favorite part hits, Ayesha and Olly group FaceTime me.

I hesitate for a minute, but then I sit up to answer.

"Hey, what's up," I say, their faces loading on my screen.

Olly's in a beanie and tank. Ayesha's wearing a red tank and has a black bonnet on her head. I can see she's in her room, pictures of all of her celebrity crushes plastered on her sunlight-orange walls—21 Savage, Mac Miller, Chris Evans, Barack Obama, and others.

"Heeeeyyyyyyy," Ayesha mutters, popping her gum.

"I'm surprised you picked up, G," Olly says.

"I am, too," I say. "But I'm more likely to pick up than Grace."

"Ha-ha. Damn!" Ayesha spurts.

"Wow, I need some IcyHot for that burn," Olly mutters. "You don't have to drag me like that."

"My bad, my bad," I say. "It just will never stop being funny to me that you're being catfished. Wait. Ayesha, what happened with your thing with Trevor?"

"Something came up for him, so we're hanging out tomorrow," she says.

"Dang," I say.

"*Anyway*. You guys studying for that quiz in Mrs. Flynn's AP Government class?" Olly asks us. I simmer my laughter down even though it's hard to do successfully.

"Hell nah," Ayesha goes.

"Nope," I say back. I don't need to study for that class.

"Why not?"

Ayesha beats me to an answer. "Mrs. Flynn trynna come work my shift at my momma and daddy's store? Didn't think so."

"Touché, I guess," Olly says.

Someone rings the doorbell to my house a bunch of times, like they're the police. Biscuit goes crazy with her barking. Usually when she's barking like this, we've got to give her bologna just to calm her down. I wait for Karina or Pops to get the door.

After a minute, I hear Karina call, "Giovanni! You have a visitor."

"Sorry, guys, I have to go," I say, kind of hesitant. I don't know who the heck it could be. The only two people it could be are on FaceTime with me, but it's definitely not them.

"See you later," Olly says.

Ayesha waves, and I click off.

My eyebrows furrow and I quickly remove my headphones. I walk down the stairs and see Karina in a closed bathrobe, a glass of wine in hand. She's opening the door wider, letting the moon's light rush in and revealing David, the new kid—the one who almost killed me on his motorcycle.

My mind races. *How the hell did he know where I live? Why is he here?*

"Hi," he says. He's holding a plate covered in aluminum foil. "Um . . . this might be weird. Well, of course it's weird. I—I still felt bad about earlier, so I just wanted to come by and say sorry again. It wasn't my intention to, you know, almost—"

"It's fine," I cut him off.

"What's this about?" Karina asks.

"Nothing. It's not important," I answer.

A quick pause.

"What do you want?" I ask him, probably sounding super-fucking rude. The wind is blowing through his red hair, which is looking even redder than the last time I saw him.

He extends his hand. "I'm David."

"Yeah, I remember your name," I say. *Rude.*

"Hi, David," Karina says, and smiles, shaking his hand.

She gives me a pointed look, so I shake his free hand, too.

"Ah, awesome. Good meeting you, Karina." His voice is all singsongy and annoying.

He looks down, then up at me.

And stares.

I stare back.

"Oh, I almost forgot! So, my folks and I just moved into the neighborhood from Kansas—right across the street, in fact. My parents sent over this crème brûlée for you guys." He hands the plate over to Karina. "We're just getting used to things here in Indiana, and we heard sweet desserts are the way to make new friends." He smiles wider.

"We should be the ones bringing over dessert for you! Welcome to Indiana and to the Haven," Karina almost cheers. "The weather here is probably a little bit more indecisive than in Kansas."

"You'd be surprised."

My mind rewinds his words. Instantly, part of me kind of wants to know his story. He's white, and ain't no white folks *choose* to live here. Some white folks just kind of end up here. I've seen lots of white kids from this neighborhood at school and they don't dress like this guy. Hmm. Maybe I shouldn't be profiling him like that.

An awkward pause.

"Great," David says sheepishly. "Well, I'll leave you two alone now. Thanks for the warm welcome. I'm sure we're going to enjoy this neighborhood. Sorry again about earlier, Gio. See you at school?"

I answer him a little too delayed. "Sure. I guess."

"Can't wait." He gives a big smile, not showing any teeth. "Also can't wait to tear it up with you on the court."

After he leaves, Karina asks, "How do you know that boy? He's very friendly."

"He's the new kid on the basketball team. Ran into him again when Olly, Ayesha, and I were out." Neither of these are lies.

"Oh. Small world. I'm surprised they're moving into that house across the street." The house across the street has been abandoned for years and looks like no one should ever live in it. Weeds and vines growing around the front, stray cats living on the porch.

"Yep." Tongue to cheek. I head back upstairs to play a few rounds of *Call of Duty: Zombies* on Xbox with Theo. After he ends up beating me with his zombie kill streak, he ends up crashing on my floor, his head resting on a pile of clean clothes I've yet to fold. Biscuit even joins him. It's adorable. It's so adorable, I take a photo and upload it to my Instagram page, where I have over a thousand followers—mainly because I'm on the basketball team. I caption the picture, Ladies, he's clearly taken.

It makes me laugh a little too hard.

Before falling asleep, I spend an hour or so scrolling through my Insta and Twitter feeds and watching all the Snapchat stories of people on my friends list, until my phone buzzes.

It's a new follower notification from Instagram.

@Not_Bowie01.

I click on the profile to see who it is.

It's David.

FIVE

♦ ♦ ♦ ♦ ♦ ♦

THE NEXT MORNING, I wake up from a nightmare drenched in sweat, huffing and puffing all the carbon dioxide out of me and all the oxygen into my lungs. I like waking up from nightmares because the feeling of realizing you're okay is amazing, even though the whole nightmare itself is fucking torture.

In it, I was a little kid again. Nine years old. I was playing at the park in the Haven. I saw Theo and Pops and my birth mom. She was helping me learn how to shoot a basketball, how to place my feet, how to set my arms in a shooting motion. I dribbled around her and then shot the ball—a layup. I turned around and Theo and Pops were gone, and it was just my birth mom with tears streaming down her face. Tiny pebbles started to funnel around her like some sort of tornado or portal until she completely faded away out of sight, replaced by rain and lightning and thunder and sirens. I woke up right after a lightning bolt struck a few yards away from me.

I take my shower and get dressed, knowing I'm getting a late start to the Saturday. As I'm putting on my sneakers, I hear three loud voices coming from the kitchen. Karina's and Pops' and one I can't quite make out. Some woman's voice. A certain amount of nervousness gets in my chest at the thought of it being Dr. McCullough, my old therapist—or worse, one of my teachers, like Mrs. Oberst, making a home visit to tell Karina and Pops about my performance.

Pops is talking. Nah. He's yelling, and I can hear all the tension in his voice. I haven't heard Pops this angry at whoever he's yelling at since the time Theo bought the latest *Grand Theft Auto* with saved-up birthday money after Pops said it was for people in satanic cults. Actually, this might even be worse than that. *Definitely* worse.

I head downstairs, to hear more.

"Do you have any idea what this is going to do to the boys?" Pops shouts.

The other voice answers, says something, but it's too soft for me to make out any words.

"You're just as clueless and careless as you were the day you left. You need to leave, Jackie."

By now I'm listening outside the kitchen. The biggest lump forms at the back of my throat and my hands get really clammy and warm at the mention of that name.

Jackie.

My birth mom.

Mom.

Ma.

She's here.

She's . . . fucking . . . here?

She's really here and this isn't one of those hallucinations or daydreams.

It's like I have to summon energy from the universe just to take a step forward into the kitchen. Eventually, my legs do what they're supposed to do.

As soon as I'm in the kitchen, my eyes lock with hers. My mom's. Jackie's. Here she is. The woman who abandoned me. I can tell my eyes pool with tears by the way her face blurs, so I blink. Everything around me goes quiet.

I'm not sure if this deep look she's giving me is because she's looking at the mistake in me or picturing all the years she's missed since she's been gone. No matter what, I want to scream. But I can't. It feels like there's a thick pillow on my face and I'm suffocating.

"G-Bug, honey," she says. "You're so big and got facial hair coming in. Wow, look at you." She tries to touch my face, but I pull back, like it's an instinct.

"What—what are you—?" I can't finish my train of thought.

"I'd like to spend some time with you, sons, and maybe . . . make things right." Her voice is all fast and filled with emotion. *Make things right?* What kind of shit—I don't even know what that means. I still can't speak, but Pops does it for me.

"Jackie! What are you talking about? You just up and left your kids behind. You left *me* behind." I can tell by the sound of my Pops' voice that he's trying so hard not to blow up. He used to tell me never to cry in front of other people—that the best time to cry is when it's just you alone in the darkness. I've noticed how since listening to him I've become more and more like Pops, the way I knowingly accept the darkness that finds me. But look at him. He's not even holding back. Not at all. These are angry, pissed-off tears.

I try to say something, anything at all, but no words come out.

Everything in my chest is numb.

I wipe the tears with my sleeve. My mo—*Jackie* swings her head around to face Pops.

"You just don't understand!" Jackie shouts. "It's compli—"

"I don't need to understand!" Pops' voice booms.

I close my eyes and take the deepest of breaths.

She turns back around. Facing me. I'm stunned.

My birth mom, no, I mean Jackie, no, I mean Mom, no . . . Jackie stares at me. I stare back harder, and I'm hating this terrible back-and-forth. I can't get over this glossy look in her eyes that's somewhere between surprise and regret. Instantly, there's an explosion in my stomach that turns it sour. I blink and blink and blink back the tears and all the screams I want to release.

She doesn't look exactly like she does in the photo Karina gave me. She's different, older. Hair cut shorter, in a small, curly natural Afro. She's wearing a sundress with tulips on it. She's got the same brown eyes from the photo, though. Same cheekbones, mouth, and empty expression.

"My boy." The words fall out of her mouth in a fat, bubbly glob. I shake my head and step back, step back, step back.

She opens her arms for a hug, but I refuse. It's the second time I've denied her this, but she denied me her love and presence all these years. I shake my head and allow myself to take a couple more steps away.

Breathe in. Breathe out, I remind myself. *What you're doing is okay.*

Theo comes downstairs and sees this woman—a woman he probably doesn't even remember or recognize. He was like four when she walked out. Theo immediately draws to my side, latching on to me like a magnet, like he knows who she is, like he needs reminding that I'm here and won't ever leave him. To him, I mean safety. To him, Jackie means . . . *stranger.*

"Theo," she says, "don't you recognize your own mother?"

She comes forward as if she's going to hug him, but he presses into me more, like he's trying to crawl inside my skin. Now he knows who this is. And neither of us are having the reaction we thought we'd have. At least, I thought I'd welcome her back with open arms the very first moment I saw her again. I didn't know it would be like this—this hard, my anxiety scarring me from the inside out. I didn't know I could feel this much anger, this much pain, this much hurt all bottled up, brightly burning inside my chest, unable to come out.

It's like I have to will the energy from the earth's core to speak up.

But I do.

"Why—What are you doing here?" I ask. I can feel myself shaking. "Where have you been all this time?"

"G-Bug, I want to answer all of your questions. I really do," she says. "Could we have some time alone?"

Theo hugs me tighter at my waistline and starts to sob into my side. Something about this tells me he's feeling every emotion I am. I shake my head. I don't trust her. I don't want to be alone with her. At least, not right now. I just can't do that right now.

She quickly wipes away some tears and gazes at us like she loves us.

"But I'm your mom," she says, and I want to smother those words. My mom? Since when does she want to be one? Rule number one on how to be a decent damn mother: Don't abandon your kids.

It's just that simple.

So simple.

I keep quiet again.

Jackie, with a trembling voice, murmurs, "I remember bringing you home from the hospital after having you, G-Bug. The doctors wrapped you up in a tiny blue blanket and let me hold you. When I saw your face—those big brown eyes, I thanked God for a beautiful baby boy. I knew that you'd grow up to be just as beautiful, and I—"

"Stop!"

"G-Bug. Are you okay?"

"Don't call me that!" I shout at her, a surge of fury rising within me.

She takes a step back and puts her hands up like she's defending herself.

"I *was* okay," I tell her. "Until you came back. Until you showed up here like nothing ever happened. Like you haven't been gone all these years and haven't said a word to any of us. I don't . . ." I gasp for air, my jaws burning. "I don't want you to come back. I handled you being gone for years. I can handle more years than that."

My birth mom just stares blankly, with wetness pooling around in her eyes, fidgeting with her hands in front of me, like she's broken to pieces by what I just said to her.

"I'm gonna go for a walk," I murmur, my voice cracking.

Theo lets go of me, but Karina grabs my arm, saying, "Gio, wait."

"Please let me go, Karina," I say. My trembling won't stop.

She runs a thumb along my arm. "Gio, just please be careful." Suddenly, she releases me at once. I grab my yellow SpongeBob SquarePants hoodie that's hanging up by the door. Theo asks if he can come with me. I nod at him and take his hand.

SIX

ONCE I GET OUTSIDE, I rip the lock that chains my bike to the side of the house. I haven't used it in years because the seat's worn all the way down the metal frame and it hurts to sit on it for too long.

Theo stands on the pegs I have coming out of the sides of my back tires. I installed them myself back when I used to bike around with Theo on my back, and they're finally coming in handy as we make what feels like a great escape.

I pedal us down the sidewalk, without any real sense of direction, no idea where I'm going, I just keep on. I didn't think it would ever be this hard to face her after all this time. I'd always thought things would be different—*way* different. That the time I saw her again, if it ever happened, would be smoother, like a little reunion—that no other feeling would matter except for the warmth of being reunited with her. It's funny how life works, how you can think and think and think things are gonna go one way, but they end up going the complete opposite way. Sadness beats and beats and beats out of us as we ride on. I almost expect the trees to bend over like they're weeping, the sidewalks to crack in a zillion parts, the sky to split open to offer a little brightness. But it doesn't happen. Only the truth that our mom is back haunts, like a dark cloud chasing us.

Despite it being cold, drizzly, and windy, we end up at a Steak 'n Shake about a mile or so away from West Haven. I hope this is far enough away from her.

"She can't find us here," I tell Theo, who's wiping away at his eyes. I can't tell if it's just rainwater or tears or a mixture of both.

He nods at me like he can't speak. We walk into Steak 'n Shake and find an open table. It's mostly empty for a Saturday. There's a family eating chili fries in one corner. In another, there's a man wearing dirty, baggy clothes. I can't see his face since he's facedown on the table, like he's sleeping. Maybe he's homeless?

I reach into my pocket for my phone to call Olly or Ayesha. Someone. I've got texts from both of them, so one of them has to answer me.

I call Olly first. It goes to voicemail.

I call Ayesha next. She picks up.

"Gio?" Surprise fills her voice. I never call her this time of day on a weekend without texting her first.

"Are you home?" I ask.

"No, I'm with Malik." She pauses. "Everything okay?"

The truth: Nothing is okay. "I'm okay" is what I tell her, though. She's with Malik and I don't know what that's all about.

"Don't lie to me, Gio. It sounds like you've been crying."

Silence. I feel like I'm falling forward with the force of years and years of heavy grief, Theo beside me.

"Gio?" Her voice leaks concern. "I've known you for too long. I know when something is wrong."

I don't even realize I sniffle into the phone. I fight for my voice.

"Sh-sh-she's back, Ayesha. My mom. And I'm—"

"Just breathe," Ayesha interrupts me, like she gets it. "Breathe. Where are you?"

I'm in this weird area between wanting to be alone for the rest of my life—or here with Theo—and wanting a human security blanket, like my best friend. Sloppily, the words fall out anyway.

"Steak 'n Shake on Washington," I say.

"On my way," she mutters pretty quick, but then hangs up.

A woman approaches me and asks if I'm ready to order. Her voice is familiar. I look up to see that it's my former math teacher, Ms. Herr, in a white uniform and black apron. She's got blond hair with pink highlights tied up in a ponytail, and a face full of makeup. Her face brightens as she recognizes me.

"Hey there, kiddo." She nudges my arm. She's called me kiddo since I had her.

"Hi, Ms. Herr." A half smile that's kind of forced.

"Who's this cutie patootie?" She pinches Theo's cheek.

"My little brother," I say.

"Well, he looks just like you. What can I get you two?"

I glance at Theo and he shakes his head. "We're okay," I say. "Could we get water, though?"

"Sure thing, kiddo."

"Are you okay, Theo?" I ask him, thumbing his cheek across

the table before trying to fix his hair. His box cut is kind of flattened a little bit from the rain.

"I'm scared" is all he says, and I get it.

I hold my hand out on the table and he places his on top. Then we do our handshake where we clasp hands, hook our fingers, and then snap, but it feels like we do it in slow motion. "I know you're scared," I say. "But I'm here and you'll be okay as long as I'm here."

Right when Ms. Herr comes back with our waters, Ayesha arrives, bursting through the Steak 'n Shake doors like she's ready to fuck some shit up. She stays ready, and I like that about her. She's brought Olly with her and they plop down at our table. I perk up a little.

"Gio!" Ayesha shouts. "Theo!" Some excitement is evident when she says his name.

"Sup, guys," I say, wiping my face.

Ayesha hugs Theo and makes a sympathetic face at him. "Poor baby." He's not a baby, but I get what she means. Olly orders some fries with Thousand Island dressing. Ayesha gets an Oreo milkshake and shares it with Theo, but I can't eat right now. For some reason, my appetite has vanished. My stomach feels empty, but I don't want to eat anything.

"So, your mom's back, huh?" Olly goes, like I somehow forgot, like it's not the very thing that landed me here at Steak 'n Shake.

"Yeah," I say. "I woke up from a nightmare and heard people screaming, and when I finally went downstairs, there she was, just standing in the kitchen like she never left. Like everything was fine, telling me how she wants to talk to me."

"She dropped you like a bad habit. That's so fucked up for her to just show up unannounced like that," Ayesha says. Ayesha knows my birth mom, from when we were growing up together. So her saying it's fucked up validates my feelings.

"Seriously. The least she could've done was explain why she left you in the first place," Olly murmurs, smashing his fries.

"I think she wanted to," I offer. "I didn't let her. I didn't want to hear it. We didn't want to hear it."

"You didn't want to hear it?" questions Olly.

"Nah," I say. "I mean . . . I do, of course, I want to know. I was just caught off guard, and I knew that no matter what she said, it wouldn't justify her leaving like she did."

"Leaving you with that DL alcoholic daddy of yours," Ayesha continues for me. She can say things like that because as awkward as it might be, she knows things about me and my family that an adopted sister would know.

"Makes sense," Olly says.

"Guys, I don't know what to do. I don't want to go back home. She might be there."

Ayesha struggles to suck some of her milkshake with a straw.

"Well, I've got a guest bedroom," Olly says. I look at him, and he goes on. "My parents would love it if you stayed with us."

I consider that. Like, for real. "Thanks, Olly. It means a lot."

"You're my best friend. Anything for you," he says, licking the salt off his fingers.

"I just don't know what to feel," I say, watching Theo use a spoon to pick out all the chunks of Oreo to pop in his mouth.

"It's okay if you don't know what to feel," Ayesha says. "It's okay because this is your life, your heart, your feelings, and changing those things take time."

I need to hear this from her. "Thanks, Yesh."

"I mean that shit, too," she continues. "When my momma left to get clean, I was pissed and excited at the same time. Weird shit, right? But when she got back, it took me so long to process everything. 'Cause on the one hand, my momma was back and clean. But on the other hand, she had to go get help for two years, and that still hurt me."

I fidget with my hands on the table, taking in her words.

Ayesha clears her throat. "Sometimes the one who left you in pieces comes back. Sometimes they're different and other times, they're the same as before, but what's important is what you make of their return. Sometimes, you just ain't ready. Ready to heal. Ready to forgive. Ready to move forward. And that's okay."

Damn, I need this, too. I sit back in my seat and fold my arms. I look at Theo and then out of the window, then back at Theo again. I tell myself I have to be strong for him. So I take a deep breath and count in my thoughts. When I was seeing Dr. McCullough, she said counting or naming the states in alphabetical order and even reverse alphabetical order helps you clear your head, helps push through anxiety and panic attacks.

I count.

And count.

And count.

In my thoughts.

But I can't shake this grief. I can't shake the weight of her return off of me. It feels like the whole world leaps away from me and I'm trapped in the sunken place, like in that Jordan Peele movie *Get Out*. I wish *she* would get out.

Ayesha wraps her arm around Theo's neck. "How far are you into *Naruto*?" she asks him. I forgot she likes anime, too. And it takes a while for me to get that she's trying to get him to think about something else. I need to do the same.

Theo slurps the rest of the milkshake from the bottom of the glass and then answers. "I'm at the Chunin Exams arc."

"That's a good arc," she says. "My favorite arc is the Sasuke Recovery Mission."

I have no idea what any of this means, but it puts a smile on Theo's face, which puts a small one on my face despite everything that's happened today.

Karina's been blowing up my phone with calls, FaceTimes, and text messages—and I haven't answered any of them. She texts me again as I hold my phone and it brings a little calm to the tsunami trapped inside of me.

Karina

She's gone. I asked her to leave. Come home, honeybunches. Please answer. Are you and Theo okay? Where are you?

I don't have any reason not to believe her, but something about going back makes me a little hesitant. Then I tell myself I need to clear my head for a little bit alone in my room and part of me wants to process things more with Karina or Pops. And I think Theo needs it, also.

Eventually, that's what we do. Ayesha and Olly got here by car. They used Olly's parents' fancy-ass BMW.

"Want a ride home?" Olly asks.

"Nah. Theo and I rode my bike," I tell them. We all say our goodbyes, and Olly and Ayesha both give me that tight best-friend hug that makes me feel so loved and comforted and at ease for a little while. Then Theo and I get back on my bike and pedal home.

Sometimes I have this dream where I'm sinking in quicksand. It's one of my biggest fears. It's always a vast and deep body of quicksand and all my weight slowly carries me to the bottom. I struggle and struggle and struggle to break free, but nothing works. I shut my eyes and repeat to myself that I'm not going to let this quicksand win, no matter how far I sink to the bottom, no matter how much sand and water gets in my mouth and stomach, no matter how much the pressure crushes me, no matter how much quicksand tires me out. I won't let it win. I won't die. I'm awake right now, which means I'm alive, but I can feel myself losing the fight the same way I do in that nightmare.

SEVEN

I CHAIN MY BIKE back to the side of the house, unsure of when I'll use it again. Hopefully, it's no time soon because my nuts are now pretty sore. But I grab Theo's hand and we slowly walk into the house. Karina attacks Theo with kisses and hugs and she tries to do the same for me, but we settle with a hug.

"Oh God! You're back and safe," she mutters mercifully. "I was worried. I didn't know where you guys were going."

Theo starts crying again. Karina rubs his back in a slow, circular motion. I hug him. There's a pause that lingers for what feels like an eternity as he sobs.

"Let it out, let it out," Karina says almost in a whisper, the syllables cracking and splitting in random places. I notice Pops is gone—maybe he had to go find a bar to get drunk enough that he forgets his problems instead of facing them.

Theo goes upstairs to his room, Biscuit following him up. He shuts his door—and I know he'll be in there for the rest of the day.

"We just went to Steak 'n Shake on Washington," I say. "And we met up with Ayesha and Olly."

"Okay, honeybunches." Her voice fills the room with concern. "Your father went to—"

"Karina." I stop her before she finishes. "Can I go lie down for a little while?" I'm not trying to be mean, just wanting a little space. Besides, I already know what she was trying to tell me.

Her lips tighten. "Yeah—yeah, of course, honeybunches."

"Thanks," I tell her with a tight-lipped somewhat smile.

"When you want to talk or if you need me, I'll just be down here reading my book."

Once I'm upstairs in my room, I lie across my bed and put a pillow across my face to muffle the sound of my crying. I cry enough that I could supply the planet with another entire body of water—the Giovanni Ocean. I let out tears over my birth mom's return. I let out tears over my life being fucked up. I let out tears about how even more messed up everything feels all of a sudden. I let out tears because I feel so, so alone.

I bet there's a scientific study out there about how if you're abandoned by a parent, all hell breaks loose inside you, all the strings break, all the ships sink. I bet there's another study about how if they try to come back, it suddenly may seem like the roots of your very existence are being violently uprooted by a stranger who hates plants. Like being jumped by a 7th Street Disciple. At least, that's how it feels right now.

I get an Instagram notification. It's a direct message. I recognize the username as David's.

David

Hey! You should give my last post a like. I'm trying to get people to see my painting of MLK. After all, it is black history month.

I ignore him once, but five minutes later he double DMs me, like he's determined.

David

Please??

Also, sorry again for almost running you over.

So I reply to him. I'm not really in the mood, but I don't want to be shitty, either.

Me

I put my phone in airplane mode so I don't receive any more notifications. I click onto my mellow-out playlist because I really, really need music to put my mind somewhere else. I have a playlist for almost every significant moment in my life. My mellow-out playlist completely relaxes me, transports me to a better place and gives me more peace.

"Foreign Hands" by George Ogilvie is the first song that plays, and it's the perfect one to get me to feel a little hope. But when I close my eyes, all hope flees me in a flash as I think about the day my birth mom walked out for the first time, the memory getting caught in my eyelids. It's like I'm a little kid all over again.

She has her bags in her hand and her thick, long black coat around her. I reach out for her hand, afraid of the thunder, afraid of the sirens. Tears cascade down her face like it's a window and there's a storm inside her. The thunder has never felt so close. The lightning comes and goes in piercing strikes, all electric purple and quick.

She picks up Theo and gets on one knee. She puts her hand on my shoulder and looks me right in the eye.

Then she says my name with a breath like it'll be her last. "Giovanni."

"Yes," I whisper, a lump wedging itself into my throat from my gut.

"I'm coming back, okay, G-Bug? Stay strong."

"Okay," I promise.

"I mean it," she says. "Do you mean it?"

I pause, feeling the world do cartwheels away from me. "Yeah," I say back.

She tells us she'll only be away for a few weeks. "I'll be in Amsterdam, helping refugees. The time will fly by, G-Bug. I'll write you letters and everything. I promise." She smiles.

I hold my breath for as long as I can. I'm used to her going away and going all over the world, helping people, like an actual superhero. I know she always comes back. But there's something about this time. This time feels different.

She kisses me on the forehead twice, her lips gentle—so gentle, feeling like cotton balls dabbing my forehead.

Our last hug feels so velvety and warm, her soft hair wrapped around my tiny, bony shoulder.

Pops watches, standing a few feet away, now shaking his head as if he knows right now, in this very moment, that none of us will ever see her again.

Tears flood my eyes as my mom opens the door, walks out into the rain, and gets into her taxi.

I snap out of it, hating that I never even got a letter from her. Not from Amsterdam. Not from anyplace she went after. She never tried to come for me or reach out to me, until now, like I was some permanently past-tense piece of her life. I turn my notifications back on and notice a new email from her.

At first, I don't open it. I don't want to hear what she has to say. And it's not like she gave me much time to respond to her last email, crashing my house before I could even think about whether I wanted to email her back.

I'm through, I tell myself.

That lasts about ten minutes. Because here's what really sucks about having a piece missing from your life: the not knowing.

I open her email because I know I wouldn't be able to stand not knowing what's inside of it.

To: GioTheGr8@gmail.com
From: missjackie01@global.net
Subject: Thinking about you

G-Bug,
If you want to talk to me, I'll be here when you're ready.
I'm so sorry for just showing up like that after all this time. There's so much for us to talk about and I have so much explaining to do. Please give me that chance.

Love, Mom

Something begins to build up inside me, pulsing through my veins. I don't know where the urge comes from, but I reach into my nightstand drawer and snatch out the photo of my birth mom that Karina gave me.

I stare at it.

A tear falls.

And then I'm furiously ripping it to shreds, piece by piece, tossing each fragment across my room. My room becomes a snow globe of paper and tears.

Fuck.

EIGHT

SUNDAY AND ANOTHER ONE of Pops' sermons on the complicated nature of forgiveness flies by and suddenly it's Monday. Despite not getting any more emails from my birth mom, it's the only thing I thought about over the weekend. And shit, man, I consider staying in bed for the rest of my life, never leaving my room. But I can't. I have to go to school and I have to do things and I have to carry on. And I damn sure can't miss basketball practice.

We've got another big game soon, and if I missed practice, Coach would either sit me out for our game as a way of punishment or completely kick me off the team. Neither are options I'm willing to risk. Me explaining to Coach that my birth mom showed up at my house after being gone half my life and how that sent me into a dark place would only get me a blank stare. He always tells me and my teammates that "personal lives stay off the court." So I don't think all of this is exactly something he'd empathize with.

I will myself to get up and out of bed. I brush my teeth and shower in the bathroom, staring at my face in the mirror afterward. Olly and Ayesha blow up my phone, checking up on me, as

I get changed into my Black Panther hoodie (#WakandaForever) and some gray joggers. I put on my Curry 5s.

Theo's downstairs, where he's eating a bowl of Cinnamon Toast Crunch mixed with Reese's Puffs. He eats some combination like this every morning.

"Morning, Theo," I say.

"Morning," he says back to me with a milk mustache.

"What are you kiddos up to?" Karina asks, walking into the dining area in her scrubs.

"Nothing," Theo answers for us.

"You doing okay, honeybunches?" Karina leans in and asks me, holding my arm and thumbing it.

I hesitate. She probably knows I've been real out of it the last couple days. "Better, I think."

I pour myself a bowl of Theo's famous mashup—Cinnamon Toast Crunch and Puffs. Unlike Theo, I put my milk in second, after the cereal. I sit at the table and eat next to him.

Pops walks into the dining area and sits at the table, wearing a suit and tie and holding a newspaper. He always turns to the obituary section first every morning. It's depressing, but he usually knows at least one person. Someone's always getting ganked in the Haven, but never anyone I know like that.

Pops doesn't say anything the whole time he reads, doesn't even acknowledge us in the same room as him.

Karina has to get him to talk. "What's going on at the church today that has you looking so fresh?" Karina's only a few years younger than Pops, but she's always trying to use slang to be cool. It makes me cringe sometimes.

"Board meeting," he says bluntly.

"Oh, okay." Karina starts to make coffee. "How long will that be? We've got Theo's parent-teacher conference tonight."

"Just a couple hours," he says. "We should be done in time." And just like that, he goes back to reading the obituary section of the newspaper.

"Theo, when you're ready for school, make sure you grab your big coat because it's cold out, okay? It's supposed to be like twenty-something degrees out," Karina tells him, kind of looking at him in a scold.

"Okaaaaay. I'm not a little kid," Theo says, sassing back a little.

"All right, all right, I'm just making sure you know," she says, sipping her coffee, which looks like it has way too much creamer.

Nobody mentions Jackie. It's like, if we don't talk about it, it never happened.

When it's time to take Theo to school, I run over my mental checklist of *Things To Not Leave At Home*—a mental checklist I go over every school morning. I make sure I always have the right textbooks, my homework, a snack so I can sneak-eat in class, gum, and my hairbrush. I'm in the process of hoping for some waves to come in, so I need my brush on hand even at school. And of course, I need gum because I always want my breath to be minty fresh because you never know what the lunch ladies might be serving—I'm not trying to have hot, stanky breath for a whole school day.

"I'm ready," Theo says, all bundled up and ready to go, backpack on and everything.

I grab for his hand and we head out, after saying our *see you later*s to Karina and Pops. Karina's really superstitious and doesn't like us to say *goodbye* because she thinks that's bad luck like we'll be gone forever, never to return home again. And the older I get, the more I think maybe there's some truth in that.

It's cold as shit outside, my phone saying it's 31 degrees out with a freeze-your-nuts-off wind chill. Thankfully, Theo's school is close, and we get there in ten minutes. And it only takes him explaining one entire anime episode to me.

"Have a good day today, li'l bro," I tell him.

He looks at me and makes a face. "You too."

I watch him walk a few feet away from me before turning back.

"Hey, Gio?" he calls out.

"Yes?"

"You think one day I'll be able to walk to school by myself?"

Something inside me breaks, and I get choked up for a minute. I know that's one of his dreams. "Yeah, Theo," I say. "I think one day, you will be able to."

He smiles at me and I have no choice but to smile back since his is infectious. I have to catch the city bus because there's no school bus that comes to our neighborhood. I check the bus app to see when the next one is as I walk back to the place where it stops, which is also conveniently closer to the direction of my school in case I need to walk the whole way there. I also notice missed texts from Olly and Ayesha in our group chat. One of the texts from Ayesha is about David's DM about some MLK painting that I still haven't looked at. Apparently, he messaged her about it, too. Another one of their texts is about how she and Olly caught an earlier bus.

I catch one of the last city buses that runs near West Haven before school starts. I sit in between a man who smells like Fritos and an old lady who keeps singing the chorus to Dolly Parton's "Jolene" over and over again. I've honestly never been so excited to step off the bus and walk the rest of the way to Ben Davis High.

The bell rings kinda quick afterward, and I brush past random people as I make my way to my locker to get my books before I'm late to take my AP Government quiz that I 100 percent didn't study for. Each of my morning classes feels like one mind punishment after another, and I'm not able to think about what the teachers are saying or what projects are about to be due. Nah. All I can think about is my birth mom. Like a thorn stuck in my side. Or, like, an annoying splinter that won't come out.

At lunchtime, I grab my food and shuffle to my seat. I never sit with my teammates, but they look over and make faces at me as I pass by, like I'm Benedict Arnold–ing them or some shit. I meet Olly and Ayesha at our usual lunch table in the Giant Café, which is the name of the cafeteria. Really, there's nothing giant about this café other than our school mascot, but it's probably one of my favorite places to be in the entire school. There's something about the paintings of famous Black people on the walls that motivates me.

When I sit down, they both are quiet.

"You okay?" Ayesha asks me. "You haven't replied to any of our messages."

"I'm fine," I say, not actually believing that. "I just haven't gotten around to them yet. Sorry."

"You don't have to apologize, yo," Olly says. "We were just worried about you. Something happen with your mom again?"

"No. Can we please talk about something else? Literally anything!" I plead.

"Yeah, that's cool with me," Olly answers.

"I got a sixty-eight on that government quiz. Would it be okay if I dropped out now?" Ayesha asks the table. It's usually just the three of us at the table, and I can tell by the way she slumps down into her chair, she's ready to for real call it quits on the whole high school thing.

"What would you do if you did?" I ask her. Leave it to me to be the sensible one. Leave it to me to ask something like this when I don't entirely feel like convincing her either way.

"I don't know. Maybe marry Channing Tatum and have beautiful, mixed, rich babies, and move somewhere nice, like Los Angeles or . . . Hawaii and live happily ever after?"

"That would be so dope," Olly intercedes, dipping french fries in mayo and barbecue sauce. "Not the marrying Magic Mike part, though. My aunt Jan lives in Hawaii."

Ayesha sighs and sits up in her seat again. "What did you guys get on that quiz?" she asks.

I load up my grade on our school's new grading portal app. I haven't checked the grade. I got a seventy, which is only two whole points higher than Ayesha's, but there's no way I'm going to announce this to make her feel worse.

Olly gladly gives up his grade, showing off because he studied. "Ninety-one," he says with pride, chest out. "Sometimes it does help that my parents are always watching Fox News and CNN."

"Nerd," I say, somewhat serious, somewhat joking.

"Shut up, Gio," he says. "Not all of us can be on the basketball team and not have to worry about grades."

"I still have to worry about my grades," I say. "I'm in high school with no guarantee to get recruited anywhere."

And just like that, Olly drops it and we move on to something else.

"Mind if I join you guys?" a familiar voice says behind me as I shove my turkey sandwich into my mouth like a heathen. I look up and of course. It's him. I almost choke on the bite of sandwich as it goes down my throat.

"Definitely!" Ayesha quickly agrees to let David sit down with us. I haven't told her or Olly how he showed up at my house after what happened and how he found my Instagram account to start following me. We make room at the table for him anyway, though, and I kind of want to pack up and eat somewhere else. Maybe even in the bathroom if I have to. I don't want to be around new people right now.

"Thanks for being so kind," David murmurs shyly. He makes this face like the lost new kid who's just made some friends.

"No problem," Olly mutters.

Everything goes quiet for a moment at our table,

conversations happening at all the tables surrounding us so loud I can make out full details. The football jocks are talking about how all of their girlfriends are forcing them to watch *Queer Eye*. The marching band nerds are talking about some contest they lost to a rival school. I think about how I used to want to be in marching band and play the flute because of my birth mom. She would play me lullabies with her flute when I'd have trouble sleeping as a kid. Now I think about how I never want to go near a flute.

"Anyway, I have an announcement," Olly blurts out, completely startling me.

"What?" I say, kind of not wanting to engage.

"If this is your way of saying that you've stupidly proposed to your imaginary girlfriend, Grace, you can keep it to yourself," Ayesha says with a neck roll.

"No, that's not it," Olly says slowly. "And Grace is definitely real, thank you very much." He's so in denial it's kind of embarrassing.

David looks up at him. "Are you a thirty-year-old man who's been eating nothing but mac and cheese for the past ten years?"

We all look at him.

"What?" Olly stares blankly.

"Sorry, that was the subject of a YouTube documentary I watched last night," David says shyly.

"I'm running for class president," Olly announces brightly, with his arms out like he wants us to cheer for him.

"That's great, Olly," Ayesha says, and they fist-bump. "I'll definitely vote for you."

"Yeah, man, that's really good," David adds. "Congrats!"

"Proud of you for doing that," I add. "First, you are the king of flag football . . . and now this. Look at you."

"Thanks, guys," Olly says. "I really feel all the love."

I place my right hand in front of him. He puts his left one out front to meet mine there and we do our handshake. Yeah, Olly, Ayesha, and I have a secret handshake that nobody else knows. My favorite part is the snap at the end of it. My birth mom was the one who taught me about secret handshakes, because we had one, too, before she left. The sad thing, though, is that I don't even remember it.

Out of nowhere David asks, "How long have you two been dating?" He points at Ayesha and me.

"No, no, no," I say, shaking my head hard. "We don't date anymore. That's in the past."

"Yep," Ayesha interjects. "Good and dead. We're better off as friends anyway."

"Oh! I'm sorry," David says. "I just assumed . . . because . . . never mind."

"You're all good," Ayesha says.

I look over at Olly, who seems like he wants to say something. "I'm actually kind of glad you two broke up. Being a third wheel fucking sucks."

David laughs. "I've been there. Can relate." The two of them dap up.

"Gisha is over for good," I say.

"Gisha?" Olly wonders, raising an eyebrow. David raises his also.

"Gisha," Ayesha explains. "Gio plus Ayesha equals Gisha."

"Ohhhh," Olly exhales.

Some silence tides in all of a sudden and almost takes me back to my dark thoughts from earlier. I need a distraction—something, anything. Luckily, Ayesha saves me.

"So, David, what school are you coming from?" she asks.

"I'm from Kansas. You've probably never heard of Soho High."

"Nope, but sounds like there were so' hoes there," Ayesha says, and cracks the hell up. Olly nearly falls out of his seat from laughing, too, high-fiving her for the joke.

"Ha. That's a good one," David says, and smiles again. "I'm really excited to be here at Ben Davis. I feel like there's so many more opportunities here. I'm glad the universe brought me this way."

"Well, welcome to Ben Davis and the coolest group of friends in the whole school," Ayesha says. I stare at her, my eyes widening. I can't believe she's inviting him to be a part of our crew. I mean, it's not like I don't like David, and it's not like our group is super exclusive or whatever, but I mean, there are things that only Olly and Ayesha know about me and I don't know *anything* about David—and right now isn't really a good time for me to just let more strangers into my life. Even if part of me wants to know his story of how he ended up in the Haven of all places.

When she finally notices my gaze, she puts a hand on mine and mouths the word "What?"

And I mouth the word "No" back at her.

"I can see you even though you're mouthing the words," David says, matter-of-fact. "I can go if you don't feel comfortable."

He starts to lift up out of his seat, packing up his tray.

"No," I insist. "Sorry. I'm just going through a lot. It's not you. It's . . . me."

David settles back into his chair, his leather jacket rubbing against the back of it and making a squeaky kind of fart noise. "Sorry things are tough."

"Yeah, me too," I say. "I wish the last week of my life would just rewind itself."

"Don't be depressing," Ayesha snaps at me. "Positive vibes only when we're in the Giant Café, remember?" I almost forget what she's referring to—then I remember a pact we made one time when we were sophomores. I wonder why she chose now to bring that up.

"Dude, you're a really, really good painter," Olly says to David. "I saw the one you did of MLK and the one you did of Rosa Parks."

"And the one of my forever crush, Barack Obama," Ayesha adds.

"Thank you, thank you," David says, his cheeks kind of turning rosy red. "I'm glad you guys like my work. I spent a lot of time on those."

"David the Painter," Ayesha goes. "That's gonna be your new name from now on."

"That's not very original," I tell her.

"But I like it," David says, smiling, showing his perfect set of teeth.

I open an apple juice and put a straw in. Ayesha asks David, "So, what all are you into?"

"Like . . . for fun?" he asks, his eyes flitting.

"Yeah," she responds.

David runs a hand through his hair. "Well, I'm into painting, playing basketball, Shakespeare, and creating playlists. Like. That's my thing."

Wait. That's *my* thing.

Ayesha notices this, too, saying, "Minus the painting and the Shakespeare, you're like the white version of Gio."

"Shut the hell up," I tell her, rolling my eyes.

Olly jumps in with "I saw on your Insta that you did a portrait of Ariana Grande. The day that I marry her, it will send me to heaven."

David chuckles. "I'm glad that you're so sure you'll end up marrying her. But yeah, I love Ari so much. She's, like, the gay icon of gay icons."

"Gay icon?" Olly and Ayesha both ask.

"Meaning a lot of gay people like her music and what she stands for," David explains.

"Oh, okay," Ayesha says.

"So, you're gay?" I swear Olly's so fucking nosy sometimes. I glance at David, expecting him to look embarrassed, but he actually looks pretty unfazed.

"No, I'm not. Bisexual, actually," he answers, and I nearly choke on my sip of apple juice. It all goes down the wrong tube—whatever wrong tube is in my throat.

"No way? Did you know Gio is also—" Olly cuts himself off when he sees my glare and my head shake.

"Is also what?" David asks.

"Is . . . uh . . . also a big fan of the Chicago Bulls," he finishes off with a lie.

"You know I'm a Golden State fan, bro," I tell him. "Steph and Klay are like my favorites."

"Oh. Right." He still pretends like he didn't know.

We get down to eating, and I'm relieved when the bell rings and lunch is over. My next couple of classes are mostly a breeze because I either drift to sleep in them or some of the jocks give the teacher a hard time, like Malik, who starts cracking jokes about Mr. Silva's camouflage crocs during chemistry. Malik even asks Mr. Silva if he prefers hunting for deer or wild geese. It's the laugh I need to get through the rest of the day. It's not until eighth period where I pull up my birth mom's email to read it again.

I'm in the middle of reading it all over again for maybe the tenth time when Mrs. Oberst comes over and forces my laptop shut. She slides over a pink piece of paper, not saying anything.

I unfold the pink piece of paper to read it. It's a detention slip. In the margin, she writes to see her after class.

The bell finally rings as she's mid-sentence about character foils. Everyone rushes up and out of the classroom, but I stay behind and walk up to her desk slowly, crumpling up the pink slip in my grasp.

"Is there something I can do to help you stay focused in my class?" Mrs. Oberst says. "College professors won't be as kind about this kind of thing as I am."

I don't know what to say. I just nod in agreement.

"You currently have a seventy-eight in my class. I'll need your full attention in class if you expect to pass, understand?"

"Yes, ma'am," I say.

She extends her hand, gesturing for the pink slip. I hand it over and watch her rip it up and put it in the trash. "I will see you tomorrow, Mr. Zander."

I turn around and walk out of her class, but before I'm out of the doorway, she calls for me again. I crane my neck around.

"Remember that I'm here to help you, Mr. Zander. If there's something going on at home or in your neighborhood, you can come to me."

I give her a tight-lipped smile, unsure of what to make of that, and walk down the hall.

The fact that I have a 78 in her class haunts me. If I get below that, I could be kicked off the basketball team. Damn.

NINE

▲▲▲▲▲▲

I MANAGE TO NOT think about my birth mom for a while. But once I get to basketball practice, all that changes. Whatever was working before suddenly stops and all kinds of images of her float around, her voice almost haunting me. I try to do my best to distract myself. I shake my head hard as I walk inside the gym, trying to get it out.

There's a strong odor in the gym as we have our shootaround, something like mildew and bleach, but it's not the only reason I want to throw up.

I'm here a few minutes early and I'm tossing up some mid-range shots with Malik. He's making all of his and I'm missing most of mine, but I keep chucking them up, hoping more fall in than rim out. A final jumper goes up and the ball barely even touches the rim. My whole game is off.

Malik clears his throat and wipes some of his lip sweat on his shoulder. "You a'ight?"

I glance around me and then at him. He's working on his three-point shot. He's already got a good one. His form looks like Kobe's—or at least, that's according to the highlights I've seen of him, since he was before my time. I don't think he needs to work on it.

I turn back to Malik to answer his question. "I'm good, man," I lie.

"You sure?"

I nod, lying once more. This time, without words.

He shrugs at me. "A'ight then, homie." His shot drains through the net and he yells out, "Damn, I'm cash!" Malik is pretty cocky, but if I shot as good of a percentage as him, I might be, too. Malik has a real chance to play in college. That's my dream. For me to play at some local school that would accept me, show the world how good I can be, and maybe qualify for the NBA draft.

Coach Campbell walks into the gym and our other teammates flood in for practice. Coach calls a team huddle near the stands like usual when he wants to brief us about what we'll be doing in practice. Practice is usually routine: We watch some film of previous games we've played to learn from our mistakes, work through some different plays, and then have a brief scrimmage. Every now and then, Coach will tell us that we'll be spending time in the weight room, working out as a team. I'm hoping today is not one of those days.

Coach blows the whistle for the scrimmage to begin. There are jerseys and there are skins. I'm skins, so I'm not wearing a shirt. David's guarding me and he's so zoned in on his game that he's not even making eye contact with me. He's so focused on the ball in my hands.

I try to dribble, maybe cross him, but he steals the ball and lays it up on the other end.

Next thing I hear is Coach Campbell's voice shout, "Come on, Zander! No easy buckets!"

Skins get the ball back and Malik brings the ball up the court. He passes to me in the corner. David's kind of sagging off me, so I could maybe do a quick jab and then shoot in his face, hopefully draining it. But that might not be good shot selection. I calculate my next move, then dribble in and do a spin move around him—something I've seen guys like Kobe or Steph Curry do in highlights. But I end up tripping over my own shoes and falling down to the ground, hard. David just steals the ball and throws it up for Savtaj, the tallest guy on our team, to catch and dunk.

"Bro, what the fuck?" Malik is getting more and more pissed with me. Even though this is just a practice, this isn't *just* a practice to Malik. He stays competitive.

I throw my hands up, surrendering like. "My bad, my bad."

Somehow Malik, with the help of Nick, the guy who's playing the role of our sixth man and backup power forward, is able to rip the ball from Jason, a big, muscular dude who was going up for a shot. Malik runs point and dribbles up the court again, calling a play for us—the same play we just learned from Coach. I already forgot the play, so I don't even know where to stand, where my feet should end up, or anything. I just hope and pray I guess correctly.

I run out to the left corner for a three-pointer. I'm usually the team's best scorer.

"What are you doing?" Coach yells, and once I make eye contact with him, I know he's talking about me. Damn. His hands are motioning for me to get in the post. I run over and wait in the paint until Malik bounce passes me the ball. I try backing David down and then doing my signature fadeaway jumper. I realize now that's what Coach wants me to do. It rattles around the rim, but then goes flying out.

"Shit!" I shout at myself, angry that I can't make anything. I'm really playing like ass.

Coach blows his whistle, and it catches me off guard at first. It's his way of stopping the scrimmage completely. "Zander, sit," he says. He points at one of the guys sitting down on the bleachers and subs him in for me.

"What is going on, Zander?" Coach asks me, cleaning the spit from his whistle with the tight shirt stuck to his round, jiggly belly.

I frown, place my head in my hands, and let out the world's deepest, most frustration-filled sigh. Then I answer him in an unassured tone, "I don't know."

"Well, you sit there and gather your thoughts. We need you hitting shots," he says. I'm not sure if that's supposed to be motivation or what, but I'm too consumed by rage and confusion.

Coach leaves me sitting in the same place for the remainder of practice and it fucking sucks because the frustration doesn't leave.

While everyone else heads to the showers to get clean clothes on and head home, I head for the band room. It's usually empty and unlocked during practice and it's my second favorite place in the whole school to go when I need a breather.

This used to be one of the spots I went to after school to buy weed from Malik. I sit behind an organ. I didn't even know bands had organs—I've never noticed it in all my times coming in here. Maybe it's new?

I sit there and count in my head slowly.

One.

Two.

Three.

I need this breather, I tell myself, sitting still, not saying a word, just listening to the sound of my inhaling and exhaling as it gets softer and softer. After a while, I'm crying, and not the ending of a sad movie crying—no, weeping hard, sobbing uncontrollably. I never cry like this, but damn, shit just feels too fucking hard not to, man. And I don't know what to do. That makes shit ten times worse. Man, fuck this.

I lift up, with my tears blurring my vision, and begin knocking over all the chairs and music stands. Each piece some sort of symbol for all the shit in my life tumbling down.

"Whoa, whoa, whoa! What's going on in here?"

I wipe my blurred eyes and see that it's David. His hair looks different and slicker and almost redder than before from the shower he took in the locker room, but he's back in that black leather jacket. "Are you okay?"

I'm really sick of those words right now. Clearly, I'm not.

"No," I say. I don't know why, but he's the first one aside from Olly and Ayesha that I admit this to.

I sit down on one of the chairs that I haven't knocked over. A sheet of music still rests on the stand. It's selections from the

Game of Thrones soundtrack. I kick the stand down and the sheet of music flies into the air like a kite at first before it swoops onto the ground.

"Everyone misses shots, dude," he says. "Nothing to beat yourself up about."

"No," I say.

But he keeps going. "I had one game back in Kansas where I seriously went zero for twelve in the first half. The coach took me out for the rest of the game."

"No," I say again. "It's not just about missing the shots. It's that I can't even focus on making the shots. I was just throwing shit up, throwing prayers up, hoping they were answered with points. But nothing."

David weaves through the fallen chairs and music stands and then sits in one that's somewhat close to the one I'm in. "Cat's got your brain?"

I make a confused face at him. I didn't think that was a thing.

"Sorry, my dad's always saying that," he says. "I know it's not right, but—"

"I just fucking hate my brain right now," I say. "It won't shut off."

"You know your brain is always processing stuff. Sometimes you've got to give yourself permission to not think."

"I wish I could stop thinking forever," I say, probably sounding really dramatic.

"Sometimes I feel that way, too." He looks away.

"It just seems like everything around me is crashing and burning all at once," I say, some amount of defeat in my voice.

Again, I'm probably being really dramatic right now.

He looks back at me. "Maybe if we keep letting all those things crash and burn before our eyes, they'll somehow fall back in place or maybe something new will come out from the ashes. Like a phoenix."

"Hmm" is all I can respond with.

"Sorry, I'll get off my deep philosophical soapbox now. Such a damn nerd, aren't I?"

"Nah," I reply after a breath. "It helps to put some of this into perspective. Somehow."

David blinks at me and I really notice his red hair, bright pink lips, and deep ocean-like blue eyes. "Oh good. I'm sorry things are tough for you right now."

"I—I should probably get going," I say. "Thanks for talking to me, man. I don't need to be sharing all my issues with you."

"It's no problem. I'm just across the street from you if you ever want to come over to hang out and talk more," David says with a welcoming smile.

"Thanks," I tell him, giving him a slight nod before he walks out of the band room and out of sight. I check the time on my phone and, shit, I'm almost late for the bus. I try to quickly straighten up the band room in a somewhat accurate way and make my own departure.

Once I'm outside I walk down the street to wait for the bus at the stop. I send a quick text to Olly and Ayesha to tell them that I just had a damn breakdown in the band room. I like that I can be vulnerable about things like that with them.

Olly

Holy fuck man. U wanna talk?

Ayesha

GIO! I'm worried about u! U sure ur ok?

Me

I'm ok now

Ayesha

Good. Good.

Olly

u two should cum over

Me

OLLY. It's C-O-M-E.

Olly

I know what I sent. The offer stands.

Ayesha

I'm in. Watch a movie? Things didn't pan out with Trevor, so I'm good to hang. Turns out, he's a real flake.

Olly

We can do that or play some 2K

I'm ok with coming over. I'll take the bus
to your place.

I quickly send a text to Pops and Karina letting them know that I won't be home in time for dinner tonight because I'm hanging out at Olly's place. Karina loves Olly's parents, so I know she'll be cool with it.

Once I'm on the bus, I look out the window and see a motorcycle going past. I know it's not David—the jacket's not right—but I think about him all the same. Then I think about what he said about the phoenix, and I wonder how that applies to me. All I feel right now is the burn. I'd really like to find the wings.

TEN

●●●●●●

THE BUS DROPS ME off about a block away from Olly's place. Olly's lived in the same house since he was in elementary school, and when we became friends, I used to make this same bus ride to his place all the time.

I make it to his huge, fancy, fenced-in house with multiple windows on each of the three stories of the house. Garden gnomes scattered all around the yard. Repotted plants on the front porch. I ring the doorbell.

Olly answers the door and lets me in. "Aye, what's up?"

"Sup."

I notice Ayesha beat me here. She greets me at the door with a hug. A huge-ass golden retriever comes scrambling, barking at me with excitement. "Hello, Spirit," I say, rubbing the top of her head. She knows me and I know her. I manage to get around her and inside to shut the door behind me before she attacks me with dog kisses.

I follow Olly and Ayesha into the living room area. I come here every now and then—definitely not as often as when we first became friends, but my favorite thing about this place is all the baby photos of Olly plastered on the walls and the smell of burnt incense, though I've never really seen any here. Netflix is pulled up already on the TV. Ayesha plops down onto the long couch against the wall and tells me, "We're trying to decide on something to watch."

"Oh, great," I say sarcastically. I hate trying to pick a movie with them. I love the two of them to death but trying to agree on a movie is like Germany trying to agree with the USA during either of the world wars. Spoiler: It doesn't work. The kitchen is close to the living room and I hear voices. Suddenly, Mrs. Robinson makes a grand entrance, dancing into the living room in her bright pink jogging suit like she's just getting back from a run or something. Her beach-blond hair has hot-pink streaks in it to match the jogging suit.

"Ayesha!!" she shouts, opening her arms and hugging her tight. She turns to me. "And Gio!!" As she wraps her arms around me, she smells like an assortment of flowers.

"Hi, Mrs. Robinson," I say, hugging her back. "It's good to see you."

Once upon a time, Olly was embarrassed by all this going down, but I don't think he cares much now.

"Always good to see you both," she says with her wide smile and pearly white teeth—so white they look bought. "Have you gotten taller, Gio?"

"Same height as the last time you saw me." I was over here at their place just a couple weeks ago. I guess to Mrs. Robinson that's like an entire season.

I look at Mrs. Robinson and then I look at Olly and then back at Mrs. Robinson and then back at Olly. It's uncanny. Olly's literally a replica of her. Same facial structure, nose, eyes, the whole deal. I know this isn't how DNA works, but, man, I swear Olly is made up of 90 percent his mom and 10 percent his dad.

"I'm so glad you two are over here," Mrs. Robinson goes.

"Gio's been having a rough time lately," Olly tells her.

"Oh, poor baby, everything all right?" Mrs. Robinson's forehead wrinkles and she gives me this real sincere, concerned look, like the loving mother she is to Olly.

I swallow hard. "Mhm," I lie.

"Well, all right. What's the plan for tonight, kiddos?"

"Just watching a movie, Mom," Olly answers. "That's why Netflix is on the TV."

"Okay, okay. I just saw that show about those five poor boys who got wrongly accused of attacking some lady in Central Park. It was good. I cried the whole way through it."

Olly rolls his eyes. *When They See Us?*

"Ah! That's what it was called!" Mrs. Robinson exclaims like she's been trying to figure this out for a while.

There's a loud clatter of something like metal hitting the ground. "Dennis?!" Mrs. Robinson calls out.

"Yes, honey?" a low voice says from the kitchen. Olly's dad.

"What was that loud noise?" she yells back, resting a hand on her hip.

"I dropped Spirit's water bowl all over the floor. It's okay," he answers.

She makes a face. "Well, I better get in there and see what he's really up to. Enjoy your movie, kiddos." She sashays back to the kitchen, but her scent still lingers.

"Okay, what are we gonna watch?" Ayesha asks, scrolling through her Instagram feed.

"My vote is *The Notebook*," I suggest. Something light-hearted.

"Duuuuude. That movie is trash. How about *The Human Centipede 2*?"

"EWWW!" Ayesha goes. "That movie is way more trash than *The Notebook*. *The Human Centipede* is a literal flaming pile of garbage."

"I've watched that like seventeen gazillion times. It's fucking amazing every time. But seven gazillion is a lot of times to watch one thing."

"How about I pick, since my birthday is coming up," Ayesha says. I definitely forgot her birthday was coming up, but it's still far enough out that it shouldn't be the reason she gets to pick the movie.

Olly and I both say, "No."

"Time for the random movie selection game," I suggest.

"Ummmm . . ." Ayesha thinks for a moment. "Rom-com . . . uh . . . fifteen."

I scroll through to find the rom-com section and then count over to the fifteenth movie. "*Hitch*."

"Not bad. At least there's Will Smith in it. What a daddy," she says, popping gum I didn't even know she was chewing on.

"Gross," Olly says. "He's old enough to actually be your dad. Anyway, horror and twenty-one."

I scroll and scroll and scroll. "*Zombieland*. Boooo!"

"Sigh," he says. "I was seriously hoping I got lucky . . . and my pick was the *Human Centipede 2*."

"My turn. I'm gonna do thriller and then nine." It's quiet as I scroll, but I can feel the rising anticipation. "*Inception!*"

"That's a classic," Olly goes. "I'll vote for *Inception*."

"*Inception*" is what I say.

Reluctantly, Ayesha whispers, "*Inception*." I'm glad I thought of this way of narrowing down our movie choices on the spot or else we would've been deciding all night long. We click play on the movie right when Mrs. Robinson comes back in with giant mixing bowls in each hand. Trail mix in one and Oreo balls in the other. "I've got some snaaaaacks for you kiddos," she sings like she's the main lady from *The Sound of Music*. The only musical I've ever watched. And the only musical I *plan* to ever watch.

"Heck yeah!" Olly shouts. "Love me some Oreo balls."

Ayesha snorts. "Me too. Me too. Thanks, Mrs. Rob."

"Oh, you sweet, sweet kiddos. I made all of it with love," she sings, and goes over to kiss Olly on the forehead.

And this makes him be all like, "Mom, no!"

She steps back and laughs at him. "My Olly Trolly's getting older." I'm holding back a laugh even when I don't feel like laughing. Olly's getting real red from her embarrassing him. This makes me want to laugh even harder. Then she heads back to the kitchen or wherever she's off to, taking Spirit with her.

Suddenly, I feel seriously jealous of Olly and how he has this perfect family with his mom who loves him so deeply that she'd do anything for him, like stay. He's got a dad who works a normal nine-to-five but still makes time for dad-son hang-outs. I mean, Olly's their only child, so he gets spoiled, and I know things aren't always this perfect, but still, being here sometimes is a reminder of what I don't have and what Olly does have. A reminder of my childhood struggle of overcoming abandonment. A reminder that maybe this is how things were supposed to be for me, even though they weren't. A reminder of my own brokenness.

We get thirty minutes into *Inception*, but all I can pay attention to is the rain falling from the sky. There's a nice window next to the TV with no curtains, so I can see cars swooshing and blurring past and I can see the sky getting darker and darker and I can see the drops of water falling and spinning and landing.

For a moment, I imagine that *I* am one of those raindrops. I think about what it might be like at first. But then, I think, maybe it's a lot like being myself. To have a destiny of being forgotten in a matter of time.

I'm sitting on the end and Ayesha is in between me and Olly. Thankfully, we're not actually making a human Oreo. She elbows me in my side and whispers, "What's wrong, Gio? Sorry. Maybe that's a stupid question. But you can tell me what you're feeling. You ain't gotta lie. Not to me."

I sigh. "Everything reminds me of her. And I can't get her out of my thoughts" is all I can say, and it kind of just slips out. But there's no going back now.

"Your mom?"

I nod.

Ayesha lets out a breath. "I feel, I feel. Does she keep emailing you?"

"Nah. Just that once after I saw her," I say, my voice rising.

"Shhhhhhh," Olly goes, trying to get us to be quiet because he's so focused on *Inception*. But his voice is muffled as he stuffs multiple Oreo balls in his mouth at once. Ayesha rolls her eyes at him.

I go on. "Part of me was almost just getting through all the what-ifs. Part of me was on the way of completely forgetting about her, I think." I don't know if that's entirely true, but I say it anyway because that's at least what things felt like.

Ayesha just nods and listens, offering no words.

"Ayesha, this fucking sucks. My head is everywhere but where I want it to be. Fuck that. More like where it *needs* to be. I fucking sucked at practice because I kept thinking about her and about what she said."

Ayesha reaches for the bowl of trail mix and puts a bunch in her mouth. She chews and then swallows before talking. "I've got a confession," she says.

"What?" I scratch at my arm.

"I always think about the time when you used to play out the day when you'd be reunited with your mom."

Damn, I almost forgot about that. That was way back when Ayesha and I were in eighth grade. I used to create these perfect scenarios where my birth mom and I would reunite and things would be fine and normal, like nothing ever happened. In science class, we learned that after a female penguin lays an egg, she leaves it with her mate, then heads back to the sea. She leaves for two whole months, embarking on a dangerous journey to feed at the sea and gather food, but she eventually returns to be with her baby . . . and then feeds it regurgitated fish. I told myself that my mom was like a female penguin—she went away to get things that I needed to survive, but she would come back, and I would be as happy as a baby penguin. Ayesha thought that was cool. She would always ask me what I wanted my mom to bring back for me from the sea.

And then once I grew out of believing that, I pieced together a whole other story in my head where I had convinced myself she was so good at helping refugees that she was hired as a secret agent working for the CIA, FBI, or some underground organization where she had to track down a bunch of bad guys and once her mission was over, she would come back, and we'd go on an epic road trip together and she'd tell me all the stories about her taking down the bad guys. Ayesha would go around telling people my mom was a secret agent so that people didn't mess with me.

I made up *anything*.

I couldn't allow myself to believe that my own mom wanted to forget me.

I convinced myself that she'd left for such a good reason, that she stayed away for such a good reason, and that I couldn't be upset with her. Slowly that turned into me thinking that maybe she would never come back and blaming myself for her leaving. I thought maybe I wasn't enough. Maybe I wasn't enough for her to come back to. Maybe I was too messed up of a kid for her to handle. Maybe she wanted a new family. Maybe she simply just didn't want me.

Not gonna lie. I always thought the moment I saw her I might've been a little mad at her, but my excitement and my happiness from her return would overpower my anger and everything would be okay. I could just go on, keeping on paddling my way through the swamp of life. But no. The very second I saw her, the bottom fell out of the boat, and I plunged right into it, helpless and furious.

All I say back to her is "Yeah." It's funny how things change just like that.

"You were so filled up with hope," she says. "The last couple days I've been so sad for my friend. For you. I've been sad to see that look in your eyes. You're like a brother to me and I know this is breaking you down."

I think for a moment. She's right. She usually is. Suddenly, I wonder if the darkness that I feel in my chest is there because I'm holding on to it rather than emptying it out. Something inside me is stirring and stirring and it feels wrong. I can't focus on anything. Shit, I can't even watch *Inception* without my mood completely failing. I remember feeling something like this when I was a sophomore, when I was meeting with Dr. McCullough. She said I had depression. She said you know it's that when you feel like you can't escape your thoughts, when even the smallest and easiest tasks in life feel as hard as climbing the tallest mountain.

Ayesha rubs my back in a slow motion that feels comforting. Something about just being with the two of them right now is helping me, and I try to focus on what's happening in the movie, not at all enjoying it as much as the first eight times I've watched it. Something in my brain just won't stop ticking.

When I get home later after *Inception* and a few rounds of *Mario Kart* on Olly's Nintendo Switch, I grab my basketball and try to throw up some shots at the end of my driveway. Basketball usually is the thing that clears my head, but it's not working. I'm wearing layers of long-sleeved shirts underneath my hoodie and there's so much restriction for my arms, so it makes my normal jump shot feel a little off. I can't even fucking make a layup on my own hoop.

It's like 46 degrees, but if I get to moving around some more, I can heat up. I practice my crossover and layups for a few minutes. Then I hear a car pull up somewhere close and then shut off. The sound of keys rattling gets closer and closer, but I don't really think anything of it—not until I hear a familiar voice.

"Hi," the voice says. I spin around. It's too dark to see clearly, but the streetlight is on, and after squinting for a second, I recognize the Converse, leather jacket, mess of red hair walking closer to me. David. Again.

"Hey," I say, nodding at him, then going in for another quick layup, watching the ball roll around the rim before going in. Finally. The first shot I've made in a minute.

"Wanna play one-on-one?" he asks. I scan him again. Leather jacket. Jeans. Converse? No way he can beat me in that. I think for a moment. I'm not really in the mood anyway, but maybe it's a last option that can help transport my brain elsewhere. A final try before I put the surrender flag in the dirt.

"I wouldn't want to embarrass you," I tell him.

He laughs and looks up at the stars, then back at me. "Sounds like a challenge. I accept."

I check him the ball, knowing good and damn well that he's about to take this L. I mean, not only is he in tight-ass skinny jeans, but he sure as hell doesn't know some of the hood tricks that I'm about to pull out on him. He checks the ball back, and before he even lets out another breath, I'm around him, going for a finger roll.

He raises an eyebrow. I pass him the ball, ready. He dribbles behind his back, trying to show off, before he attempts to nut-meg me, which is when someone tries to throw the ball through your legs—but I rip it, take it out, and then dunk it as hard as I can. Feels so good I almost let out a scream. But some people in this neighborhood are asleep.

I'm smiling hard, and I don't realize it until David says, "Oh, you're just going to smile in my face now, huh?" His face is so intense, like mine is fueling him.

He gets the ball again and dribbles it, alternating hands, over to the shed, which I'd consider a three-point line. He makes a rainbow shot that looks so crisp and fresh, like a shot Steph Curry or Kevin Durant would make. All net. This dude has some game. I mean, I've seen him play on a real court, but playing against him is something completely different. Malik was right. White boy has some game for sure.

Next round, and he shoots a three-pointer again.

And again.

And again.

They say the three-pointer is the white boy's shot. Black people made the dunk popular. But the fact that he's hitting all these shots kind of pisses me off. I try not to be an asshole, because it's not his fault. He's done nothing to me except cook me. I'm glad we're done.

I sneak back into the house and grab two bottles of water out of the fridge for us, making sure I pet Biscuit on the head before I head back out.

I toss one to David, and we're out of breath as we unscrew our bottles and chug our water. Cicadas buzz symphonically in the distance.

"That was . . . awesome," David says, huffing and puffing. "I'm glad you have a court in your driveway."

I attempt a laugh that becomes almost like a small wheeze for air. "It was." I mean it, and what's funny is, he's so unaware of how much this helped me.

He stares at me and smiles again. I smile back before quickly wiping it away. Police sirens echo in the distance somewhere. I know they're coming to the Haven. I'm sure somebody's called them on one of the 7th Street Disciples. Some of them are up to no good, but a lot of them are innocent and sometimes get swept up in some bad situations. I throw up a quick prayer to God, or whoever listens to me above, for things to go smoothly. I've seen too many reports on TV about Black and brown people getting shot and killed.

"You pray?" David asks me when my eyes open. "I'm Catholic."

"Oh, umm, yeah," I say, super embarrassed. I don't know

why I am. Plenty of people in the world pray. "And Catholic? I don't think I've met anyone Catholic before."

"I pray, too," he says. "That's cool."

"Yeah," I respond. "Real cool. I was just prayin' for my hood. For the Disciples."

"The Disciples? Like Jesus's disciples?"

"Ha-ha," I laugh, kind of fragmentedly. I totally forgot about that reference. "Nah, I mean the Seventh Street Disciples. They're a gang that kind of runs this neighborhood. They're more like the Avengers of the hood. All they want to do is protect the Haven, but sometimes they make some bad choices and fuck shit up. But so did Cap and Iron Man and Thor."

It's quiet for a moment, the sirens getting closer and closer—so close I can see the flashing and then all of a sudden, they stop. David and I are just looking at each other and I can see the gears in his head processing what I mean.

"Hey, would you want to, uh, come over to my place?" he asks. "I recorded the Pacers–Golden State game tonight and was going to watch it now."

I'm so quick to agree to this. "Sure," I say.

"Awesome," he says, and turns around to walk toward his house. I neatly put my ball near the back door to my house where it was before and follow. We cross the street in silence and suddenly we're at his door. He slides it open gently because his parents are asleep, apparently, even this early.

We walk in and I'm hit with this huge waft of something like maple or cinnamon or brown sugar—whatever it is, it's really sweet, and I like it.

"Your house has a nice smell," I say. It comes out pretty awkward.

He kind of snorts. "My mom's really big on baking. It's why she made you a crème brûlée."

I follow him up the stairs that creak louder and louder the higher we climb up, which makes us both laugh out loud. There's no way anyone can really sleep through that sound.

Finally, we get to his room and he opens the door. I don't know what I was expecting his room to look like but it's still a surprise. He's got paintings plastered all over his room. Some really cool ones like a melting sun that's exploding into rainbow colors. Another one is a painting of Lady Gaga in her meat dress. That one makes me laugh.

"Wow, these are so good," I tell him, amazed.

He blushes. "Thanks. They're mine."

"You ever try to sell some of your work?" I ask. Middle-school Gio is coming out all of a sudden. Back in middle school, I went through this phase where every week I had some new side hustle. One week, I'd be the guy who would sell a piece of gum for fifty cents. The next week, I'd be selling Flamin' Hot Cheetos and Takis for two dollars a bag. I was all about making money. But his paintings—they for real deserve to be sold and hung in people's homes everywhere. They're that good.

He answers, "No, I don't think so. I mean, someday maybe I will. But not right now. I'm not *that* good at it yet. It's just something that I like to do for fun. It relaxes me."

"That's dope," I say.

He smiles. "My paintings are such loyal companions. They

make me laugh and smile and break down and want to under-stand life more and more."

Hmm. That's pretty deep, but I get it. For a brief moment, I try to think if I have anything in my life that makes me feel like that, and the only thing that I can think of are my playlists.

He sits on his bed and pats the spot next to him. His bed has black and white squares on it like a checkerboard, and he grabs for the remote to turn on the TV. He starts playing the game.

"So, you're really a Golden State fan, eh?" David asks me. He slips out of his jacket and takes off his shirt. I try not to look. He changes into a different shirt. One that has Baby Yoda on it. I haven't seen *Star Wars* yet—like, any of them, so I hope we don't talk about it. But I've seen all the hilarious Baby Yoda memes on Twitter and Instagram.

"Yeah," I say. "I am. I love Steph Curry and Klay Thompson, man. The Splash Brothers are legit."

"They're awesome to watch," he says. "But sadly, I'm a New York Knicks fan."

"Sorry, bro. That's a very sorry-ass franchise," I say, and he laughs.

"I know, I know. I wish they were good again."

"Why do you like them?"

"My dad is a New York Knicks fan, so he got to watch Patrick Ewing and then later on he got to see Carmelo Anthony. He grew up in Harlem."

"Harlem? For real? I thought only Black people and brown people lived there." I worry I sound stupid, but that's for real all

I thought. I've never been there, though, so I wouldn't really know.

"Mostly," David answers, staring at the TV. "But my dad said there were a couple of white families around other than his."

"Hmm, interesting," I murmur, resting my hands in my lap. What he says sounds believable. I mean, if he's in West Haven, there really must be white folks living in Harlem.

"Baaaaaaaaang!" the announcer shouts as someone hits a shot.

I glance back at the game playing on the screen and see a replay of Steph hitting a three-pointer from the logo.

"Whoa. That man is something special," David says. "I'd kill to have him on the Knicks."

"Did you know that's where he really wanted to be when he got drafted?"

"That's what my dad told me," he says. "But every time I think about it, I get a little bit sad."

"I feel you, man," I say.

I play with the strings of my hoodie. I'm suddenly feeling really warm and my heart is still thudding in my chest a little.

"You can relax and kick back if you want, man," David offers. "Get comfortable."

"I—I'm . . . good," I say. I hope that didn't come out like I'm being a dickhead.

We're quiet for a long while, just the two of us paying attention to the game. I see Steph and Klay go back and forth with hitting shots from waaaaay deep, even see a couple dunks from our new center.

"You okay?" David asks out of nowhere. "It seems like you're being weird. I don't like weird."

We lock eyes for once. "I . . . umm . . . no, sorry, I'm not trying to be weird right now."

"Is it because I'm bi? Because I thought we were just two dudes hanging out, but if you're some homophobic prick, let me know now, so I—"

"Nah, nah, nah," I say to him, shaking my head, trying to get him to calm down. "It's not that. I'm bi, too." I say it matter-of-factly, waiting for his reaction.

His blue eyes get real wide. "What? Really?"

I nod at him. "Olly was trying to tell you that at lunch, but I stopped him. I wanted to be the one to tell you when I wanted to. *If* . . . I wanted to."

"Great, now I feel like a dick for kind of putting shit on you," he goes, slapping himself on the leg so hard *I* can feel the sting.

"Nah, man, it's okay," I say. "It's fine. And I'm sorry that it seems like I've been weird or avoidant. I mean, you're super chill and all, but I don't really know you that well and I'm dealing with so much shit right now."

David doesn't say anything. He just blinks and remains still. I don't blame him.

"Lately I've felt so much like all my emotions are so exposed to the world and I feel like I've got no place to hide." As if to prove my point, my voice cracks as I say this.

I close my eyes to stop any tears, but I can tell David scoots closer to me by how the mattress moves. He puts a hand on my arm and says, "You should eat some M&M's. You can't be sad anymore if you eat M&M's, especially the peanut butter ones." I open my eyes and find him wrestling in the night-stand, until he finds what he's looking for and tosses me a shareable-sized package of peanut butter M&M's.

I stare at the bag and then stare at him.

"Sorry, I was just trying to make you laugh right then," he says. "Epic fail, David."

I rip open the bag of M&M's and grab a few, popping them all in my mouth at once. They taste amazing. I haven't had any in a minute. I've missed them. I don't care what Olly might argue, these are definitely superior to the plain ones.

"Anyway, I don't know exactly what you're going through right now, but I understand," David says, diverting his eyes to look away. I trace his eyes and he's staring at a painting above the TV. I didn't even notice this one before for some reason. The painting is of someone's face. It's real abstract and there are so many blends of colors that I can't tell if it's a man or woman. *Maybe it's not meant to be either?* I think for a moment, in awe of his work.

David's quiet for a beat and I'm quiet, too. It's a quiet that's almost too loud, so I fake cough and clear my throat.

David lifts up off the bed and walks over to the painting. He takes slow steps to it, but once he gets in front of it, he brushes the painting with the back of his hand like he's petting an animal of some sort. "This is a painting I did of Kayla. My sister."

"She older or younger?" I ask.

"We were twins," he says.

"Were?" I can feel my eyebrows furrowing.

"She died by suicide a couple years ago," he says slowly, drawing in a deep breath when he finishes.

"Man, David, I'm so sorry to hear that. I—"

"Me too," he says back. "I think about her every day. I think about all the things that could've gone differently. I think about what *I* could have done differently. I think about our last conversation and was it nice enough or too mean." He keeps going on, but I let him have his moment to rant to me. I'm just feeling so consumed and overwhelmed by the grief I can see still shackled to him. It's a thing I can relate with to an extent. Damn, grief is already hard. But being exposed to someone else's just takes it to another level, man, and I feel so sad right now.

"David—"

He doesn't let me go on, but I don't think it's intentional. He's just got a lot to say, clearly. "You know . . . the last time I told her that I loved her was two whole months before she died? No one should wait that long to say I love you to someone they really do love. She died doing what she loved: swimming."

"Damn." All my other words have left me. I don't know what to say right now.

He sniffles a bit and brings himself back over to sit next to me on the bed. "But I'm not going to take away from what you're going through right now. I just wanted you to know that I understand hard shit."

"Thank you for that, man," I say.

He holds out his hand in the shape of a fist and I dab him there. "Of course. Sometimes I do this thing where I overshare, but I feel like I can trust you."

I fidget with my hands a little as the game goes to commercial. "Yeah," I say. "Same here." I don't know where that came from, but I think it's true.

"Really?" He looks at me with these big puppy eyes or like that cat from *Shrek*. Puss in Boots.

"I mean, you're just really real, man. Real recognizes real," I say.

He grins widely. There's a beat of silence, but then the game comes back from commercial and Golden State starts bringing the ball up the court. I'm only mildly focused on this game.

I brush my sweaty palms on my pants. "My mom walked out on my family when I was a little kid," I say almost in one breath, like it takes a herculean effort just to tell him. Even after I admitted that he seems really, well, *real*.

He puts a hand on my shoulder and listens, not saying a single thing. But his eyes say everything words can't right now, and that's enough.

A pang emerges in my chest. "It fucked me up, David. And I'm still fucked up from it." Something thick crawls up my throat, but I swallow hard.

"No kidding," he finally says. "Parental abandonment can really wreck you in a million different ways."

"What are you if the people who are supposed to love you can just leave you like you're nothing?" I stop for a second and think, *Oh shit*. "I'm talking about my birth mom here. Not your sister."

"It's okay," he says. "I mean, I've asked myself that question, for sure. I'm not sure there's an answer."

"I hear that. With my mom, sometimes it would just make me feel like I was lost and didn't belong and that hurt. Like I was always wearing someone else's clothes that didn't quite fit or, like, leading this life that was someone else's all along. But now she's come back. And now I feel even more lost."

He draws in some oxygen. "That feels hard, Gio."

"Yeah."

"I don't know what the right thing to tell you is, but Kayla read a lot of books and one day she shared something with me that gave me the courage to end a really toxic relationship. She said sometimes you have to leave people where they left you. Sometimes you have to reintroduce yourself to the pain they caused you so you can grieve and heal. Sometimes those people come back around, and the cycle goes on. But at the end, there's always more and more joy."

More silence as we both turn our gazes back to the TV. Golden State is crushing the Pacers. It's not worth watching anymore. I scoot back on the bed a little bit. Not too much, so it isn't weird.

"So, you make playlists, too, huh? I remember you mentioning that at lunch," I say.

"I do. Music is life. And I think my playlists are always saving me."

"Facts," I say back. "I feel the same."

"No kidding?"

"Nope. You wanna listen to one of mine right now?"

"I'd like that."

I pull out my phone, open up Spotify, and click on my playlist titled "Chillax." It's one that I go to a lot when I'm just kicking back with Olly and Ayesha and we're playing *Mario Kart* or *NBA 2K*.

Chillax

1. "Simmer" by Hayley Williams
2. "Forgiveness" by Paramore
3. "Outta My Head" by Khalid and John Mayer
4. "Dead and Gone" by Yola
5. "I Got 5 on It" by Luniz
6. "Train Wreck" by James Arthur
7. "Sparks" by James Bay
8. "Gimme All Your Love" by Alabama Shakes
9. "Butterfly" by Josh Garrels and Latifah Alattas
10. "Dreams" by Fleetwood Mac

I hit shuffle and the first song that plays is "I Got 5 on It" by Luniz. It's an old-school one that was waaaaay before my time. It's still a bop all these years later.

David bobs his head up and down. He's on beat, too, and I'm slightly impressed.

"Fiiiiiiive on it," he sings, like he's heard this song somewhere before.

"What you know about this?" I ask him, a grin easing up on my face.

"I saw that Jordan Peele movie," he says, turning red a little bit more and more. "And my dad, believe it or not, really loves that song. What are those odds, right?"

I nod. "Jordan Peele movies are great. And my Pops used to jam out to this song, before my mom left. He became a totally different person after that. I don't even think I've heard him listen to any music besides the church choir." I'm seriously wondering about this, and the more I do, the more it feels like such a sad fact.

"Church choir?" David ponders.

"My Pops is a pastor in this neighborhood," I say, probably saying it a little quietly. It's not something I broadcast to the whole world or would feel comfortable telling an average stranger, but David now lives in the Haven, he'll find out somehow. Besides, the more I talk to him, the more and more he doesn't feel like a stranger. "Our—I mean, Pops' church is on Seventh Street." I almost say *our* church, but it's not *ours*. It's *his*.

"What is it like to be a pastor's kid?" David asks.

"Weird. Because people 'round here claim to have known you and have changed your diapers and there's all these expectations for me to live a certain way, and I don't like it."

"I get that. I can tell you all about being a carpenter's son."

"True story: I thought a carpenter was a person who put carpet in houses till I was like twelve."

David laughs. "Not quite."

My phone buzzes and it's a text from Karina. She's asking me where I'm at. I text her that I'm only across the street, and she calms down. I shove my phone back in my pocket.

"Who's that?" David asks.

"My stepmom. Wondering where I am."

"You gotta go?"

"I probably should."

David lifts up and turns off his TV. "Thanks for hanging out," he says.

"No problem. I had fun," I say . . . which doesn't feel like enough. Even if there were moments that were awkward or silent or whatever, it was just so nice to be able to open up to him and to not really become this anxious mess, thinking about my birth mom, crying about it, and beating myself up. It's nice that he can relate to the weight of the grief I feel somewhat. That's something that I don't know I can say about Ayesha or Olly. I love them both, but I know they haven't experienced anything like that. And that's okay. I just think sometimes it's just nice when someone can just . . . know and understand. Like David can.

He says, "I can walk you down," then takes me through the dark hallway and down the creaky stairs and to the front door. He even opens it for me, and I walk out, noticing that it's raining again. He cuts on the porch light, so the raindrops splashing against his house meet the light and look more like golden coins raining from the sky.

"We should hang out again," he says shyly, again running a hand through his hair. I've noticed that he does that a lot. He's got great hair, so I don't entirely blame him.

In return, I say, "Yeah, I think we should."

When I get home, I'm met with kisses from Biscuit and questions from Pops and Karina. But once they figure that I'm okay and was just across the street for real, they let me go upstairs and get in my bed.

Alone again, I sit and stare at the darkness of my room, the black hole on my ceiling. I think and think and think. At one point, I actually reread the email she sent and end up crying myself to sleep.

I dream one of my nightmares. The one where I sink and drown in quicksand. None of my limbs move and I can't breathe. I sink and sink and sink, never making it to the bottom, but one thing's different about the nightmare. I hear my mom's voice, echoing around me. "G-Bug! Where are you?"

I call out to her. "Mom! Ma! Momma! Help me!" I cry out over and over again. But she doesn't find me. Her voice fades away.

ELEVEN

♦♦♦♦♦♦

BEFORE LUNCH THE NEXT day, I rush to my locker to collect my books for the next few classes I have so I don't have to stop again after lunch. Malik walks past me and I nod sup to him.

"What it do? What it do?" he says, waddling kind of like a penguin because his pants are hanging so low they're damn near at his ankles, showing his white boxers. He comes over to talk to me. As he approaches, I'm dazzled by those diamonds in his ear and chain around his neck.

"Not much. You?" I offer him, and we shake up once we're close enough.

"Same old. Same old. You been practicing your shot?"

"I did last night," I say. "Practice yesterday was real bad. Had a lot on my mind is all."

"I feel that, bruh. Don't let whatever it is ruin what gives you joy. I don't let my momma's sickness get to me when I'm hoopin'," he says. "I let hoopin' completely drown out all the bullshit."

All I can do is nod. I know he's being real with me. "Respect, bro," I say to him, putting more bass in my voice than normal.

"How is Ms. Diane, though?" I feel like I ask him this a lot, and I hope I don't annoy him when I do.

"She doin' good. She cussin' out them doctors every chance she gets, though. They keep trynna put her on different medications and shit and she ain't with all of that."

I laugh a big laugh. "Sounds like Ms. Diane. I might stop by her store after practice."

"I don't know if she'll be there. Tatiana might be in there, though." Tatiana is his baby sister. She got pregnant last year by a 7th Street Disciple who was like five years older than her. Rumor has it: She's pregnant again by a different Disciple.

"A'ight," I say. "I might visit her at the crib, then."

"A'ight, bet," he says. "I got other things to do after practice, but you go."

"Bet." We shake up and he keeps it moving, waddling down to wherever he's going next, his backpack hanging around his shoulder like he's protecting it. I know what might be in it.

At lunch, David's already sitting at our table, waiting for the three of us to get there. It catches me by surprise, but I don't mind. I think after our talk last night he can sit here and be part of the squad.

"What's up, David?" I ask.

He smiles widely. "Hey," he says.

He and Olly shake up and Ayesha waves at him.

"Y'all heard what Penelope shared on Facebook?" Ayesha asks, craning her neck before she sits down in her usual seat.

"Nah, what happened?" I ask.

Olly opens up a bag of Cool Ranch Doritos in the loudest way he possibly can. Just Olly being Olly, right? He offers me some, and since I can't turn down the Cool Ranch kind, I reach in and grab a few.

Ayesha drinks some of her drink and continues her story. "She shared this video of some guy holding up this old Asian lady in an elevator."

"Okay?" I question.

"But she commented something about, like, how this is why Black people are scary. If I see that skinny ol' trick, I'mma knock her ass out."

"Damn, she's really racist," Olly says.

"For sure," I say, shaking my head. Staring at my tray, unsure if I should eat my hamburger first or my fries.

"Remember freshman year when she asked Thomas Zheng if he ate puppies and kittens for the holidays because he's Chinese?" Ayesha goes.

"Ah. Shit," I say. "Yeah, I remember that mess. She claimed it was a joke and laughed it off, but I can't believe she got away with that shit, man. She always does."

"Are you talking about Penelope Roe?" David asks.

"Yeah," Ayesha says. "You know her?"

"I'm supposed to be working with her on a project in physics," he says. "But now . . . I don't know if I can even do that without feeling terrible. That's really shitty and racist what she did."

Ayesha points a fry at him. "You know what, David? You real cool. You part of the squad now."

David just looks at me and looks back at her, smiling nearly from ear to ear. "Eh, thanks, Ayesha."

Olly smacks his lips when he eats, so that's all we hear for a few seconds until Ayesha calls him out. "Close. Your. Damn. Mouth."

Olly gets all defensive and says, "Hey, hey, hey, get off my ass, will you?"

"Act like you got some home training," she replies.

"What am I? A dog?" Olly and Ayesha start fighting about what that saying really means and they're not really trying to hear each other out.

David looks at me, forking through his salad. "I had fun last night," he says.

Part of me is embarrassed that he says that out loud. But I don't know why because I had fun, too. "Same," I tell him quietly. I haven't told Olly or Ayesha about what happened.

"How do you feel about the NCAA?" he asks next. Whew. College basketball. I've got thoughts, for sure.

"Worse than the NBA, but still watchable, I guess. What about you?"

He kind of chuckles. "Depends on the day." I watch him put a forkful of lettuce and kale and tomato in his mouth. "I think Duke is fucking fantastic, but nothing can beat the kind of talent that's in the NBA."

"I agree with that," I say. "The NCAA just has so many stupid rules and they need to start paying their players when they're putting so much pressure on them."

"Yeah," David says back. Putting more salad up to his mouth.

"It just seems really unfair to have the college players essentially work and risk injury for free. That's real trash."

"Hmm. I guess I never really considered that part. Yeah, NBA's better, now that I think of it," David says. He smiles, and of course, I notice a piece of lettuce or spinach—something green—on his tooth.

I try and gesture by pointing to my mouth.

He looks serious all of a sudden. "Oh, shit, do I have—" He wipes at his teeth feverishly, trying to get it. "Did I get it?"

I look for him. "Yeah. You're good."

"Thanks," he says. "That's how you know when you've met someone genuine. When they point out that you have something in your teeth."

"Ha-ha. I guess so." I smile back.

It goes quiet, and out of the corner of my eye, I notice Olly and Ayesha with their heads propped up in their hands, listening in, and this lunchroom suddenly feels like someone just cranked the heat all the way up.

"What?" I go.

"Nothing. What were you guys talking about?" Olly asks, finally giving up on arguing with Ayesha. He will always lose at that, but he never learns. I tell him that we've been talking about college basketball versus the NBA.

"NBA's better," Ayesha gives her take.

"No, no, no. Definitely college," Olly says. He's had this take for so long, and every time he brings it up, Ayesha and I explain to him all of the ways he's wrong. I'm honestly surprised he still has this take.

Ayesha's all like, "What? Boy, you is crazy."

And then Olly's like, "Crazy because I prefer to watch

basketball where there aren't super teams that everyone knows will win it all from the very beginning of the season?"

Suddenly, their second argument commences. Ayesha and Olly start arguing about their NCAA brackets and the Final Four, and I'm not entirely sure why since the Final Four's not for a few more weeks, but they're extra prepared. We watch a lot of NCAA and all the tournaments together every year, but really only as a way to show that we love Olly even when his hot takes are actually ice cold takes. I'll ride for Duke until I die because that's where I wanna get recruited and I think they're good, but I'd take any NBA team to beat any Duke team on any day.

David appears to be enjoying being at our table, but to be honest, every time I look at him, I think about just how much I might've overshared when I was with him. It felt nice to open up to him, but today, I just feel off. I don't wanna make it a habit of opening up to him and hiding it from Olly and Ayesha.

Luckily, the lunch-is-over bell sounds and we all hop up from the table. Also, luckily, Ayesha and Olly drop it.

Most of my afternoon classes kind of fly by, and it's the first time in a long time where each one doesn't feel like doing one 5K after another.

Then I get to Mrs. Oberst's class. She starts talking about how we'll soon be wrapping up *To Kill a Mockingbird* and next will read a book about police brutality. She doesn't tell us what it's called, but I just hope it's not another one written by somebody white who doesn't know what the hell it even looks like to live in the hood or deal with police brutality.

Mrs. Oberst grabs a big box from beneath her desk and begins passing out our copies of the book. Once I get my copy, I can't help but sigh at the cover of it.

She whips her head around, her bob cut flipping in the air. "Is there a problem, Mr. Zander?"

I can't take back my sigh and I don't entirely want to cause a scene right now, but I just can't help myself. "There's a white guy on the cover of this book," I tell her. "First, you made us read *To Kill a Mockingbird*, now this?"

"Mr. Zander, I don't seem to be following. Harper Lee is very fine literature. She's one of the greatest authors who ever lived. She lived through an intense time of racial tension and her work shows us up close the effects of racism and Jim Crow in the South."

"No," I fight back. "Her work shows us racism from the white gaze, which isn't actually that helpful."

The rest of the class erupts in "oohs" like I just roasted her or something. She clutches the box of books to her side and looks around the classroom.

"English class is all about learning to appreciate different perspectives," Mrs. Oberst says to the class, some amount of frustration in her voice. "We're reading the assigned texts that I teach every year. You won't get to complain about what your professors are teaching in college. They won't care. I'm just preparing you for that. But thank you for the feedback anyway."

What kind of passive-aggressive bull is this?

When she looks away, I roll my eyes. Man, sometimes she can get on my last nerve.

Her class always feels long as shit. The seconds and minutes feel more and more like hours each time I'm in here. Ayesha's scrolling on her phone underneath her desk, and by the look of the screen, it looks like either Instagram or MatchUp. Olly's in the back, listening and paying attention. He's always paying attention in this class since he has, like, this weird crush on Mrs. Oberst. That's another thing about Olly: He has a shit ton of weird crushes on older women.

I remember he had the biggest one on Karina before I had to check him and tell him about how weird that was.

Finally, the bell rings, and she dismisses the class. I hate that that's a rule of hers. She's always trying to prove a point.

Practice is relatively chill. All Coach has us do is run some drills and practice setting screens to get shooters open. That's something I can't mess up, since literally all I have to do is stand in place with my feet spread a little bit apart.

I still haven't pinpointed why I'm feeling worried about last night all of a sudden. I don't know if it's just weird having someone who's kind of a stranger know things about me or if it's my fear of getting close to someone only for them to leave. There's nothing about David that screams that he would take all of my secrets and publish them in the school newspaper for the whole school to see. He's just the world's hardest game of sudoku. I can't figure him out. I don't really know what he wants with me and I don't really know what I want from him.

At the end of practice, everyone gets showered and then we meet out on the bleachers since Coach Campbell wants to give us a pep talk about our upcoming game against a rival school nearby.

I sit in between David and Malik on the bleachers.

"Some of you are moving a little slow out there, so keep pushing the pace," Coach says. "We want them to go at our pace when we're on the floor, not the other way around. We play Center Grove next and they're a good team. But we're a better team, right?"

Everyone on the bleachers shouts back, "Yes, Coach!"

"And we're going to kill it on Friday during the game, right?" he asks.

Again, everyone shouts, "Yes, Coach!"

"What's our motto?" Coach asks.

"Great spirits often receive fierce opposition from mediocre minds," everyone shouts in almost an emotionless blur of voices. We have to shout this every now and then. It's really just a rip-off of an Albert Einstein quote, but Coach Campbell wants us to believe he came up with it himself. A lot of us know that, but we recite it anyway.

Coach blows his whistle to dismiss us from practice and I gather my things—my backpack, my headphones, and my sports bag. Then I wave bye to David as I head toward the doors.

I get a few steps in before I feel someone pull me back gently. I turn around at once, and realize David's grabbing my elbow.

"Would you want to, uh, maybe grab dinner tonight?" he asks. He scratches his forehead and completely aborts all eye contact with me for a brief moment.

Wait. Is this . . . ? Is he asking me on a date? Or am I over-thinking this?

Before I can give him any sort of an answer, he adds, "It's cool if not. That's okay. I just thought I would ask."

"Nah," I say. "I mean yes—yes, I'll go to dinner." It's just dinner. I don't need to make this out to be something it's not.

"Awesome!" He half smiles, but his cheeks are flushed and red and his voice kind of shakes a little bit.

"Where at?" I ask.

"Do you like pizza?"

"Who doesn't?"

"True, true. I know a great pizza spot just a few blocks away from West Haven. They've got a great mac-and-cheese pizza. I can pick you up in a couple hours?"

It's funny that he's just moved to town and is already trying to show off restaurants to me, a person who was born here. But I don't want to embarrass him when he already seems a little nervous, so I just say, "Sounds good. But for the record, mac and cheese doesn't belong on pizza."

"Okay, that's fair—see you then!"

I nod at him. "You catching the bus back? I can walk to the bus stop with you."

"Actually, I rode here. Want a ride?" he asks.

"Nah, I'm okay," I say. "I've gotta make a stop before I go home anyway."

"Okay, cool. So, I don't have your number . . ." He tosses me his phone to enter mine.

I put in my phone number and pass him his phone back

before waving goodbye. Outside I walk to the bus stop and stand there, waiting for the bus to come. It only takes about five minutes for it to arrive, but when it does, I'm, like, the only person on it, so I sit all the way at the back and plug in my headphones. I click on my playlist called "Fall Forward," which has all the perfect songs for me to relax right now. "Let Me Down Slowly" by Alec Benjamin is the first song that plays. Alec Benjamin is such a good artist and he's probably in my top-ten favorite artists lately.

I get FaceTime calls from Olly and Ayesha, but I decline them. I'm just wanting to listen to my music right now. They both text me asking why I declined them, and I tell them that I'm on the bus. Olly invites me over, but I tell him that I'm going over to Ms. Diane's.

Olly
Why are you going over there?

Me
I wanna ask her about my mom.

Ayesha
You sure that's a good idea, Gio?

Me
I don't know. But it's something.

I get off the bus at a stop that's before my usual one. I walk up the sidewalk, passing along somebody grilling even though it's the end of winter and it's still cold out, passing several stray cats scurrying away, and passing a bunch of kids playing at the playground. I pass the area where I used to play Cops and Robbers with Ayesha and Malik. Back when I was closer with Malik.

It's been a minute since I've been to Ms. Diane's house, but I know that I'm at her house when I see that she has red tape on her front door in the shape of a cross. The last time I asked her about it she said it was her way of keeping the demons out. She only wants good spirits in her house. I try to knock in a certain way that doesn't make her feel anxious.

Ms. Diane answers the door in a bright pink head wrap, some sweatpants, and in a wheelchair. This is a version of Ms. Diane I'm not all that familiar with, but it's her, nonetheless.

"Heyyy, sweet thing," Ms. Diane says. "What brings you over here?"

"Just wanted to come by and say hey," I answer. I *did* want to check up on her. Malik only tells me so much. I'm sure he's not wanting me to know the truth. He hasn't said *anything* about her being in a damn wheelchair. I'm having to find this out on my own.

"Well, come in, come in," she says. She yells for her oldest son, July. He owns the barbershop in the Haven. Ms. Diane's real nice to let July stay with her even though he's a whole-ass adult.

"What, Ma?" July asks, wearing a do-rag, a plain white T-shirt, and some joggers. He's wearing a headset and is holding a PlayStation controller. He notices me and nods what's up at me.

"Sup, July?" I say. "I need to come up to the shop at some point."

"Yeah, bro, I'll squeeze you in. You know I got you," he says, coming over to give me dap.

"I called you in here to fix Gio some of that tea I just made," Ms. Diane says, wheeling herself closer to the couch.

"A'ight," July says back.

"I'm okay," I tell them both, stopping July before he goes into the kitchen. "I just finished a bottle of Gatorade after practice, so I'm okay."

"You sure?" July asks me, wrinkling his forehead.

"I'm good. Thanks, though, July."

"A'ight, let me know if y'all need something. I'm just back here on *Fortnite*. I'm really out here working these dudes."

"Okay, whatever," Ms. Diane says, waving him off, and suddenly July disappears into the back again. "Come and make yourself at home, Gio. This place will always be your second home."

I sit down on the couch next to her. "Thanks, Ms. Diane. You been doin' okay? I didn't know you were in a wheelchair." Shit. Why did I say that? Malik told me she was cussing folks out just over some medication. What about the wheelchair?

"Doctors say I'll get worse and worse as the days go by, but I think I'm okay. I've lived a good life and have done all I think the good Lord wanted me to do."

"Yeah?"

"If it's my time, then it's my time. Ain't nothin' I can do about that," she says. Ms. Diane's originally from Louisiana. Every now and then I can hear it in her voice, even though all of my life she's lived in the Haven.

"I'm sorry to hear about you being sick," I tell her. I don't know if that's any comfort—probably not, but I really am sorry.

"Ah, it's okay, sugar. Ms. Diane will be okay." She looks so sadly up at the ceiling. I look around the room, too, and everything feels so weird. This living room looks exactly like it did the very first day Malik invited me and Ayesha over for a game of hide-and-seek back when we were little.

I'm quiet, my leg's just shaking as I tap my foot against the wool rug.

"Y'all grew up so fast on me," Ms. Diane says. "Stand up, let me look at you." I do as she says and stand up.

"Yeah, I grew a lot over the last summer," I tell her. "I didn't know you could still be growing when you're more than halfway through high school."

"Yeah, you and Malik just keep getting taller and taller," she says. "Mhmm."

"I don't know if Malik will be home anytime soon," I tell her.

"I already know that, child," she says, tossing up a hand. "He's been dealing that stuff out there. I done told him several times about that stuff. He either gon' end up in the state pen or dead. I done told him over and over to stop selling and hanging out with them no-good Disciples."

"Yeah" is all I can say back to her.

She sighs loudly. I can feel her sadness. "Gio, you ever talk to him about getting out of these streets? I look at you and I know y'all used to be real close and somewhere along the way you two split up like two peas from the same pod."

"I don't know what happened with us," I tell her. "I try to tell 'Lik to stop selling, but he keeps giving me excuses about how he needs money."

Ms. Diane rolls her eyes. "That boy got a lot of nerve. I just don't know what he gon' do when I'm gone."

My heart breaks just thinking about that. I don't want to think about Ms. Diane not being here. I don't say anything to her, just nod at her that I'm listening, hearing her out.

"I just keep thinking what if I raised him in the suburbs or—" Ms. Diane covers her mouth with her hand. I notice there's a hospital band still on her wrist. "Oh well. Maybe one day, he'll get it through his thick head. That's why I'm trying to get him to start applying for college."

Still just nodding and listening.

"I remember yelling at y'all when you, Malik, and Ayesha would be running through my house, breaking all kinds of stuff," Ms. Diane says, a big smile on her face like she's reliving the moments.

"Those were good times for sure," I tell her. It's kind of crazy how now Malik and I don't talk all that much and it's like Olly's replaced him in our squad.

"Your momma and I used to be sipping on wine coolers in the kitchen while the three of y'all was just tearing up my house, playing whatever games y'all would come up with."

I stare at my hands for a moment. My heartbeat picking up speed. The two of us sit in silence for a moment, like we're both trying to transport ourselves back to one of those specific memories. I swallow hard and then take a deep breath before asking a question that's now burning the back of my throat.

"Have you kept in contact with her over the years?" I ask her. I try to be vague because I kind of don't want to let Ms. Diane know that she's come back. I don't know how she would react, and I don't want to add to the stress I know she's already feeling about everything going on in her life—her kids and her health.

"Your momma?"

I nod.

"No, we talked probably once or twice when she first left the Haven, but then I never heard from her again."

"Damn—sorry, I mean, dang."

"You're okay, sugar," she says. "I'd call her and call her and wouldn't get anything but voicemail. Eventually, the number just stopped ringing altogether."

"Wow."

"Your momma was my best friend, but even your best friend can be a mystery," she says. "The thing about it is, I'm not even mad at her. I would've left the Haven, too."

"But would you have left Tatiana, Malik, and July behind?"

Ms. Diane grabs my hand, thumbing it. "I would never leave my kids behind unless I had a good reason to do that. I was a single mom. Nobody was gonna take care of my kids if I did that."

"Oh," I say, and kind of sink in the couch a little bit. I lock eyes with Ms. Diane, and I can see my own anguish reflected back at me.

"I knew your momma for a long, long time. She wouldn't have done what she did unless she had to."

My breathing gets a little heavy. I try and try and try to think about what Ms. Diane is saying, but I don't know if there's any scenario where it makes sense for my mom to leave us. Maybe I'm being unfair, maybe I'm not thinking about this from the right angle. I just don't get it, I guess.

Tears are forming in my eyes and actually falling and falling and falling. I'm trying to hold back before I make more of a watery mess. I wipe my face hard with my sleeve and then stand to my feet.

"I should get going," I tell her.

"Oh, okay, sugar" is all she's like. "It was so, so good to see you."

"Good to see you, too, Ms. Diane."

"I'll have to tell Malik you came over when he gets home," she says.

"Yeah," I say. "You should come to our game on Friday, if you can."

"I told Malik I would be there, but I don't know. Now that I'm in this wheelchair, it's not always the easiest to get around these days."

"I see. That makes sense."

"Yeah, but I told July that if I can't make it to go and record it for me."

"Ah. Well, I'll see you later, then," I say.

"Give me a hug before you go, sweet pea."

I bend down to hug her in her wheelchair. She still smells the same as I remember—whatever perfume that reminds me of lavender or roses, or both.

I reach into my pocket and grab out a twenty-dollar bill. I sit it across Ms. Diane's lap. "I want you to have this."

She looks at me and then the money and then back at me. "I can't take this from you, Gio."

"Please," I tell her, pleading. "I want you to have it. It's a gift."

She folds it up and holds it close to her chest. "Well, thank you, sweet pea. Awfully nice of you." She offers me a wide smile that I return quickly.

I open the door and wave at her as I head out and begin my walk back to my place. It's cold, and the whole way back, I'm holding my arms together, shivering, thinking about what Ms. Diane said about my birth mom.

My phone blows up with notifications from David about tonight. Shit. I totally forgot about going to dinner with him.

When I get home, Karina's sitting at the dining room table drinking a glass of red wine and petting Biscuit. She offers me a glass of lemonade. David's still currently blowing up my phone, so I answer him by telling him that I just got to my house and haven't even gotten ready yet.

"Where were you?"

"I went over to Ms. Diane's and she said that she knew my mom really well and that she would've only left if she had no other choice." I take a sip of lemonade.

"Ms. Diane said that?" Karina asks me, putting Biscuit down on the floor.

"Yeah," I say. "She said she would've left the Haven, too, if she had the chance, but she wouldn't have left her kids."

"Oh, okay. I see," Karina responds, stands up, and comes to my side of the table. "Listen, honeybunches, I know you want answers, but there's only one way to get them."

I stare up at her. "What do you mean?"

She palms my chin in a nurturing way. "You have to talk to her."

I sigh and something falls from my chest to my stomach. I'm unsure of what it is, but it's heavy and I don't like it. I look away, knowing that Karina's right. Of course she is, but I really, really hate that she's right about this right now.

"Want to help me make dinner tonight?" Karina asks. "It's just going to be the two of us—your Pops and Theo have that youth group thing." I used to help her make dinner a lot when I was younger, but not so much anymore.

"I wish I could," I tell her. "I'm going out."

"Really? Where? With who?"

"David, from across the street," I answer. "I think he asked me on a kind-of date. He says he knows a really good pizza place, so we're gonna go there."

"Ah, I see. Well . . . have fun with him," Karina says, and kisses the top of my forehead.

"I kind of want to skip, though," I confess.

"Why?"

"All this thinking about my mom. I'm kind of not in the mood for pizza or dates or kind-of dates or whatever this is."

"Just go," Karina says. "It'll be good for you, honey-bunches."

"Fine," I groan, and head upstairs to my room to get showered and changed into some clean, more date-appropriate clothes. I pick out my Paramore hoodie, some skinny jeans, and a pair of matching Jordans. Then I hear someone knocking on my bedroom door as I'm slipping on my skinny jeans and Jordans.

"Who is it?" I ask, expecting it to be Theo asking me to play multi-player on some game on his Xbox. But a head pops through a crack and it's Karina.

"Hey, I have something for you," she says. Her voice is steady, but her hands shake.

"Come in," I say. "What is it?"

She opens the door wider. I don't know why I'm just noticing that she's already in her nighttime robe. She's holding something that looks like a shoebox, and I'm wondering when she bought me a new pair of shoes and why.

"I thought it was time for you to have this," she says, still holding on to the box tightly. "Your dad and I have been fighting over this for years. I thought he should've given it to you sooner, but he made me promise not to ever bring it up with you."

"Bring what up?" I ask. I'm feeling clammy and warm all of a sudden. I don't like wherever this is going.

"You should've known about this a long time ago, but your dad thought he was protecting you from getting hurt more,"

Karina says, her lips trembling. She hands over the box and I don't want to even open it.

"What is this?" I ask a final time, but she just shakes her head and offers apologies.

"I'm sorry you didn't get to know about this sooner, honey-bunches," she says, her voice cracking in several places. "I've just seen you so beaten up about her that I couldn't—" She just completely stops and walks out of the room, closing the door behind her.

Now all of a sudden, I'm left in my room with this strange box that I don't know what I want to do with. I can tell that my hands are shaking.

Slowly but surely, I open up the lid to the box and I don't see any shoes. All I see are loose pieces of paper. I pick some out to investigate them. And after reading the first line of one of the papers, I'm instantly a mess of tears.

Dear G-Bug,

Happy thirteenth birthday! You're growing up so fast. Look at you, you're a whole teenager now. I wish I could be there with you to celebrate with you. I may not be there right now, but one day, I'll come back for you and Theo. Hope you're taking care of him for me. Stay strong. Both of you.
Love you so, so much.

Mom

Hands and lips trembling, I reach for another one to read it. I don't know if I *should* read another, but I do.

Dear G-Bug,

You're in high school now? Where has the time gone? When I was your age, I had just joined the girls' basketball team, started taking driver's ed, met your dad, and had my first real kiss. I know you probably don't want to know about your mom's first kiss, but I hope you can experience your own firsts, my son. How are things with you? Please write to me. I'd love to hear from you. You and Theo getting along? Does he ever ask about me? I love you so much, G-Bug. Never forget that. Don't forget me.

Mom

I read and read and read the letters my mom wrote to me. All this time, she's been writing to me over the years, but they've been kept away from me. But for what? I feel angry, pissed off, confused. I throw the box on the ground and scream and wail to the top of my lungs like someone's giving me open heart surgery without any anesthesia. My thoughts are banging up on each other until they aren't really thoughts anymore, but more like clouds landing punches on me from the inside.

I don't know why she wrote me so many letters but didn't just come back. She never did. I mean, until now. Now she's back, but for the last week, I've not been wanting to have anything to do with her because I thought she didn't care. I mean, until now. I mean, at least she wrote to me. I mean, she's been trying to talk to me. Suddenly, Karina's voice echoes around in my head. That I should talk to her. That she could have answers.

I curl up in my bed, underneath my blankets. And I shut my eyes tight, my breathing getting heavier and heavier before it becomes almost wheezing, like before I outgrew asthma. Someone's blowing up my phone, and I know that it's David, but I ignore the texts and the calls and the Instagram DMs because I just want to be alone right now. I *need* to be left alone with my thoughts.

I can't sleep. I'm not sure if it's because it's still kind of earlier in the night or because I can't get my mind to power down or stop crying or what, but I know that I remain still for hours and hours and periodically a head pops through the crack of my door. I know it's Karina—only she would be that worried about me. I just remain on my side, staring straight out my window. I'm able to see the moon and the stars there for a long-ass time, but I stay awake long enough to see the sun come up and the stars disappear.

TWELVE

●●●●●●

POPS AND KARINA ARE having a screaming match when I come down for breakfast with Theo before I walk him to school. Theo's eating a combination of Lucky Charms and Frosted Flakes, but in between bites, he covers his ears because they're so loud. I walk over to kiss his forehead.

When they realize I'm downstairs, they both go completely quiet. They're just staring at me, like I'm some stranger walking around in their house. Then Karina walks over to me and rubs my arm and says, "Look who's up. How are you, honeybunches?"

I don't know what to say, so I just shrug. I stare at Pops and he stares back at me. By the way he does this, I know why they were arguing.

Theo gets ready and Karina volunteers to walk him there today in my place. They're leaving a little early, I think so Karina can get Theo out of here. When they leave, I try to leave, too, but Pops stops me.

"Come back here," he says. "We need to talk."

I don't know if I want to talk to him right now, but I turn back and take a seat. There's a bottle of Jack on the table and he pours a little bit into his coffee.

"Why didn't you give me the letters?" I ask him, my voice shaking. "I don't understand."

"I did it for your own damn good, Gio!" he nearly barks, taking a drink of his spiked coffee.

"What do you mean? I just—How could you know that?"

He smacks his newspaper against the table, and I jump back. "I was married to your mother for a long time. She ain't who I thought she was."

"That doesn't make her a terrible person. That doesn't give you the right to keep her letters away from me all this time!" My voice is rising, and I don't even care.

"Boy! I had every right to do what I did," Pops shouts, standing to his feet, a snarl on his face. "I did it so you wouldn't be hurt by her anymore. She's the one who walked out on you—on us! Not me!" He starts pacing around in the dining area and living room.

I sit there and sulk in this chair, watching him. I can't argue with that last part. As distant as Pops has become over the years, he never abandoned me or Theo. Still, I can't help but think things would've been a lot different for me growing up if I had the chance to even write to her. I didn't get to read any of her letters—and this made me think that I was something she wanted to forget, something she lost interest in and wanted to drop, like a bad habit. Everything that I believed is in question. Everything I've been told might've been such a terrible lie.

I don't know what to think.

What to believe.

What to feel.

What to do.

But I know one thing: I'm so hurt and beat up about the fact that this whole time I could've had some sort of relationship with her, some sort of contact. Maybe I wouldn't have needed to go through counseling with Dr. McCullough back when I was a freshman and sophomore. At least, not as often as I did. Or maybe at least her absence wouldn't have felt as heavy. Maybe I would have the answers to all the questions written on my heart that I don't even know to ask. Maybe the grief I experience in waves and seasons wouldn't be as heavy as a tsunami tiding over me, completely consuming every inch of my body until I, too, am something to be grieved.

Don't forget me, she wrote. And I didn't.

But I thought she'd forgotten me because there weren't any words telling me otherwise.

Now there are words, frozen in time but now thawing out. I've only read a couple letters so far, but that's enough. I now know the words are there.

I stay seated, lost in my thoughts. It feels like time's no longer moving, but it must be, because Karina comes walking back through the door, wearing her thick winter coat even though it's supposed to be warmer out today. Pops returns to the room when he hears her come in.

"What's going on in here?" she asks once she sees how tensely Pops is looking at me.

"I'm trying to fix the mess you started by giving him that box, Karina—what do you *think* is happening?" Pops fires back.

"The mess *I* started?" Karina yells back, her drawn-on eyebrows furrowed and pointy.

"Yes! Those letters are just Jackie's way of trying to manipulate him into believing that she actually gave a damn about any of us."

Something stings inside. "But she did!" I shout, like I'm fighting for my voice to be heard. Once upon a time I would've only said something like that to Theo as a way of comforting him—or as a way of convincing myself of it, too. But now . . . I don't know. Maybe she cared. Maybe something happened that she had no other choice but to go? Suddenly, I'm thinking about what Ms. Diane said to me last night and I think I actually believe what she said.

Pops gives me this look like he doesn't want to deal with my foolishness. Instead, he continues the fight with Karina, and they go back and forth arguing about whose fault it is. But none of that really matters. I feel lied to and betrayed. That's what's important at this moment.

"I'm going back to my room," I tell them. "I don't want to talk to you right now."

Pops sits down aggressively and throws his hands up like he's giving up, and I take that as a sign to head upstairs and shut the door behind me.

I sink onto my bed and consider FaceTiming Olly or Ayesha, but one look at my phone and I see so many notifications from David, I start to cry. Maybe I'm a lot like Pops after all, the way I run away from facing hard shit and just shut down. I can't be mad at him for turning to alcohol, can I? I feel like the worst person in the world. I consider staying in bed all day just to cry and return all of David's calls and texts, but I can't miss practice tonight. It's the day before the big game against Center Grove, so there's no way I can miss it if I want to remain on the team. I figure I'll see David in person at school and then again at practice. I'll have many opportunities to apologize for what I did in person.

I sit at my desk, open my laptop, and pull up the last email I got from my mom. I read it and reread it. Then I plan out my response to her. For the longest time I stumble on the very first word.

Mom?

Jackie?

Mom?

Jackie?

I don't know which to use. I swallow hard and trust my gut that whatever I type is meant to be there. Still, I'm surprised by the one I choose.

To: missjackie01@global.net
From: GioTheGr8@gmail.com
Subject: UNTITLED

Mom,
It's Gio. I'm writing to you because I don't know what to do. I'm writing to you because I feel like I'm stuck, and I know you're the only one who can help. I just got a box of all the letters you wrote to me over the years. Pops kept

them from me, which is why I never responded. I know you at least wanted to hear from me, even if you were gone. After talking with Ms. Diane yesterday, I know that you wouldn't have left unless you had a good reason to do it. I don't know if there's any scenario that I can think of that would cause you to leave, but I trust Ms. Diane and therefore I think I would want to hear you out. I don't know where you've gone, but I have a basketball game tomorrow and it would be cool if you came, if you could. We can maybe talk afterward, if you're up for it? I don't know. If not, that's okay. I just thought I would try to write you back for the very first time.

I hope to hear back from you soon.

I'll be waiting.

Gio

It takes me a little bit to pull myself together, but eventually, I get ready for school. I put on some joggers, one of my floral-patterned shirts, and the pair of Curry 7s I got for my birthday last year. Karina got them customized for me, so my name is etched on the inside of the shoes. I go through my mental checklist of things not to forget and decide that the first thing I'll do when I get to school is find David. I want to tell him that I didn't mean to ditch, and I want to tell him about the box. I don't know why, but a part of me just senses he'll understand. He'll get it.

I head downstairs and walk past Karina and Pops, who are still sitting at the table. I tell them that I'll see them later and I head out for the bus stop. I meet Olly and Ayesha waiting for me there, even though I'm running a little late. When I see them, I open up about the letters and about my argument with Pops. I want them to know what's been going on. I don't want them to be in the dark about this.

Ayesha looks shocked. "What did she say in the letters? Did she say why she left you and Theo?"

"I haven't read all of them yet. And to be honest, I don't know if I want to," I say. "All I know is that she's been writing to me."

"Yo. That's wild that you're just now finding out about the letters," Olly says. "Let me know if you ever want to set them on fire. We have a firepit at my house."

"Thanks, Olly."

"I'm serious."

"I know you are."

"Good."

We get to school after the first bell rings. The hallways are all empty, except for the three of us. Mr. Dickey is in the hallway walking our way. *Shit*. I've done such a good job avoiding him in the last week, but he sees us. The three of us look at each other and then lower our heads as we walk toward our lockers.

"Hold up, hold up!" Mr. Dickey shouts from a ways away. When he's closer he's vomiting questions on us. "Why are you three late? Where you coming from? Where are you going?" He squints his eyes that kind of are too big to be squinted. The air smells like weed and instead of finding the source of it, he's asking us about why we're late. Ain't that some BS.

Olly answers first. "Our bus was late taking us to school," he says.

"He's telling the truth," Ayesha says. "Besides, we ain't even that late."

Mr. Dickey twists his lips. "Late is late, Miss Chamberlain. Get to class, you three."

After he walks away, Ayesha's all like, "Goddamn. Mr. Dickey's always trying to kill somebody's vibe."

"Straight up," I say. "He got eyes like a hawk, too."

"He looks like he can see into my soul," Olly adds, and we all laugh.

Olly, Ayesha, and I exchange books from our lockers and Ayesha takes an extra-long time, using the mirror on the inside of hers to apply lipstick and eyeshadow. We all have the same class right now, so Olly and I have to wait for her to finish before we can go.

She puckers up her lips, making like a popping sound. "How do I look?" she asks, also fluttering her long eyelashes.

"Great," I tell her, and I'm not lying.

"You look like that girl from *Charlie and the Chocolate Factory*," Olly jokes, and I'm not gonna lie, I laugh a little bit at it.

Ayesha slams her locker shut, rolling her eyes, and leads the way to AP Gov. When we arrive, Mrs. Flynn is showing a movie of some sort, so we have to awkwardly shuffle into our seats near the back. I try not to make eye contact with her, but when I do it anyway, her eyes are narrowing in on me and she doesn't blink. But after a moment, she goes back to watching the documentary on Nixon and Watergate with the rest of the class, like she's gonna let this one slide.

I like sitting in the back of the class. You can be kinda invisible if you try hard enough. Some people put up books in front of them to hide the fact that they're asleep. Others scroll on their phones underneath their desks.

I click on Instagram and I noticed David posted a photo thirty seconds ago. It's a picture of him and a girl who looks so identical to him it's scary. The caption says: missing you a lot today, K.

I'm assuming it's Kayla. She's really pretty, but the photo feels sad. I double-tap to like the photo right as Mrs. Flynn clears her throat to have us put away our phones. All the lights are off and it's dark, but somehow, she still manages to catch us.

I try to focus on the documentary, but I'm suddenly wondering about what David's feeling. Not only did I bail on him, but it looks like he's thinking about Kayla today.

Lunchtime comes and David's a no-show. I can't make him out anywhere. I even glance over at the table where some of the basketball team sits. I see Erick, Jason, and Savtaj. All of them have their arms around their girlfriends. But David's not with them.

I wonder if my bailing on him completely ruined whatever friendship was blossoming between us. I mean, I'd hate it if someone bailed on me, so I can't expect him to have been okay with it.

"Where's David?"

Ayesha looks around, searching for him, and then shrugs. "I don't know. He posted one of his paintings this morning on Instagram, but that was before school even started."

I turn down the brightness on my phone and pull up his Instagram on my phone. It says that an hour ago, he posted a painting of a motorcycle. I think it's the exact one he was driving when he almost ran me over. Maybe it's a jab at me for ditching him? Or not. But I can't help but think that he's upset. Maybe he wishes he actually ran me over. I wouldn't blame him, if I'm being real.

I sigh and almost melt into my seat.

"What's wrong with you?" Olly asks me, holding a chicken sandwich and taking a bite.

"What? Nothing? What do you mean?"

"You look like you're holding in a really big fart. I've known you for a while now. I can tell that you're anxious about something."

I roll my eyes. "I think he asked me out on a date yesterday," I whisper across the table to her and Olly like it's a juicy secret.

"He WHAT?" Ayesha gets a little too loud and Penelope Roe and some other girls at a nearby table crane their necks and stare at us.

"I didn't go, though," I say. "I had too much on my mind."

"GIO!" Ayesha nearly shouts, and I motion for her to be quiet.

"Shhhh!" Penelope hisses at us from a table in front of us, whipping her head over like she's annoyed at us. I recognize some of the girls she's sitting with because they're cheerleaders and sometimes travel with the basketball team.

"Oh, hell nah," Ayesha says, rolling her neck around in a circle. "Don't shush me. I'll clothesline your white ass!"

"Enough, ladies!" Mr. Dickey shouts across the way since he's on lunch duty. "Either of you want to spend detention with me tonight?"

"No, sir," Penelope and Ayesha take turns responding back to him.

Penelope and Ayesha settle down. Mr. Dickey goes back to talking to another teacher.

"'Clothesline your white ass,' Ayesha?" I repeat her words, holding back a laugh.

"Yes, fuck her. You know I'd do it, too," Ayesha says, rolling her eyes and laughing.

"That was so damn hilarious. Anyway, let's rewind. So, David asked you out and you ditched?" Olly asks.

I swallow air. "Like I said. It was a lot when Karina dropped those letters on me. I didn't even feel like leaving my room, let alone leaving my house."

Olly nods. "Fair."

"Yeah, that's fair," Ayesha adds. "I'm sure David would understand that."

"I hope," I say. "I just can't help but think that he's pissed at me, though."

Each of my classes are kind of the same—teachers assigning unnecessarily ridiculous amounts of homework, teaching stuff many of us will never use again after graduation, making predictions about our futures and all that. David's still nowhere to be found. I'm convinced he's avoiding me. And he's good at it, too. A little too good at it.

I just want to say sorry to his face. I stare at my phone, not seeing any notifications or messages from him. I debate in my head on shooting him a quick text, but that feels cheap. If I was going to do that, I should've done it this morning. Damn, I'm such a dickhead for bailing and I feel like an even bigger dickhead because it seems like I don't even care. It seems like I'm playing the wrong card every turn I get. And now I can't make it up to him because he's nowhere to be found.

Shit.

Shit.

Shit.

Practice.

I forgot all about practice. I'll have to see him there, right? It's not the ideal place to have this conversation, so maybe it'll have to wait even longer.

I stand in the hallway for the entire duration of the passing period, hoping to get a glimpse of him so I can run after him just to explain myself. But again . . . nothing.

I check in on my email as the late bell rings, and my mom hasn't responded to the email I sent her. Damn. Maybe I ruined my only chance at getting answers from her. Maybe she's really packed up her shit and left for good, cutting ties with me forever. Hell, maybe David's already done the same. It's only a matter of time at this point, isn't it? But the thing is, David would have every right to do that. I fucked up for sure. I just hope I get a chance to talk to him. I know nothing I say will make it okay or right, but I want him to know what happened anyway.

After school, I head to basketball practice, hoping David at least shows up to that. He can miss school, but he can't miss practice, right?

When I get there, David is there already, chucking up shots with some of the other guys on the team. Has he been here all along, but has been skipping classes to avoid me? My mind always works in worst-case scenarios. I walk near him, and he doesn't even look at me. He exhales really loudly each shot he tosses up. He tosses up another shot and the ball bounces off the rim and goes flying. I run after it to bring it to him and he doesn't even say thank you. It's official: I've royally fucked things up here. He's pissed with me. *Dammit, Gio.*

"David—"

"What?"

"Hey, I, um . . . I'm sorry. Okay?"

He gives me a cold stare and just shakes his head. I know he doesn't want to talk right now, surrounded by most of the team. Or maybe that's the story I want myself to believe. Either way, I can take a hint.

"We can talk later," David says, and walks off.

Well, shit. "Okay."

I walk into the locker room to put my stuff in my locker for after practice. Malik's in there. He's changing into his jersey and basketball shorts.

"Hey, 'Lik," I say.

"Sup, bruh," he says back. "Ma told me you ended up stopping by."

"Yeah," I say, shoving my sports bag into my small, compact locker. "I saw July, too."

"July's lazy ass was prolly playing that damn game, wasn't he?" he asks with a laugh.

I kind of chuckle, too. "Yeah," I say. "He was. Headset and all. He still hanging with the Seventh Street Disciples?" Maybe I'm being too nosy.

"July puts most of his attention in his barbershop. Every now and then he'll come around and Disciple. Because he's been out here Discipling for so long, he don't have to be out in the streets as much as somebody like me."

"Hmm," I say. "I don't know how all that works. I'm glad I didn't get caught up in that."

Damn. Did I just say that out loud? Malik gives me a glare, and I know I *did* just say that out loud. I'm such an asshole for that one. It's unfair for me to say that, especially to him, because he felt like he didn't have a choice.

"Not all of us can be like you, Gio" is all he says back. I don't know what that means, but it's probably a good idea for me not to press him on it.

"I didn't mean that," I say as some sort of half-assed apology.

"Whatever, bro. It's cool, it's cool."

He puts some baby powder in his shorts and under his armpits. I've never seen anyone do this but Malik, and it feels normal to watch him do it.

"'Lik, you didn't tell me Ms. Diane is in a wheelchair," I say. I don't know why I have to throw that out at him right now. Somebody needs to duct-tape my mouth shut.

"Because I don't want everybody to know," Malik snaps.

I turn away to take off my pants and change into my basketball shorts and jersey, but I keep talking. "'Lik, I'm here for you if you want to talk or need anything."

Malik doesn't respond for what feels like an eternity. I have to look back just to make sure he's still in the locker room with me and didn't just walk out. He's there, all right—crying but trying to be tough at the same time.

I walk over, and he opens his mouth and says, with trembling lips, "I don't want to lose my mom, man." He punches his locker.

"Ms. Diane will be okay," I say. "She's one of the strongest people I've ever known. And that's truth right there."

"It feels like each day she's getting worse," he says. "That ain't cool, man. That ain't cool at all."

I just nod and listen.

He goes on. "Life's too short, man. You gotta remind people that you love them. You gotta be there for them. You gotta do everything to provide for them."

I nod again. "Yeah, you're right." Something—no, everything about this rings true. I think about Karina and even Pops. I think about Theo. I think about Ayesha and Olly. I even think about David. And my mom. I don't know what to do with that, but they all come to mind.

Some of the other guys come into the locker room, so Malik wipes away at his face. "Anyway, bro, I appreciate you. I appreciate you wanting to help me. But I got us."

I know he does. I know he's taking care of himself and Ms. Diane. I just hate how he's doing it.

I follow Malik out into the gym, where Coach blows his whistle to begin practice. He lets us know that we'll be practicing how to run the triangle offense tonight. Some people get excited because that's the system that Phil Jackson ran with Michael Jordan.

Coach starts me out on the bench, but when he puts me in, he assigns me to guard David. He won't even make eye contact with me, which feels like pouring rubbing alcohol on an open wound. There's no way he can see how sorry I am if he still won't even look at me. Next, we practice switching onto bigger players on defense. At one point, Coach calls us to stop so he can make some adjustments.

"Zander," he calls. Since he uses my last name, I know he doesn't like what he sees from me. If I'm not fucking up one thing, it's another.

"Yes?"

He snaps his fingers. "You're switching a little too slowly. We need some more aggression. Pretend you're a hungry lion and the person you're guarding is a gazelle."

"Yes, sir," I respond. Even though I'm annoyed and tired of getting singled out, I take his advice.

Coach blows his whistle again and practice continues on for the next hour and a half, and we just run the triangle over and over again, until eventually we get it right and Coach is happy with us.

After practice I catch David after he finishes showering. We're the only two left inside the locker room. He's sitting on the bench near his locker and putting on a clean shirt.

"Hey," I say, walking over to sit next to him.

One look at me and then he looks away. "Hey," he responds plainly. I know he's still upset with me. Man, I really must've hurt him by what I did.

"David—I—"

"Gio, I want you and I know you don't want me," David snaps. "But do me a favor: Don't give me these mixed signals, okay? Please. I don't want you to play me like you play basketball."

"No, let me explain," I say quickly. "Please."

He sighs and scoots over, putting his head back on his locker. "I'm listening."

"Last night, my stepmom gave me this box that contained letters that my birth mom wrote to me. Letters that I never got. I was wrecked. Confused. Hurt. I just kind of . . . shut down. And I know that's not a good way to respond, but that's what happened, and I . . . I couldn't let you see me like that," I say, my chest heaving. Tears gathering.

He doesn't say anything, just listens. He finally makes eye contact that sticks. And his face changes from bitter and distant to sincere and empathetic.

"I'm just . . . so sorry for bailing, David," I say, staring at the dirty black-and-white tile on the locker room's floor. "That was such a shitty dickhole thing for me to do, but it felt like I had no other choice. I was a mess when Karina just dropped those letters on me, and all of a sudden, I realized my birth mom had written to me all along."

"It's okay," David says, but it's like I don't hear him because I keep ranting anyway.

"I'm a child of abandonment. It's been hardwired in my very existence since I was a little kid—since the moment I watched her walk out that door," I say, slowing up a bit. "David, when I say that moment fucked me up, I mean it. It really fucked me up, until this very day. You deserve better than what I am. I hurt people because things can get too hard, because I'm so fucked up from her, because I'm always waiting for everyone to walk out. And they should! I don't deserve good things, I don't deserve my friends, and I definitely don't deserve someone like you." I'm sobbing now and David wraps his arms around me, pulling me in close. When I regain my composure, I wipe away every tear from my eyes and scoot over a bit from him.

"Y'know, I wish I could paint you how I see you," David says. "Because what you're saying isn't how I see you at all. I see a boy with the most contagious smile in the universe, the gentlest hands. Your eyes are somewhat sad because of the broken cards you've been dealt . . . but they're still the warmest and kindest eyes I've ever seen. Loss fucks you up, but it doesn't change who you are. I have to believe that. It forces you to be brave and strong so you can hold your life together, and the lives of the people you love together—the ones who are still here. I'd paint that. I'd paint a boy who deserves his own planet."

Brave? I don't feel that word at all.

But look at David. Look at what he's living through. This isn't Olly or Ayesha telling me about loss based on things they've heard. No, David knows it for real. He's sharing what he knows with me, because he gets that I need to know it, too.

What we've been through is so different. But what we have to do to get through it is a lot the same. Or that's how it feels right now.

He leans forward next to me, and I'm leaning in, too. Once upon a time I would've pulled back, but not now. Suddenly our lips are touching. Everything in my head goes quiet and I kiss him back, like he's oxygen and I'm desperately breathing him in. His lips are soft and warm against mine, and they taste sweet—sweetly understanding. Man, I need this.

"Whoa, whoa, whoa!" a voice says somewhere around us. We break away quick, busted. I crane my neck around to see Malik.

"Man!" I say, jumping to my feet. "I—uh . . ."

Malik puts his hands up. "Y'all cool." He looks at me and then at David and then back at me. "I ain't gon' tell nobody."

I'm kind of thrown off by how he's reacting. I expected something else—I don't know *what* exactly, but not this. Definitely not this.

"Thanks, 'Lik," I say.

He just nods, grabs some things from his locker, and then heads out of the locker room, leaving me and David there, alone. Again.

"Well, that was weird," David says when Malik is gone.

My heart is racing in my chest from the adrenaline. "Yeah," I say. "Thank God it wasn't Coach."

"If Coach Campbell tried to kick us off the team for kissing, then I don't think I want to play on this team."

"I don't know that he'd do that. But I don't want to test him."

David exhales. I can see his chest release all the air.

"Then, for your sake, I hope Coach doesn't find out."

I don't know if that's a jab or not, but I just respond with "Yeah. I trust Malik to keep a secret. I grew up with him and till this day, he's kept secrets."

"I probably shouldn't have done it in the first place," David says sadly.

"But I wanted to," I say back.

"Really?"

"I wouldn't have gone in for it if I didn't want to, man."

"Oh?" He kind of grins. "Good."

"You're a good kisser," I tell him. He's not the first boy I've kissed since breaking up with Ayesha, but he's the best boy I've kissed since breaking up with Ayesha.

"Thanks," he says, showing teeth now. His pale skin turns red from him blushing, and I like it. I like that about him. How compliments can stain his skin.

I'm all nodding and smiling.

"Want a ride back home?" He throws his bag over his shoulder.

I think for a moment. "Yeah, sure," I say. I think Olly and Ayesha caught an earlier bus. At least, they haven't texted me about riding with them. Sometimes they wait for me until practice is over. Other times, they don't.

I follow him outside to his car. It's a white Honda Civic with a license plate that says his name, but some of the letters are numbers.

"Cool car," I say when I get in. One whiff and it smells like those lemon tree air fresheners.

"Thanks," he says. "It was a gift from my parents. It was theirs, but then they bought a better one for the two of them to share."

"Smells good, too."

"My mom drives this car a lot still and I swear every time she uses it she uses a zillion kinds of air fresheners."

"Ha-ha. My stepmom is like that but for our house. She puts those little plug-ins everywhere."

He turns the car on, the engine roars to life, and we take off toward West Haven. The car ride is quiet, except for a little music playing in the background. For a while I don't recognize any of the songs that play, but finally one does play that I do kind of vaguely recognize from somewhere.

"Who is this?" I ask him.

"Seriously?" He looks at me with a smirk, like I didn't recognize Beyoncé or something.

"Yeah." I laugh the word. "I think I know this song, but I'm blanking on who sings it at the moment."

"It's called 'Summer Love' by Carly Rae Jepsen," he answers. "Man, she's like the hottest pop artist out right now."

"Debatable," I say.

"Who would you say is hotter?"

"Hmm, I don't even have to think about that one," I say. "I'd probably say Ariana or Billie Eilish."

"Okay, that's a fair answer. I thought you were going to say T-Swift."

"Naaah! I would never say T-Swift," I tell him, kind of laughing. "Damn. I can't believe you got me saying the name T-Swift now."

"Okay, now, you've got to give *some* props to old T-Swift. Before she kind of lost her marbles."

"Lost her marbles?"

"Yeah. She lost them."

"Is that, like, a white people saying?" I ask. "'Cause I don't know what that means."

"You've never heard that?"

"Nope."

"Then, maybe," he answers, and looks back at the road as we pull to a red light.

I focus on the cars and buildings that blur past us once we get driving again. I can see my reflection in the window, and for the first time I see my birth mom in me. We've got the same eyes, the same eyelashes, the same mouth and jawline. The main thing that's different is our noses—I got mine from Pops.

"So, did you figure out what you're doing about your mom being back?" David asks me out of nowhere, taking me away from staring at my reflection.

"I emailed her about tomorrow's game. I told her I'd want to talk to her. I hope she comes" is all I say, my head leaning against the window.

"I hope she comes for you, too," David says. His tone is serious, but his words are tender.

"Thanks, David. I appreciate that."

A few minutes slip by and we stop at a stop sign. I watch David ease out of his black leather jacket and decide to ask him about it. "You wear that black leather jacket a lot," I tell him. The way the words come out it sounds like I'm judging him, but I'm not. "That came out wrong. Sorry!"

"It was Kayla's. She saved all her money to buy it from this secondhand store. She always said it made her feel tough and invincible when she wore it, but now I get that she didn't really feel that way. I started wearing it after she died. I don't know, I guess I like to know she's with me. Still out in the world."

Damn. Most of my life, I tried to mask my grief and pain the best I could so I wouldn't draw in any attention, so no one had to offer their words of sympathy to try and make me feel better about myself. But look at him. He chooses to wear his as a jacket.

"Sorry you went through that," I tell him. "So, when you wear that jacket you remember her?"

"Every time," he says.

"Damn. I think I know what you mean. Why was she so sad?" I ask, my breathing picking up. "You don't have to answer that if you don't want."

David grips the steering wheel tight. "No, it's fine. It's just . . . complicated."

"Trust me. Complicated is my middle name."

"Kayla was hurt by a lot of the people in her life, and she just couldn't find her way out of that hurt. I tried to help her. But the hurt . . . it was just much deeper than what was visible on the surface, you know?" His voice breaks up in so many places.

"That has to be really hard."

There's a brief quiet that passes between us. "My old therapist once told me that one day I'll forget the painful things about my sister, but I don't think that's how it works. I think you just learn to live with them. It's like grief is a backpack we wear through life, and we're constantly putting hard things inside it. Not to ignore those things, but to carry them with us as we go on. Well, that's in my grief backpack, Gio. What happened will stick with me forever. This jacket means everything to me."

I offer a thin smile, nodding my understanding to him. And I sit there, staring at the side of his face, lost in my thoughts. I'm really looking forward to that day where there will be no more crying or pain or death or mothers who abandon you or sisters who die by suicide. I'm really looking forward to everything being turned upside down—or right side up, and all I can feel is the deepest happiness any human can feel in the presence of love and love *alone*.

Olly FaceTimes me. I answer it and somehow Ayesha clicks on, too. This whole group FaceTime thing is weird.

"Sup," I tell them.

"Hey," Ayesha says, and I notice she's filing her nails down.

"What are you up to?" Olly asks me. His beach-blond hair is styled to one side of his head.

"I'm in the car with David on my way home," I say.

"Are you guys talking about the date you didn't show up for?" Olly asks.

I look at David and then my screen. "I'm not wearing headphones, Olly, so he can hear you."

"Shit, my bad," Olly says. "Hi, David!"

"How's it going, Olly? Hey, Ayesha," he says to them as he

drives. I kind of pan my front camera toward him a little so they can see his face.

"You two want to come to Kreamy Kones with me and Ayesha?" Olly asks.

I look over at David and his eyes meet mine. "I'll go, if you go," he says.

I think for a brief moment and tell them that we're in.

THIRTEEN

ONCE WE PULL UP to Kreamy Kones, my phone dings. I pull it out to check where the notification's coming from and my eyes get wide from what it is. It's a reply from my mom. She's finally read my email and she's finally replied. Instantly, I lose all the breath in my lungs.

To: GioTheGr8@gmail.com
From: missjackie01@global.net
Subject: RE: UNTITLED

G-Bug,
Sorry I'm just now responding to you. I'm so glad you emailed me. And I'm so glad you got my letters even if you never got to read them before. I would love to talk. I'm not sure if I can make it to your game. Is there another place/time that works?

Mom

"What's wrong?" David asks, cutting the engine.
"I . . . umm . . ." I can't get the words out.

I just show him the email response and his eyes match the wideness of mine. "Wow," he says. "It's like we spoke it into existence. That's awesome. How're you feeling?"

"I don't know," I say. "All the emotions at once at full intensity." I draw in a breath.

"Don't overthink it. You should respond," David says. "Don't get caught up worrying about whether she will stay or worrying about what you want to say. Just go. Be with her. Enjoy the time with her for what it is. Trust your heart."

"You're right. It's annoying that you're right."

"Besides, tomorrow's going to be a huge day."

"Yeah," I say. "Maybe when I talk to her, I'll need another round of therapy by the end. Or maybe not. Maybe our conversation will be therapeutic enough."

When we walk into Kreamy Kones, we find Olly and Ayesha at the counter ordering. When they see me, their faces illuminate with excitement. I shake up with Olly and then Ayesha.

"Hey, David," Ayesha goes, looking at me with raised eyebrows.

"Hi, Ayesha. Hi, Olly," David says.

"Yo! Looks like you guys are cool again, huh?" Olly says.

"Oh. Right. I meant to text you guys that we, uh, made up. Sorry. It all happened just a little bit ago. Anyway . . . I just got an email."

They take turns reading it on my phone.

"Aw, Gio," Ayesha says. I'm not sure if that's sympathy or more excitement, but I take it.

"That's cool, Gio," Olly says. "Now, order since we have

something to kind of celebrate." Celebrate? I don't if that's the word I would go with. I mean, I am looking forward to talking to my mom, but I don't know if there's really anything about it to celebrate.

I ask for my usual. Mint chocolate chip ice cream with cookie dough and sprinkles. David orders chocolate ice cream with Oreos on top. We all go and find an open table for four in the back near where the entrance to the back freezers is.

I'm picking through to find all the cookie dough pieces in my ice cream when Ayesha asks me what would be the first thing I ask my birth mom when I meet up with her.

"I think I really just want to know the truth," I say. "Pops hasn't really ever told me much. And I don't know if he ever would."

Suddenly, I think about the very moment my mom stopped loving me. I don't know if that ever happened, but at one point that's what I convinced myself. I wanna ask her about that, too.

The chimes ring above the door, signaling a new customer. We all look back almost simultaneously. We gotta watch our backs. It's Tatiana, Ms. Diane's daughter, who's pregnant again at sixteen. She comes with some tall, skinny light-skinned boy with a red bandanna on his head.

Tatiana makes eye contact and comes over toward us. "Hey, Ayesha! Hey, Gio!" She knows the two of us, but she doesn't really know Olly and she doesn't know David at all.

I wave at her, but Ayesha's all like, "Heyyyy, girl. How's it going?" There she go, being fake. "How long you got left until you're due?"

"Just a few more months, girl," Tatiana tells her. "I'm ready to get this thing out of me. I'm tired of throwing up every night."

"Oh, I bet," Ayesha says back. "You know the baby's gender?"

"Nah," Tatiana says. "I want it to be a surprise. I'm just excited Imani's gon' have somebody to play with."

"Where's she at?"

"Imani's at my momma's house right now. I'm about to go get her."

"Aw, that's cool," Ayesha says, faking like she's actually interested.

"This is Bunny, by the way," Tatiana says, introducing the Black guy she walked in with. "He's my new baby daddy."

We all shake his hand, introduce ourselves to him. Tatiana and Ayesha exchange phone numbers and then Tatiana and this Bunny dude go and find their own table.

David goes, "Sorry if this is offensive, but what kind of name is Bunny?"

"It's not his real name," I explain.

"Really?" His face bunches up a little and he scrapes at the bottom of his bowl.

"Some people in the hood have nicknames or, well, gang names for their own protection," Ayesha explains for me. "Like my real name isn't Ayesha. It's Queen Latifah."

"Really?" David looks shook. And I hold in my laughter.

"Nah, I'm just fucking with you," Ayesha says to him, and busts out laughing her ass off.

"Oh, okay," David exhales.

Ayesha changes the topic completely. "You guys see that the Migos are coming to town in a few months?"

"Whoa. Like the same Migos that sing 'Bad and Boujee'?" Olly's intrigued. What does Olly know about "Bad and Boujee"?

"Yeah. They're doing a concert at Lucas Oil Stadium. And I'm thinking about getting tickets. Mainly to see my husband, Quavo."

"Who do you think is the best Migo, Gio?" Olly asks. "I prefer Takeoff more than the others."

"Hmm . . . Quavo is the best hook Migo. Offset is the best flow Migo. Takeoff is the best lyrical Migo," I say. "Overall, Offset can do everything, in my opinion, so he has my vote."

We all look at David for his answer and he shrugs. "I'm going to be honest. I have no clue who you're talking about. What's a Migo?"

We all laugh together for a bit. Even David joins in, laughing. It's good to laugh with him and not at him.

Eventually, Olly and Ayesha have a side debate about which Migo album was the best. I use the opportunity to ask David if he's okay.

"I'm fine," he says through a smile, and he moves his foot over to me, kind of almost playing footsie underneath the table. "I'm just happy to be with you."

It's weird that he's hanging out with me and my best friends as my kind of date. It's strange because I've never been in a position like this before. Back when I dated Ayesha, Olly was our third wheel. I think David's taken that place now, but it doesn't seem like he cares.

He's fully himself here. He laughs and offers jokes and tells stories like he's been in our squad for years. I like that he's so comfortable even if it's probably going to take a while for me to get used to this. I'm just so glad that he's here. By my side.

He smiles at me. His smile could bring world peace, cure any disease, mend broken hearts together over and over again.

After Kreamy Kones, David drops off Olly, Ayesha, and then me last. When he pulls up in front of my house, he invites me over to his place to hang out.

"You can make up for bailing on me," he says, and winks at me.

"How about we meet up later tonight, like in a couple hours?"

"Sounds good." He smiles, then gets serious. "Just . . . if something comes up or if you're not in a good place, let me know, okay?"

"Yeah, okay," I tell him. "I'll do that."

Karina and Pops are chilling in the living room watching *Family Feud*. I take it they've made up about the whole situation with the box of letters that Karina gave me. Biscuit greets me with kisses when I sit on the couch with them.

"Hey, honeybunches, how was practice?" Karina asks. Her voice is soft, but I can always tell that she's happy to see me.

"It was good," I say. "Coach was just trying to prepare us for our big game."

"Oh, good, good," she says. "I made some blueberry muffins if you want one. They're in the oven now."

"No thank you," I say. "I went to Kreamy Kones after practice."

Pops clears his throat and interrupts our conversation. "You're on the schedule to serve at church this Sunday. You're running communion."

"I—What? I don't know if I can." What I really mean is: I don't want to.

"You heard me," he says. "It wasn't a request."

I fidget with my hands and then look at Karina. It's like we've developed telepathy because she turns back to Pops and says, "I can do it, Charles, if Gio can't. Maybe he has something with basketball."

"I don't give a damn about no basketball," Pops goes. "People at the church keep asking me if you even a Christian anymore."

I should've known. This isn't about me. Everything is always about him. Never about me or what I want, but about him and his reputation.

"No," I say, standing to my feet. "I won't do it."

Pops stands to his feet, also, and he comes close—real close like he's gonna hit me. But he doesn't. He just balls up his fists and I remain still. Even though I'll get paid for it, even though it doesn't require that much work to pass out the bread and the grape juice at church, I don't know if I want that. Pops always talks like I'm gonna take over the church when he's gone, but I wanna play basketball. Honestly, I'd rather study rocket science or engineering or manage a McDonald's before I take over his church.

"Come Sunday morning, if you don't have your Black behind up at that church and—"

"I'm seeing her tomorrow," I interrupt. "My . . . my mom."

"What did you just say?!" He takes a step in.

Karina clutches her chest at first, but then walks over to me. She puts her hand on the small of my back, supporting me in this.

"After my game, we're gonna talk, and then I'll know the truth about why you didn't want me to have her letters and why you haven't talked about her and why she left and all the other questions I have. I wanna know why she left me with such a terrible person, like you."

"Gio!" Karina attempts, patting my back.

I turn away to head upstairs to my room and Pops goes, "Come back here! I'm still talkin' to you!"

Ignoring him, I go to my room and shut my door, locking it so he won't come in. Man, it felt so good to stand up to him like that. It felt good to not just take whatever he says. I sit on my bed and make a quick playlist for tomorrow. I take my time thinking about songs that I want to include for this playlist. It's a special one—I mean, all of my playlists are special because they are about specific moments in my life, like making it to high school, breaking up with Ayesha, figuring out that I'm bisexual, the day Olly and I became best friends—but this one feels like it'll be one of the more important ones, so it has to be good.

The first song I add to the playlist is "All We Ever Knew" by The Head and the Heart. I study the rest of my saved songs closely, carefully selecting just the right songs for this particular playlist. The last thing I have to do is come up with a name for it, but I'll think about that later. For now, my only worry is that I'm picking the right songs.

1. "All We Ever Knew" by The Head and the Heart
2. "Babybird" by Chloe x Halle
3. "Part II" by Paramore
4. "Moments Passed" by Dermot Kennedy
5. "Lonely Girl" by Tonight Alive
6. "Happy" by Wande
7. "Royals" by Lorde
8. "Just Breathe" by Don Brownrigg
9. "Change" by J. Cole
10. "Heal" by Tom Odell

Someone knocks on my door. The knocks are soft, so I know it's not an angry Pops.

"Karina?" I say.

"Yes, honeybunches," she says softly. "I just wanna check in on you."

"I'm okay," I tell her.

"All right. Let me know if you need anything, okay?"

"Okay," I tell her.

A few minutes later, I hear Biscuit growling at my door. I unlock it to let her in and Theo's waiting there, also.

"Hey, man." I rub the top of his head and let them both come in and jump on my bed.

"Wanna play *Halo*?" he asks me. "I just downloaded some new weapons."

"Of course, buddy," I tell him even though I'm not really in the mood to play games, but I'll do anything for Theo, no matter what.

Theo gets *Halo* started in his room. We've got headsets on and we're fighting squadrons and helping each other out as best we can. I wonder if I should tell Theo about what's going on. I think he should know. She's been emailing me but hasn't said much about Theo. On top of that, she wants to meet with me alone. Maybe she wants to figure things out with me first, but I can't go see her and not tell him. I can't hide something like that from him. I pause the game to tell him. "Theo, I'm hanging out with Mom tomorrow."

He just looks at me. "Really? Are you gonna ask her why she didn't want us?" There's so much sadness evident in his voice, and it makes me want to burst into tears.

I stare into his eyes and I know he means it. "Yeah, I'll ask for you, Theo."

He resumes *Halo*, not saying anything else, and we keep playing for a while.

FOURTEEN

POPS FINDS ME IN my room right before I head out to meet David. I'm at my desk, staring at my mom's last email and listening to "Eastside" by Benny Blanco featuring Halsey and Khalid. He grabs my shoulder and I jump back, caught off guard by his cold, hard hands.

"What do you want?" I ask him, spinning around in my desk chair. I sound real grumpy.

"We need to talk," he says. "I told Karina I wouldn't get angry. I'm trying to work on that. But there's been so many bad things happening up at the church and then all the stuff with Jackie and . . ."

"What's happening at the church?" I ask. I know I don't really like it or care too much about being a pastor's kid, but I know how much this church means to Pops—and no matter what, he's my Pops, so I wanna know what's going on.

"Somebody's been stealing money from the tithes and offerings account," he says. "If we don't come up with the money, we might have to close the church."

"Oh crap, that sucks."

"Yeah," he says, sitting on the edge of my bed, putting his

head in his hands. "I know it was one of the deacons or deacon-esses. I'm just trying to figure out which one it was."

"You know Deaconess Lisa's real slick," I tell him.

"I know," he says, kind of with a grin. "She's my first target."

Some silence floods in my room.

"Anyway, I just wanted say you're right. You're right. I am a terrible person. I am a terrible parent. I've been so . . . terrible to you and Theo."

I swallow and listen to him, unsure what to do with my hands and arms. This is a big moment. I've never heard him own up to something like this before.

"Growing up, my dad was real hard on me, overly control-ling. When I was your age, my dream was to have my own business. I didn't care what kind of business it was. I just wanted to have something that was all mine. All I had was a dollar and a dream. But my dad didn't think that was realistic enough for me. He had me start reading the Bible every day, trying to convince me to go into preaching. He would always say that a man is only as good as his legacy," he says, then takes a breath before continuing. "I gave up all my dreams to follow his. Even changed who I was so that I could show him just how good of a legacy he would have with me. You see, son, a boy's greatest desire is his father's heart, so I did whatever I could to make him proud, even if it meant forgetting who I was entirely along the way. I've seen myself become this bitter, cold, con-niving drunk who has done nothing but push you and Theo and Karina and, at one point, your mom away every chance I get. And I'm sorry, Gio. I really am. I didn't realize until now just how me being so hard on you, keeping things from you, never showing you how proud I am of you was actually making me into my father. That's not what I want for my kids."

"What are you trying to say to me?" I ask, but it comes out too snappy.

"Listen. I'm sorry. I just thought . . . that being hard on you was easier than telling you the truth."

"Yeah" is all I can say. Suddenly, I can't even form real sentences. I don't know what's happening. All sorts of emotions build within me from listening to him explain himself. I heard Grandpa Rick was so focused on himself that he didn't really have time for Pops. And I know Pops spent so long trying to get Grandpa Rick to notice him—to really see him. There are pictures around the house of him as a kid wearing overalls and playing with toys and Grandma Ruby is in them, but Grandpa Rick is not.

He puts a hand on his forehead, like he's stressing out about what he's telling me. "The thing about Jackie—your mom—is that she's not who you think she is, son. Your mother is broken."

"But aren't we all?"

I almost hear him bite his lower lip. "The Bible says so. My daddy used to tell me that sometimes in life you have to figure out what people you're going to give up. He would say that sometimes it's your own flesh and blood you gotta leave in the past."

That feels really harsh, but I think I get what he means.

He goes on. "Son, it's my job to protect you, to keep you safe, no matter what. Sometimes, the way I go about that isn't always the best. But, at the end of the day, I always get the job done. But your mother . . . she's the one thing I can't protect you from."

I swallow hard. "What do you mean? Why would you need to protect me from her?"

He stands up and paces the length of my room. "I can't say, but I'm sorry. Over the years, I've tried and tried and tried to keep you from knowing things about her, hoping that you wouldn't be curious about her or ask about her. But you always did. You always wanted to know about her. Karina and I had this big fight about her giving you the letters because I thought they would hurt you. I thought they would make you want to ask more questions. And today, I've realized just how much more that must've hurt you than the fact that she was gone."

"Yeah," I say. Again. Just a single word.

"I can't stop you from hearing her out. After all, she brought you into this world just as much as I did."

I'm so confused where this sudden burst of understanding and father-like-ness is coming from, but I like it, and I want this to be how things are between us more and more. This isn't the Pops I've known for the last several years, since Mom walked out, but I like this version—this is the version that I want to stay around.

My phone's buzzing. It's David calling me. I let his call go to my voicemail but shoot him a quick text that I'm not bailing on him. He texts back that he's waiting for me outside when I'm ready.

Somewhere inside me I find a way to tell Pops, "Thanks, Pops, for saying all that. It means a lot to hear."

"Of course, Gio. Did you read all those letters?"

"No," I say. And that's the truth. I really only read the two, or three. I really wanted to read the other ones, but I didn't want to either torture myself or give myself this unrealistic hope that my life would suddenly change now that I'd read them. But I'm talking with her tomorrow—surely that might at least change *something* about my life.

"I read them as soon as we'd get them in the mail. She just wanted to live a life that . . . well . . . you'll find out what. I'll leave that up to her to tell you about that."

"Why didn't you just throw them away?" I ask.

He looks around my room like he's thinking of an answer before looking at me with these big, sincere eyes. "I love Karina to death, but your mom was my very first love. There are letters in the box for me, also."

Wow. Hearing him talk about the letters, I see more emotion and empathy in him than I ever have, and I don't know what to make of it.

"I'm sorry, Pops," I tell him. I don't know what I'm apologizing for or whatever, but I do it and it feels right, and it causes Pops to smile.

"You don't have to apologize to me. That's my job right now." Pops opens his arms and I meet him there, and it's warm and perfect and fatherly and I kind of melt there for a while before I'm mended again.

* * *

"Before pizza, I have to take you somewhere" is the first thing David says to me when I get in his car. I don't argue, and we head downtown.

There's a light dusting of snow on the streets. We park in one of the two-hour parking spaces and walk along the canal, where there are couples walking dogs and young kids trying to collect the melting snow.

We turn a corner and David sort of circles me, looking me up and down. "You look really nice with all that drip."

"*Drip?* Who taught you that word?" I joke with him. "Thanks, David."

"Those Kyries?"

I almost side-eye him. "Definitely Curry 7s."

"I'm wearing my LeBron Soldier 12s," he says. I look at them. They're black and yellow.

"I can't stand LeBron and I can't stand his shoes, either. But I'm honestly surprised you're not wearing Converse."

"Wow. Hate for the king and hate for me, huh?"

"Hater is my middle name," I lie, and then add, "And MJ is the real king. He made basketball popular in a totally different way."

"Can't argue with that one. But I must say, I'm taking LeBron in a one-on-one with MJ."

"MJ got skills, though."

"Also can't argue with that one."

"Good. Because I have all the receipts on my phone of videos of MJ just embarrassing dudes on the court," I say.

"Whatever, whatever."

"So, where are we going?" I ask him after a minute or two of walking.

"DeeJay's," he answers.

"Isn't that, like, a record store or something?"

"Mhmm," David says. "I figured since you like playlists as much as I do maybe going to DeeJay's could be a good first thing to do on a first date."

I look at him and he winks at me. The boy loves his winks. "Date, huh?" I say. That word *date*. It feels like a Sour Patch Kid on my tongue. Sour, for sure, but nice.

"Sorry," he says, motioning his apologies. "I thought . . ."

"I'm just kidding. We're chilling. *Date* is just a word."

He goes back to being his normal self again. Walking alongside me. But honestly, there is something about the word that feels weird. This is new territory for me. I mean, there were times where I, like, saw a couple guys in secret—purely text message exchanges or social media DMs late at night of our junk—but that's not what I have with David. I don't know exactly what I have with him or what I want with him, but it's not *that*. Ayesha was the first person who I dated—actually dated, doing things like going out, spending real time together like human beings should. Whatever's happening here, I'm cool with it. Focusing on my grief and all that stuff that's happening with my mom has prevented me from truly appreciating what David's bringing to my life. I mean, he's been kind and present and real and there for me over and over, even when I didn't deserve it. He's a real G for that, looking out for me and walking me through the darkness.

He moves to hold my hand, and I allow them to come together, and we carry on walking downtown. My heart pounds in my chest at the fact that he's holding my hand because I'm now worrying about if someone will see us and force me to be out at school before I'm ready. I walk closer to his side to almost hide our hands, like I'm trying to camouflage my feelings for him.

"You're so warm," he says. "Like, your hands are really warm."

"Oh . . . sorry."

"No, it's a good thing."

"Oh, then, dope."

Finally, we get to DeeJay's record store. We get inside and the first aisle we go down is the rock/alternative section. The place smells like old wood. An older woman at the cash register looks up when we come in, but doesn't say anything.

I watch David flip through the band names that start with the letter *P*. Then he pulls out a disc and flashes it to me. "It's Paramore's first-ever album."

My eyes get really wide and I nearly snatch it out of his hands.

"I've gotta buy this," I tell him. "This is seriously limited edition."

"I called ahead to make sure they had it here," David says, grinning sneakily.

I hold it close to my chest. "This is so damn dope, David."

He walks down the aisle a little bit more. "I really want My Chemical Romance's first album."

"*Danger Days?*"

He makes this surprised face. "*I Brought You My Bullets*, actually."

The woman who was at the cash register follows me around. Every time I look back at her as a way to show her that I see that she's following me, she looks away.

Almost like it's an instinct, I keep behind David as we make our way through the aisles. There are huge bins that don't conform to alphabetical order, and David's scanning them for My Chemical Romance's first album, frenzying through the records like he's trying to pick apart the ugliness of the world to find a treasure or something.

"Sleeping with Sirens!" he shouts, flashing me this medium-sized record with a brown lettering. "Another classic band and another great album by them."

I look at the price tag. "Fifty dollars?!" I can feel my eyebrows furrow. I check the Paramore album I'm holding. Luckily, it's about half the price of this Sleeping with Sirens one. I don't have a lot of money left in my wallet and buying this record might just kill whatever remaining dollars I've got. But if I can sacrifice going out to eat with Ayesha and Olly or spending money anywhere else, I can get this record and feel like it isn't going to be the worst decision I've made all week.

"Records can be pricey," David says, "but some are worth every dollar for the history."

"Hmm . . . I never really thought about it like that, but yeah. You're right."

"What about this one?" David asks me, holding up a Taylor Swift record.

"Absolutely not." My eyes roll.

"But it's T-Swift!"

"David."

He laughs a small laugh. "Fine. I'll just get it for your birthday and wrap it up so you won't know what it is. Sorry, I just have really gay DNA."

"I'll burn it," I tease him. "And, yes, I can tell about the DNA thing."

"Wow. That's how much you care, huh?"

"David."

"Okay."

I watch David scan all the racks of records, flipping through old rock bands all the way to newer, young rappers that make him go, "What the hell is a 21 Savage?"

I laugh at him. "You're straight-up uncultured," I say, teasing him some more.

"Look." He points to his pale arms and then his face.

"What?"

"I'm white as hell. Some people use the peach crayon to color white people, but you need the white crayon to color *me* in."

"Oh, David."

"I'm being for real."

He goes back to flipping through the records. Before I do the same, I look him up and down. His black leather jacket. His red curls. His tight skinny jeans that show his ass nicely. His Lebron Soldier 12s. This boy is such a mystery, but I can't help but feel like I'm on top of the world when I'm near him. I can't help but feel every butterfly in a fifty-mile radius flutter in my stomach. I don't take my eyes off of him—I can't. His ivory-white skin, like a blank but beautiful canvas, his long eyelashes like mini fanning feathers, his full lips. Everything about him—it's cute.

The white lady who's been following me around steps in between David and me. "Can I help you with anything?" she asks.

We both look at each other and then at her. "No, thanks."

Instead of walking away and not coming back, she goes into another aisle and follows us again. I'm not sure if David notices or not, but I do, and I'm weirded out.

"What about this one?! It's on sale for half price," he says, flashing me another record. "To be honest, this one will be even hotter than any Taylor Swift record one day."

"BTS! Jungkook and Jimin are very beautiful men."

"Agreed."

"A'ight. Are you ready to check out?" I ask him. I wouldn't mind staying in this shop with David for hours and hours and hours, but it's getting kind of late and we still need to get pizza.

"I want to look for one more thing," he says. "I'll be right back."

"Okay, no rush," I tell him as he turns away to go into another aisle. I stay put and look around me for a rack that piques my interest.

I slip the Paramore record under my arm so I can scroll through the '80s Funk section better.

"Hey, stop! Young man! Stop!" someone yells from behind me. I whirl around. It's the white woman.

"Um . . . sorry," I say. "Stop what?" My stomach twists.

"Put that record down if you're not going to buy it," the woman says. "Don't make me call the cops."

"I didn't do anything," I say. My fists clench at my sides on instinct. "I just put the record there so I could keep looking around."

David comes back into the aisle I'm in. "What's going on?"

"This woman is threatening me," I tell him. "She thinks I'm stealing from this place."

"What?" David asks, confused. "That's stupid. Why would you think that, lady?"

"You are on video camera." The lady points up to a camera attached to the ceiling, ignoring David's question. "I'm tired of people like you thinking you can come into my store and steal."

WHAT.

THE.

ACTUAL.

FUCK.

"Huh?!" I shout, turning my head sideways. "People like me? I ain't trying to steal nothing!" My hood side is about to jump all the way out, and I'm not about to stop it. My fists clench even tighter at my sides.

I breathe out.

Thump. Thump. Thump.

My pulse speeds up.

"People like you. Thugs."

My eyes nearly pop right out my head with how big they just got. I look back at David and he's not doing anything, like he's frozen in place. Then he puts the records he's holding down. His face goes red.

My voice is thick. "Lady. I ain't trynna steal anything from you or anyone." I try to remember what Karina and Pops told me when talking to white folks—to be proper. I squint to read her name on the tag on her shirt. "Ms. Jillian, I think there's been a mistake."

The white woman places a finger in my face. "Did you think you'd just run out of here and get away with it?"

"What? No!" David steps forward to get between me and her.

"Look, lady, you need to chill before I lose my shit," I go.

"Gio, it's okay." David tries his best to keep me calm and to keep this lady calm, like some sort of mediator. I'm not trying to mediate shit. She came at me. I'm coming back twice as hard.

"Fuck that." I let the record fall to the ground.

I can hear the thumping of my heart against my chest. It just got so hot in here.

The lady pulls out a walkie-talkie and calls for security. Within seconds, a tall, bald white man comes running over. He's in a legit police officer's outfit. Gun, Taser, everything.

I look behind me, noticing other people staring our way. It hits me that this might not end well. It hits me that this lady is racist. It hits me that she's siccing this cop on us—no, on me. She hasn't said a thing to David. Ain't this some shit?

Fuck. I don't want to go to jail. I don't want to get hurt. All I want is to just go home.

Standing completely still, I imagine tomorrow's headline: *Black Hoodlum from West Haven Detained for Stealing at*

Record Store Night Before He Sees His Birth Mother. It wouldn't be the first time a headline like that has been all over the news. I start to shake in my Curry 7s.

"What's the problem?" the guard asks.

"I think this young man was trying to steal from us," the lady answers, clipping her walkie-talkie back to her hip.

I grab David's hand and squeeze it tight. I send up a single prayer. *God, please make this right.* It's the first time I've prayed in a minute, but I throw it up with desperation.

"Step forward," the guard barks at us. It takes everything for me to move.

I glance at David before complying. He looks scared for me and his lips tremble. Almost as much as mine. "Just do it, Gio."

I exhale and take a step forward, closer to the officer.

"I have to search you," he says, raising his eyebrow at us. "Get against the wall there." He points to the one filled with Nirvana and Spice Girls records.

He searches me first, starting in my shoes. He places his fingers in my socks and feels around in there. His hands move up my legs, into my pockets and waistline, then inside my shirt, until he says, "Nothing! All clean."

There's nothing fucking there. I'm not some goddamn random thug who wants to rob this place, I think to myself. My stomach squeezes harder and all I want to do is scream. All I want to do is go home. It takes a shit ton of effort not to do it. I'm so heated you can use me for kindling.

The lady and I are staring at each other now. I want to call her a racist bitch so badly, but I'm not gonna do that or give this cop a reason to say that I was resisting. I'm not trying to give him any reason why he should shoot me in this record store. Hell, why does a guard even need to be armed in a record store?

"Please leave my store," the white lady says.

"I want to go home," I tell David. We walk straight out and head back for his parents' car.

"Are you okay?" he asks me. "That was messed up."

There's a hand on my constricting chest. I can't say anything. Still shaking, though.

In the car for most of the ride, I still can't say anything. David tries to reach for my hand, but I pull away. It's not David's fault what happened back at that record store—none of it was his fault. But he's still white and it kind of felt like he was more on the side of peace than having my back when I needed him to.

Eventually, I open up to him. "I'm never going back in that place. Ain't worth it." I tuck my hands in between my legs.

"Yeah. I'm sorry. I just—"

"It's not your fault, David. It's okay."

"They were an average record store anyway," he says, trying to calm me down some more. When I don't say anything else, he asks again, "Are you okay?"

"I'm fine. You?"

"I'm good."

I pull out my phone and post in our group chat. I just need to let them know about it and that I'm safe.

Olly

Fuck racist assholes.

WHAT THE HELL??

David keeps his eyes on the road. I stare out the window at all the cars and buildings that blur as we pass, thinking about that lady who followed me and that cop over and over again.

David reaches over to poke my shoulder. "You sure you're okay? Y'know it's okay to not be okay, right?"

I keep staring out the window and look up at the starry sky. Clearing my airways, I sneak a glance at him. I don't know if I'm crying, but I get that dryness in my throat like I'm about to.

"I just . . . I feel like you weren't on my side," I say.

"What?"

"I know you were scared for me—I know that."

"I was just really shocked it was happening. I don't know what you're trying to tell me."

"What I'm saying is that you didn't fight for me."

"Fight for you? I was scared also," David answers.

"But you weren't being searched by a fake cop, David. You weren't the one who was being profiled. You don't know what it's like to go through that."

"I'm queer, Gio," he says. "I think I know what it feels like to be harassed."

"You know what it's like to be queer in this country, but you'll never know what it's like to be a person of color. David, I'm bisexual, but I'm still Black. Before anything else, I'm Black."

David is silent for a moment.

"I don't think I'm in the mood for pizza anymore. I just want to go home," I say.

"Yeah, sure. Okay."

It's so painfully quiet in this car for the rest of the ride.

Out the window, the buildings we pass turn from fancy-looking and five stars to abandoned and run-down, and the roads get bumpier from all the potholes, so I know we're getting closer to West Haven.

He drops me off in front of my house. Before I hop out of his car, David grabs for my arm and I get a glance at his face. It's a sad one, but I look away quickly.

"I just—"

"It's okay, David," I say, interrupting him and undercutting my words with the bitterness of my tone. "You don't have to say anything else."

I get out and shut the door behind me. It takes everything in me not to look back at him, but I manage not to. Once I'm inside the house, Biscuit attacks me with licks and I pick her up and hold her close, almost like I did with the Paramore record in that store. I rub the top of her head, between her ears, and she squeals and squirms in my arms like she wants to play. She completely puts me in a better mood. I love that about Biscuit.

I bring her up to Theo's room. He's up late with his gaming headset on, playing *Halo*. Biscuit runs in and curls up on his bed.

"What's up, Theo?" I ask.

I don't know if he can hear me, but he looks back in perfect timing. "Hey!" He waves.

"You playing online?"

"Mhmm. With some friends."

"Nice."

"Gio, what's a fruitcake?"

My eyes are big, reminding me of that time I got called that in the third grade and asked my birth mom and pops. "It's a dessert," I answer. "Why?"

"Someone keeps calling me that on the game."

"Tell them that fruitcakes are delicious and so what if you are one."

He smiles at me.

And I smile back.

I'm not sure if he needs to hear this more or if I do, but something about saying it feels good.

Olly and Ayesha FaceTime me when I'm back in my room. I spend most of the rest of the night talking to them about what happened at DeeJay's and whether or not I should be up front with David about the two of us—whatever is really going on between us.

"So . . . what you're saying is you can't see you and David as a *thing* thing?" Olly asks, after everything. I can tell he's wearing his *Star Wars* bathrobe.

"It's just . . . it would be so much easier if we weren't," I answer.

Ayesha clears her throat. "Whaaaat? What do you mean? I see the way you look at him, like he's something good to eat or some shit."

"Exactly," Olly says. "So what if he messed up? Sometimes it takes white people a little more time to learn how to be an ally.

Like an actual one." The fact that Olly says this makes me feel mixed feelings. On one hand, I like it. On the other, he's not the one who should be telling me what a good ally is.

"It's just that it's already hard enough dealing with the fact that I'm bi and am kind of falling for a dude when Pops has told me time and time again growing up that being gay or bi was a sin and that he wouldn't allow it under his roof." I don't know if he feels differently about that after our conversation. But nothing leads me to think so. After all, he's still the pastor of the neighborhood church.

"I hear you," Olly says. "But maybe you're overreacting?"

Ayesha just says "Hmm" and smacks her lips as she eats some graham crackers and peanut butter.

I twirl my headphones around and continue talking to them. "Sometimes you can't explain what you see in people or what makes you fall for them. I can name a zillion reasons why David is great. But there's one thing that makes me feel like there's this giant divide between us I can't ever get past. I've never liked anybody white in that way."

Olly adds, "You wouldn't be the world's first gay interracial couple."

"It's not just that. Pops doesn't want me to just date a girl. He wants me to date a Black girl."

Ayesha interjects with "But this is *your* life. *Your* happiness, Gio. Not his. No matter what, you deserve to be happy." She's the second person to tell me this, after David, and still it feels strangely foreign. That word. *Happy.* Something I haven't been in a long time.

"You're right," I say. "I just don't even know what that looks like."

"That's okay. You'll figure it out. You always do," Ayesha adds, crunching on some graham crackers again.

"Thanks, Yesh. Means so much to have you two by my side."

Olly puts a finger up. "All I'll say now is if you feel that strongly about being with him, tell him that. Don't dick him over and keep him waiting around, waiting for you. You two are grown-ups and can figure out whatever this is that's going on between you two."

"I know. I know. I hear you." As true as that is, I'm not wanting to hear it.

Ayesha changes the topic. "Tomorrow will be here before you know it."

"I know," I say. "I'll be talking to my mom in less than twenty-four hours."

"You think you're ready?" Ayesha asks, trying to shove an entire peanut-butter-covered graham cracker in her mouth.

At the thought of it right now, I don't feel like I'll explode or fade into ash like from a Thanos snap, and something about that feels like progress. "I think so," I answer them. "I . . . think so."

"Good," Ayesha replies. "If not, you can always back out."

That's reassuring as hell. And I nod at her on the screen. After a few minutes of watching Ayesha chew and Olly pretend to be masturbating, I decide to maybe call it quits on our nighttime FaceTime call. "I think I'm about to hit the sack."

"Me too," Ayesha says. "Good night."

"Night," Olly says.

"Night, guys."

David's blowing up my phone with texts about how he's sorry, but I just want to relax and clear my head, so I don't reply. I click airplane mode on my phone and shove it underneath my pillow so I don't hear any pings from notifications.

I look at the pieces of the photo I tore up of my birth mom scattered across my floor. I've not picked them up or put them in the trash. They remain there, like they're decoration or something. Then I stare at the box of letters on my desk. Part of me wants to stay up all night reading them. The other part wants me to wait until I talk to her first, but still, staring at the box does something inside me. I wouldn't say I'm, like, looking forward to tomorrow or anything, but I'm definitely looking forward to asking all of my questions and saying all the things I couldn't say when she randomly showed back up. Maybe enough time has passed that I can do that without bursting like a hot air balloon that flew too high. All my thoughts popcorn around in my head.

FIFTEEN

●●●●●●

I SEE MALIK DEALING in the boys' bathroom when I get to school the following day. Some freshman who's dressed like he's a lot harder than he really is tosses Malik a twenty-dollar bill and they shake up before the transaction is all the way over.

"Sup, Malik?"

"Sup, broski?"

"Not much."

"That's what's up. You ain't see nothing, right?"

I know how to answer that. He's not the first 7th Street Disciple who's caught me watching a deal and asked me to keep quiet. "I didn't see anything."

"That's my dawg." We shake up as well. "I know your secrets, too."

Before he walks out, I tell him, "You should think about stopping that, Malik." I don't see why he can't work at July's barbershop or take over Ms. Diane's store before it has to close down to make money instead.

And he makes this face like I just offended him. "You don't know what you're talking about, Gio. It's hard out here."

"I know it's hard, but—"

"Nah, you don't. You got a family and shit. All I got is my momma and July and Tatiana and pretty soon if that ALS bullshit takes my momma, I'll only have Tatiana and July. We need money, man."

I'm quiet now like I can't say anything else after that. I feel him, though. "Yeah, okay. I hear you. Sorry I said that." I know my place. I know when to stop pushing around him. He's always had a temper since we were kids. I ask, "Any updates on the store?"

Malik licks his lips and brushes his hair with a hairbrush he pulls from his pocket. "Nah."

"Well, okay. Just keep me posted, 'Lik," I say.

"I got you, bro," he says back. "Anyway, I'll catch you at practice later tonight?"

"Yeah, 'Lik."

David's waiting for me at my locker with something wrapped in wrapping paper and a bow. He has this saddened puppy-dog look on his face and he's even twisting his body, rocking side to side, like he's trying to make me fall for him all over again.

"David, what are you doing?" I ask him nonchalantly, looking around. People are staring at us and I don't like this attention. No one has their phones out, recording us, but I'm sure some people might think it's a little suspicious that David, who's out and proud, is in front of my locker with a gift in his hands for me. My eyes search the hallways for Coach.

"I'm sorry," he says.

"People are watching now."

"Sorry. I really wasn't trying to make a big scene."

I sigh. "Follow me," I tell him. And I lead him all the way to the band room. I come in here to chill and get away when I need to, and I know no one is ever using it this time of day. We sit on a bench behind the percussion section.

"This is for you," he says, giving me the wrapped package.

"What is this?"

"Just open it."

Slowly, I unwrap the package and I see some green lettering, and I think I know what this is. When all the paper is off, I realize it's the Paramore record I didn't get to buy from DeeJay's.

"Don't worry. I didn't get it from DeeJay's. I won't ever support that place again after what they did to you."

"Where did you get it?"

"I searched everywhere for it last night and this morning. I finally found it on Facebook Marketplace. Some thirty-year-old emo guy met me at a gas station and all he wanted was a hand job."

I make a face. "What?"

"Kidding. Kidding," he says back.

I regain my composure. "Wow. Thanks, David," I say, grinning but trying to brush it off quickly.

"And no, I'm not trying to win back your trust or whatever by giving you this. I just wanted to do it because I care about you a lot and what I did was shitty."

I look into his eyes and they hold me in place. I let him speak. He scoots closer to me on this bench and places his hand on my knee. I hope no one comes in and sees us.

"I'm such a dumb idiot for not standing up for you more last night, Gio. I realize that now. You needed me to do something and I didn't because of my own fear. I didn't even realize that I put my own feelings before yours even though you were the one in danger. And that was shitty and racist. I'm so, so sorry, Gio. Please forgive me."

"Yeah," I say. *Super shitty* is what I want to say.

He looks defeated at first. "I'm Team You. Not Team Anyone Else. Let me make it up to you."

He raises his hand up my thigh. "Man, you make me weird" is all I say to him at first.

"I what?"

"You make me weird. All I did last night before I drifted to sleep was lie there thinking about my feelings until my eyes shut and then I even dreamed about them, thinking and dreaming about playing basketball and winning, but in all of them, you were there. Even when I'm pissed at you, I want you there. I'm pissed at you that I can't even be totally pissed at you like that."

He kind of chuckles into his hand. "So does that mean you forgive me?"

"I forgive you, but that doesn't make anything right."

He wraps his arm around my neck and kind of gives me a side hug. "I understand that, and I'm wanting to learn how I can be better. I don't know what it's like to be in your shoes and I'll never know, but at the very least I can understand better." The bell rings and we're late again.

"Fuck. Beat you to class?" David says. And we both race our asses to our classes.

* * *

Later at lunch, Olly's attempting to entertain the table with some new hot take about how *The OA* is a better Netflix show than *Stranger Things*.

"They're so different. You can't even compare them like that," I tell him between mouthfuls of Flamin' Hot Cheetos.

"Yeah, but if you had to rank all the shows on Netflix from best to worst, *The OA* will always come before *Stranger Things*," he argues.

"Hard disagree," I push back.

"Yeah, I can't get with that, either," Ayesha says.

The three of us look at David. "What do you think?" I ask him.

He makes this face like he's pondering it. "I'm a huge-ass fan of *Stranger Things*. But I really like *The OA* as well."

Olly kind of pouts that none of us agree with his trash take. "Fine. Look, for our next movie night, we're watching *The OA*."

Ayesha drinks some grapefruit juice and clears her throat. "I've got something to say."

"Do you have a ridiculous hot take, too?" I ask.

"Ha-ha. No. Not a hot take."

I sit up in my seat, leaning in. "What's up, then?"

"I stopped talking to Trevor," she says, and pushes some natural brown curls out of her face. "I'm talking to Malik again."

"I knew it!" Olly snaps. "I totally fucking called that. I knew it was about to happen."

"What?" is all that comes out of my mouth. "Malik?" Malik my ex-crush. Malik our childhood friend. Malik the Disciple.

I knew they've been hanging out, but it's been the least of my worries the past few weeks.

"Yeah, we're gonna try us again. We've been hanging out for a while now, too," Ayesha goes, flipping her hair over to the other side of her neck.

I can't help but feel betrayed that she didn't tell me. "But you realize he's still a Disciple, right?"

"Mhmm. I know," she says. "I might not like it, but even folks in gangs deserve love, Gio."

"Yeah, I guess," I mumble. I'm probably being shitty, but I don't know if I particularly like the idea of Ayesha and Malik together. My two childhood best friends. What would that mean for *us*? I can't even think straight right now. I'm meeting with my mom tonight and I should be looking forward to what that time might be like, but now this whole situation steals all that away from me.

"What?" Ayesha asks me. "You're making a face at me."

I bunch up the muscles in my face. "Nothing," I answer, and stare down at my tray.

Ayesha smacks her lips. "Okay, good. Malik might be a hood-ass dude, but he's just as charming and funny and sweet."

My phone buzzes and it's an email notification from my mom. She's excited to see me tonight, she says. She can't wait.

When I head to Mrs. Oberst's class, she's standing at the door with an armful of stapled packets. She hands each of us one as we walk in and take our seats.

The bell rings and she walks in to begin class. "Good afternoon, ladies and gentlemen. The packets I handed you at the door is your midterm. It's a take-home midterm, meaning you will have to complete it on your own time over the remainder of the marking period."

"Yes!" Some people cheer and celebrate.

"This is about to be a piece of cake!" Olly whispers behind me, but I guess Mrs. Oberst hears because she turns her head around and sits on the edge of her desk.

"Not so fast. The last five pages is an essay portion," she adds. "You'll have to select one of the prompts about *To Kill a Mockingbird* on page twenty-five."

The class groans at the mention of an essay. Damn. An essay feels like the last thing I want on my plate right now. But especially an essay about some racist-ass book.

"Let's flip over to page twenty-five to go over those discussion questions!"

Papers shuffle and turn as the groans continue.

I stare at the essay prompt questions but tune out everything Mrs. Oberst has to say for the time being.

- Discuss the role of family in *To Kill a Mockingbird*.

- Discuss and analyze the author's descriptions of Maycomb. What is the town's role in the novel and how does it compare to the role your neighborhood or town plays in your life?

- Discuss the concept of fear as presented in the novel, keeping in mind the many fears faced over the course of the story.

- Follow the theme of the mockingbird throughout the novel and analyze what the bird may symbolize or represent.

I accidentally let out a pretty deep sigh.

"Mr. Zander, do you have something you'd like to share with the class?"

There's a lot I want to share, but I don't really have the energy to waste talking to her about how ridiculous I think it is that we still have to study this book as if it's the last word on race relations in America. Trying to talk to her and get her to see where I'm coming from sometimes is like trying to catch a fish in the deepest part of the ocean using dental floss: impossible.

I shake my head so that we can keep it moving. The minutes drag along like hours, but finally I'm saved by the bell.

At basketball practice, after our usual warm-up shootaround, Coach has us run warm-up drills that loosen all my muscles, but I'm confident I'll be sore tomorrow.

Erick is doing high kicks beside me as I do air squats. "This is hell. I hate this so much."

"Same," I say. Sweat leaks into my eyes and rolls from my nose to mouth.

"Dude. I would gladly and wholeheartedly toss a brick at the person who invented stretching," he adds.

I nod and keep squatting before I move into planking to get blood flowing. I need to save all the oxygen in my body that I can.

Erick moves into doing kickbacks and groans out of discomfort.

"Erick! Bro!" I shout. "Keep going. You got this!"

David comes over and starts planking right next to me. "Hmm . . . I wonder who has the better form between the two of us?" he says between deep gasps. We've been warming up for fifteen minutes, but David never gives up or makes it look like he's struggling. I'm all out of breath and for some reason, it feels like my entire body is stuck in molasses, but David looks so unfazed by his warm-ups.

Erick puts in his AirPods (because he's rich) and starts jogging around the track, taking huge leaps forward. 'Lik's jogging, too. But once he sees Erick, he sprints harder. 'Lik hates being challenged because he's gonna do whatever it takes no matter what.

David and I now get up and help each other do sit-ups.

He wipes sweat from above his lips and then holds my ankles while I'm on the ground. "When was the last time you did something fun, like genuinely, insanely fun, like skydiving or bungee jumping?"

I genuinely have to think about that. I've not even been to the movies in a while. "I don't know," I say. My stomach feels like a zillion bees are attacking it. My body feels like someone has taken a cheese grater to every single muscle. *This hurts so badly.*

"Wanna do something Saturday or Sunday night?"

"I might have to work at my dad's church on Sunday, but maybe we could chill on Saturday? Just know that bungee jumping and skydiving are vetoed out of the discussion. That's for white people."

David and I switch places, so that now I'm holding on to his ankles. I try not to stare at his sweaty upper thighs by telling myself that would be unholy. Watching David do these sit-ups so effortlessly, though, kind of gives me even more energy to power through the rest of today's warm-up. Maybe it's not *energy* at all. Maybe it's freedom that turns into the extra motivation I need to get through this.

Coach blows the five-minute whistle. *Hell yes! Only five more minutes.*

Coach blows the last whistle for the team to run back to the bench and wait for the next instruction. Everyone looks tired and wheezes for air, panting like dogs for water. Except for David.

"Five-minute water break before our next set," Coach says, blowing the whistle once more. *Next set?* I think to myself.

The whole squad goes inside to the weight room after chugging two, three, four cups of water each. Coach has created an individual workout plan for everyone. Mine involves bench pressing and pull-ups. Maybe it's his subtle-not-so-subtle way of telling me I need more muscles or upper-body strength. I don't care, but I'm slightly offended.

I do a couple sets of pull-ups before going to start bench pressing. I'm pretty drained from running, so this whole bench-pressing thing takes a godly amount of effort.

David lifts weights next to my bench-pressing station, his biceps flexing, looking bigger than when I last saw him shirtless.

Practice lasts for another hour. Coach passes us all snacks, like kettle chips and protein bars, before our last group activity: showering.

Everyone files into the locker room to claim their own shower station. Some of them work better than others, so it's always a race. Savtaj and Jason usually fight for the one in the corner, since it stays hot the longest. David and I hover outside the showers for a minute.

"I seriously can't wait for Saturday," he says to me.

"It'll be fun," I say, looking around the corners.

David winks at me and tries to hug me, but I pull away. "What, do I smell that bad?" he asks, sniffing himself.

"No," I whisper, signaling around us. "The guys could see us."

He backs away slowly. "Right. You don't want people to know."

"I'm sorry, David," I kind of whisper, pulling him to the side.

His face goes stiff and he rolls his eyes, a towel over his shoulder. "Gio, I don't like being your little secret. Let me know when you're not afraid of being who you are."

He leaves me standing here in the middle of the locker room as everyone heads to the showers to get cleaned up and changed.

I feel hurt by what David just said, but I can't blame him. It's just, I was trying not to show that I liked David in any way, so I don't make things weird on the team, and I don't want any of this getting back to Pops. I just don't want attention drawn to us or the fact that I like him. And really, I think someday in the future, I wouldn't care if everyone here knew about David and me. Because, you know what? There's something really good happening with the two of us, I think. I can't articulate the kind of sweet feeling I get when I look into those blue eyes. It's magic. Something like that.

David's been more like a firm foundation lately. I can come to him and know that he'll be there to support me no matter what. There are feelings that I have when I'm with him—they're all so messy and complicated and lovely.

But right now? I'm still not ready for the other students at Ben Davis to figure out that I like him, outside of Ayesha and Olly.

SIXTEEN

THE TEAM HUDDLES UP in our same old way when Coach Campbell tells us to. Scanning around the gym, I see just how packed this place is. It's full of Ben Davis fans in purple-and-white face paint and it's full of Center Grove High School fans wearing red face paint, which feels kind of racial and problematic. If we win, we get home court advantage against North Central or Mt. Vernon, depending on which one of them wins their game tonight.

"This is your night. Play your heart out. Give this all you've got, and we will win. Remember: Great spirts often receive fierce opposition from mediocre minds," Coach says.

I feel nervous all of a sudden. I haven't practiced at home like I normally do before a big game like this. I know I've been so distracted by everything lately that I haven't been on my A game, but I'll need to bring it tonight. I keep looking back to try and find my mom out in the crowd. There are just too many people. I'm nervous that she came. I'm also nervous that she didn't.

Coach designates Malik to lead the team chant. We put our hands together in the middle of our circle. David puts his on top of mine and I lock eyes with him.

"One, two, three," Malik counts down.

We all roar, "GO, GIANTS!"

The referee blows her whistle to kick off tonight's game. I'm one of the starters again—Malik, Jason, Savtaj, David, and me. Savtaj goes up against the center for Center Grove to win the tip-off for us. This is a good sign, for sure, because winning tip-offs always feels like you're immediately granted good game luck, but as I cut across the floor to get in position for a corner three, Coach's words slip back in my thoughts and linger.

Give this all you've got, and we will win. I draw in a deep breath.

I suddenly feel sick.

I look down at my foot tapping as I wait.

Malik tosses me the ball in the paint. I dribble through a guy's legs and go up for a layup, but I miss it. *Fuck. Who misses a layup?* I want to punch myself in the face for that one. I throw my hand up and mouth the words "My bad" to Coach and then to my teammates.

We lose the rebound to Center Grove.

Heading back on defense, I pick up my man. Their point guard, #11. He's trying his best to cross me up, but I try even harder to keep up, to stay in a good enough of a stance that he doesn't take my ankles. But sure enough, I fail, and that's exactly what he does. He blows straight past me and cocks up an alley-oop. *DUNK!* The sound of the hit to the rim is so damn loud, it almost feels amplified up close.

Every sound, every movement feels intensified right now. My heart is racing in my chest. *Shit.*

Shit.

Shit.

We're back on offense again. Savtaj passes me the ball inbounds and I dribble up the court, trying to make a play. I signal with my head for everyone to get David open for a shot. When I get close enough, Malik attempts a screen and then I go around him and trip, the ball falling out of my hands, and it gets taken by #30 on the Center Grove team.

I look up at the stands once, the crowd still cheering, no, nearly roaring. I'm not sure if that's Center Grove's crowd celebrating because of my fuckup or not. But they score on us. Again.

And again.

And again.

And again.

I run over to the left side of the three-point line. #11 follows, guarding me tight. This has been such a slow start to the game, yet we're already down by ten points.

I run over near the paint, close to the basket, and call for the ball after getting open thanks to a double screen by Malik and David.

Savtaj gives me the ball with a nice bounce pass. I see David in the corner and he's wide open. Jason's wide open in the other corner. David's a better shooter, I know that for a fact, but for some reason it's like my muscles force me to pass to Jason. I panic. And I end up turning the ball over when #2 on the Center Grove team catches my pass. Already, I've got two damn turnovers.

I feel like throwing up. My jaws clench up. It's getting harder and harder to breathe. I try to count to five in my head without closing my eyes.

One.

Two.

Three.

Four.

Five.

Before I get any further with ruining this play, Coach calls an emergency time-out. We've already used a couple of them in the first half because we're doing so poorly, and I can't help but blame myself. Everyone knows it's my fault. *I* know it's my fault. I don't even have to be convinced of that at all.

Coach looks disappointed at me, but then starts screaming at all of us. He's looking each and every one of us in the eye, but I can't help but think he looks at me longer than everyone else. "We are playing like second graders out there. Center Grove's guys are getting clear paths to the rim, shooting wide-open threes, and they're getting really comfortable being here. This is a home game. I don't intend to leave tonight humiliated for getting killed on our home court. You all don't seem to get it. If we lose this game, we're done. Our season might as well be over."

"What should we be doing differently, Coach?" David asks. He looks at me and I take it as a passive-aggressive sign, but I'm sure he's just trying to make a joke, so I don't feel as bad. Then we break eye contact.

"Tighten up the defense and stop being afraid to foul when you need to," he replies, lines showing on his forehead. "Now all of you, get out there and show these punks whose court they're on."

Malik leads our team chant again. "One, two, three."

"GO, GIANTS!" everyone in our huddle erupts.

As everyone else walks back onto the court to resume the game, Coach pulls me over to the side for a while longer. "I don't want to have to put you on the bench. I will do that if I have to, Zander."

I nod. "I hear you, Coach." I don't know if that was meant to be a threat or motivation or both, but there's something weirdly comforting about being barked at by Coach. Like I've been here before and I know what to do with it. All thoughts of anything but winning this game slip out of my head.

The game resumes and I get the ball open in the corner. I throw it up with a prayer and it swishes in. I hear Ayesha and Olly shout my name.

I get the ball a few more times, scoring a pair of threes from deep range and even dunking on #22. We've got the lead now and I'm feeling good. There are a few minutes left in the second quarter, and if we blow this lead, we deserve this loss. Everyone's on their A game now, even me.

We're in rhythm and we got shots going in now all around and back-to-back for us.

I set a screen for Jason to get open. Then I run toward the basket, calling for the ball so I can make an easy layup. I notice David getting open for a corner three. I pass out to him.

Out of the corner of my eye, over David's shoulder, I see her. She actually came.

Instantly, I lose all the air in my lungs and everything

around me goes so quiet, this game suddenly moving in slow motion, and all my focus has gone down the drain right where this game is about to head. I look back at her and then see Karina next to her. And next to Karina, Ayesha and Olly. It's weird seeing my mom and Karina sitting by each other, but I feel calmer just seeing Karina's face. I don't see Pops or Theo anywhere. They're not sitting with them.

Jason passes me the ball. I dribble once, twice, and then go up and shoot and *SWOOSH!* It goes in. Half the crowd cheers. The other half—the Center Grove crowd—boos. Because they're haters. Center Grove gets the ball back, but it's quickly ripped away by David.

Savtaj sets a screen to get me an open look in the right corner. "Shoot that," he tells me. And I do just that.

The announcer's voice booms out of some unseen speaker, "GIOVANNI ZANDER FOR THE TRIPLE!"

The score's 33–26 and we lead going into the third quarter. David's racking up a good amount of steals. He's doing the dirty work for us on the defensive end, for sure. He's keeping us ahead big-time with the pressure he's putting on these boys.

We make a smooth switch so I can guard #11 and prove that I'm not the one for him to act like that with.

I get low in my defensive stance the next time #11 has the ball, and he pretends like he's looking for an open lane before driving straight to the rim. I meet him underneath the basket and block his shot from going in. It's all so very epic.

"Foul!" #11 shouts to the refs, complaining like a little kid. "That was a foul."

"That was definitely a block," I say.

#11 smacks his lips and throws his arms up like he's being treated unfairly.

He stays tight on me when I get the ball next. David sets yet another screen for me because I'm on fire and haven't missed yet this quarter and have hardly missed this whole game other than the fuckups early on.

It feels so tense in here and everything is still—so still—as I dribble.

When I release the three, it splashes it—all net and no rim. The crowd's screaming loud now—so loud it almost feels like even Center Grove's fans have started to cheer for us.

I shimmy in his face like Steph Curry. A pretty disrespectful move, but I don't have time to second-guess things.

Minutes later, everyone on our bench is going wild at David's dunk. "Dav-id! Dav-id! Dav-id! Dav-id! Dav-id!"

The rest of the game goes a lot like the last two quarters: Center Grove tries, but they're no match for us when we're playing at our best. When there's barely a minute left, the score's 59–39. Center Grove really should call a time-out and talk things over, but no, their coaches keep things moving along like they believe they have a chance at actually winning this. Even on the cusp of a blowout.

The end-of-regulation buzzer blares to life in all directions, signifying that this game is a wrap! AAAAAAAAAAAAAGH!

We won. We won. We fucking won. And the crowd goes wild. I feel so infinite and whole and free and David and I are hugging in the middle of the basketball court.

We join everyone in a huddle at the bench and we take turns giving each other hugs, high fives, and slaps on the butt. I hug David again and keep him tight in my arms for a while before we break apart, forgetting to be secretive in my excitement. I think about breaking away so people won't think something's up, but I decide to just hug him tighter instead. I think David sees these thoughts flash across my face, because he smiles in this way that I know isn't just about the game.

"That was so awesome!" I shout. We're both soaked in sweat.

"You were amazing out there!"

"You were *more* amazing," I say. He was. He scored the most points out of anyone on the floor. A whole thirty piece. That's like an NBA-level-type night.

We line up to shake the hands of the opposing team's players as the whole gym clears out. They all tell us we played well, and their coaches come over to congratulate us.

Back in the locker room, Coach Campbell can't stop beaming and telling us how proud of us he is. He looks more excited than the time he told us he was getting married to his third wife, so all this to say: This win right here means everything to Coach Campbell.

We all get showered and changed before going outside to meet people where our families and loved ones are waiting. As we walk out the doors, I look over at David.

"Text you later?"

"Yeah, I'd like that," he says with a shy smile.

David runs over to hug his parents, and then I make out Pops farther into the parking lot, standing next to his truck with Theo in front of him.

"Hey," I tell him when I get there. "I didn't think you came."

"Yeah," Pops says. "We did. You can thank your brother for that."

Theo runs up to me and attacks me with a hug. "Gio! BAAANG!" he shouts.

"Oh, you like that, huh?" I say. He makes me laugh.

"You were beast mode," he says.

"Beast mode?" I make a face at him. I haven't heard that phrase in a long time. But I like it and it makes me laugh.

Olly and Ayesha find me somehow and nearly tackle me while screaming. Olly's wearing purple-and-white face paint. Ayesha's wearing a shirt with my jersey number on it.

"Hey, guys."

"That was so dope," Ayesha cheers.

"You killed that, yo," Olly shouts, jumping up and down, so excited for me. "Such a fucking awesome game. At one point, I was all like, yikes, this game is going to overtime, but you all blew them the hell away. Straight up like Christopher Columbus."

"Um. Olly. No," Ayesha says. She's right for that.

"Shit. I'm sorry, you guys," Olly repents.

Karina walks up beyond Ayesha with a huge smile on her face. "Great game, honeybunches! You really turned things around out there. I never doubted you had it in you." She gives me a hug so warm and strong I could live the rest of my life inside it.

I don't let go till Pops clears his throat. "Gio, we're going to take your brother home. We need to walk Biscuit before she pees in the house again. We'll see you there later, right?"

I give Pops and Theo hugs. But before Theo pulls away, he looks up to me with wide eyes. "Are you gonna see our mom?"

I nod at him. "Yeah, li'l bro. I am."

"Can you give this to her?" Theo asks, pulling a piece of folded-up paper from his back pocket. I open it to see what it is. It's his Christmas list. It's so long until Christmas, but it makes me laugh that he's already prepared a list for her.

"Yeah, I can give it to her, bro."

I wave as Pops takes Theo back toward the truck, turning back to Ayesha and Olly.

"Yo. You still ready for tonight?" Olly asks me.

"Yeah," I say.

"Good luck. I know you got this," Ayesha says. They both hug me, too.

"G-Bug," I hear a soft voice say somewhere around me. My heart falls into my stomach and I swallow hard as I turn my head around. Mom—no, Jackie—no, Mom. She has this look on her face like she just witnessed me graduate from Harvard.

"Hey," I stare at her, somewhat speechless, somewhat not. I don't have the words to describe how I feel.

"Hi, Mrs. Zander," Ayesha says.

"Is that you . . . Ayesha?" my mom says.

"Yep. It's me!" Ayesha says back.

"Oh my gosh. Look at you. You're so beautiful and all grown up. Looking just like your momma. How are your parents doing?"

"They're good. Real good. I'll have to tell them I saw you."

"Yeah, do that for me, will you? I'll have to stop by their store sometime," Mom says.

"Oh, this is Olly," I say, introducing my mom to him. Olly waves awkwardly.

"Very nice to meet you, Olly," she says.

There's an awkward silence that passes quickly.

"Well, G-Bug. You want to grab some coffee or tea somewhere?" she asks.

"How about ice cream?" I recommend.

"Yeah. That sounds good," she says, and smiles.

SEVENTEEN

THERE ARE ONLY A few people in Kreamy Kones this time of night. There's an elderly Black couple in the corner feeding each other sherbet, which I think is cute, but also kind of sad to watch. There's also another lady who looks like she's in her late twenties sitting up at the counter with her headphones in and eating an ice cream sandwich.

I barely touch my bowl of mint chocolate chip ice cream with cookie dough and sprinkles when we get seated. After a mostly quiet car ride, my mom begins to talk.

"The last time I was here, your father and I sat right there." She points over in the distance near the elderly couple. Part of me wonders if they'd look like that couple if they'd just stayed together and grown old together. I'll never know.

"Dang."

"Yeah. I ordered vanilla custard with butterscotch chips," she says. I'd forgotten about her love for butterscotch. "Your father would mooch off mine after he ate all his strawberry shortcake ice cream."

And all I say is "Yeah." I try to mix my ice cream up and put a spoonful in my mouth, but it needs to melt a little bit first.

"We ran into some friends that we went to high school with," she says. "I remember that day like it was yesterday."

"Wow." I'm noticing I'm being really short and not at all on purpose. This is just . . . a lot. There are so many things that demand to be said right now, but they're all trapped by the weight of my tongue. Where did she go? Did she ever think about Theo and me? What would she do when she did? Did she know that her leaving fucked me up? Is she here to stay for good? Or will she be packing up her bags one last time?

She closes her eyes, like she's holding on to a moment in her thoughts, trying hard to recall every detail, almost reliving it.

"Gio, I loved your dad. He was this hopeless romantic, and he treated me like I was the queen of the universe. But one day something, like a string, snapped inside the both of us. Slowly, we started drifting apart, becoming these two different people with different interests and aspirations and no way to keep up or hold on to each other. I just had to go."

Damn. Already, I want to cry or throw up or both. I can't even say anything back to her.

"Some days you might snap. Other days, you might snap together."

Deep breath. "Wh-where did you go?" I ask her. This takes such a herculean effort.

"I used to tell you that I was doing mission work in the Middle East," she says. "But I met someone and moved to the Netherlands."

"The Netherlands?" I ask. "That sounds far." Suddenly, I'm like a little kid in basic geography.

"It is," she says. "I moved to Amsterdam."

"Wow" is all I can say again. "Why Amsterdam?"

"I felt safe over there," she says back, kind of quick.

"You didn't feel safe in the Haven?" I ask.

"It wasn't the Haven that didn't make me feel safe." She pauses and looks at me. "Being with your father, I felt like there was always this dark cloud above my head that never went away. I was slowly losing who I was."

A beat. I don't know what that means, but my mind's trying to process that to figure it out, like her words are a thousand-piece puzzle that I have a limited amount of time to solve.

"Can I ask you another question?" I breathe in and out. My chest gets really tight, so I place a hand there.

She casts a glance at me. "Of course. You can ask me anything, G-Bug." Her eyes are wide, hands folded in front of her, a part of her dress laced between her fingers. She leans forward a bit.

"Why—why didn't you want us? You didn't take us with you." The words fall out naturally like they've been hibernating within me, waiting years to come out. There's a blanket in my throat.

"G-Bug . . . my leaving was everything to do with me and your father, nothing to do with you or Theo." She pauses and looks at a dove flying above. "I left because I thought I was protecting you. I thought that if I was gone, I wouldn't hurt any of you, or that you all wouldn't be disappointed in me. I was afraid, and I thought that was my only option. As much as it killed me. As much as it kills me even now, to see you hurting like this in front of me. To think that maybe Theo doesn't want to speak to me. To know that I did this to you both."

"Protecting us from what?" I ask, my voice soft and fragile. "What were you afraid of?" One thing I do remember was how much Theo and I adored her, loved her, trusted her. I, at least, was convinced mothers could do no wrong. I was sold that she was there to stay, to cradle, nurture, and protect Theo and me forever. My fists ball up at my sides, like I'm angry, but I don't think I am. There're just so many feelings bouncing around inside me right now and I can't land on one for enough to have a reaction. I can't get myself to look at her in the eye for longer than a second.

"Ever wake up one day and feel like everything you've ever known about yourself was just a lie?" It's almost funny that she says this. This is exactly how I've been feeling lately . . . mostly because of her.

I nod.

She pulls out her phone and scrolls through her photo album. She hands me the phone. I'm staring at a photo of a woman with thin, dark brown eyebrows, brown eyes, and skin medium-dark like ours. I swipe over to see more pictures of them together and happy.

"Her name is Monica. I met her shortly before I left. I used to go to this dance studio a few blocks away from the Haven to work on stuff with other dancers." She swallows, and I do the same. "Monica was the studio manager there."

I remember my mom dancing when she would clean the house when I was a little kid. I remember her dancing with me in the living room to whatever random song she'd play. I never thought that she would dance her way right out of my life.

She continues. "When I met her I felt a feeling that I'd never ever experienced before and that showed me something about myself no words could ever explain."

I chew away at the inside of my lip, hands getting clammy. "What happened?"

"Sometimes the universe leaves doors open for you, and you have to make a choice to walk through or not. So I did. I told your father about my feelings for Monica and how it was all me and not anything he had done. But he was a pastor and I was a pastor's wife. Things got messy fast."

"Damn. I mean, dang."

"He took it really hard, and for months we tried to make our marriage make sense for your and Theo's sake, but God wouldn't let it. I thought time would heal these feelings and desires. That they would all go away and I would love being with your father more than I loved being with Monica. Nothing changed. Before I left, I told your father to promise me that he wouldn't tell you the truth. I was afraid that being who I am was something that needed to be kept secret and hidden, even from my own children. I was so ashamed at who I was and didn't want you and Theo to grow up with a mother like me. I didn't want you and Theo to grow up being disappointed in me. In a moment of panic and bad judgment, I packed my bags."

A beat. Sitting here in this quiet place where I can hear news anchors reporting on crime in the area on the TV, I think I'm feeling that melancholy you get at the end of a school break.

I wipe a single tear that rolls down my cheek as I listen to my birth mom explain the reason why she left was to be with a woman. Out of all the possibilities I'd imagined over the years for why she'd abandoned us, this wasn't one of them. And it makes me sad. Sad because of the decision she felt like she had to make. Sad because I kind of get it. Sad because she realized her mistake and took so long to come back. Sad because she could've helped me come out sooner.

Suddenly, I'm a little kid again, reliving some of my childhood wounds. Like, when I was ten, I was really obsessed with the X-Men comics. I loved Wolverine and Magneto and Nightcrawler and Cyclops and Iceman and Beast and Professor X. But I really wanted to be Storm. Or at least, I wanted her powers because she was the most powerful out of all the X-Men.

I put a gray towel around my head and patted baby powder over my eyelids to match Storm's eyes. Then I walked down the stairs where Pops was on the couch watching some TV show on Animal Planet, drinking a cold one.

I waved my arms in the air and bent one of my legs, like I was about to take off into the air like Storm does. I shut my eyelids, showing the white powder.

"What are you doing?" Pops had said, so strangely detached and angry.

"I'm being Storm!" I shouted cheerfully. It was worth cheering, really. "She's a superhero."

His eyes got super big and lips went tight. "Go upstairs and take that off right now. Girls won't like you in the future if you act like that. Why aren't you playing with those G.I. Joes I bought you last year or outside playing with some of the other boys in the neighborhood?"

Crushed, I went back to my room, snatched the towel from my head and powder from my eyes, and cried, cried, cried.

This is one of those memories I've tried to forget . . . or maybe not *forget*, but press down? It's been a rather successful attempt. Until now.

And when I was fourteen, Angela Aberdeen asked me to be her boyfriend during the school carnival. I remember that day clearly—the way when I was going in for a kiss, I accidentally headbutted her. The way she loved hand-holding and I hated the thought of holding her hand, but she was attractive enough and nice enough for me to brag about to the school because she was mine and nobody else's, even though she cheated. The first day we started dating was also the time I got my first boner in gym class, when I was partnered with Seth Martin, taking turns holding each other's feet while doing sit-ups.

And then there was that one time during summer break between freshman and sophomore year where Pops burst into my room and saw my laptop with side-by-side shirtless photos of John Boyega and Chris Evans, and a photo of some random girl with the smallest layers of clothing, my hand in my boxer briefs. He took away my laptop for a month, made me pray and memorize several pages of the Bible where it talks about Adam and Eve.

I come back to this moment with my mom. There's no use thinking about what things would've been like if she would've been here to walk me through.

"I know what my leaving did to you and your brother, and I know it was so wrong, but at the time it also felt so necessary to my happiness. I don't know if those two sentences can even come after each other in that way, but that's the truth." She wipes makeup from underneath her eyelids. "And when I met Monica, I experienced every color of the rainbow."

I'm biting my lip and shaking so damn hard. I wonder if she notices. She's describing exactly what I feel around David. It's uncanny. Kissing girls felt more mechanical and ordinary—each time, it was like doing something and flipping a switch while expecting light to shine. It never happened. And it didn't happen with the guys I hooked up with, either. There wasn't that connection. When I kissed David for the first time, though, everything went quiet and every switch flipped, and light rained down.

I want to tell her that I'm bisexual because I haven't gotten to tell her that. I never got the chance to write to her. I never got the chance to be comfortable enough to say that word to her. I take a deep breath and prepare myself. *You got this, Gio*, I tell myself.

"I'm . . . I'm bi," I say at once, not making eye contact with her, just staring into my ice cream that's now a little too melted.

"I know," she says. "Your father told me."

"Really?"

"The day you told him was the day he told me. He left me a voicemail, blaming me for corrupting you."

I don't say anything, but I feel that choking sensation in the back of my throat that feels like sandpaper when you're about to cry.

But instead of crying, I let the words out. "I met this guy at school. He's on the basketball team. David. The white boy who managed that dunk at the beginning of the third quarter. I like him, I think, but I don't know. I can't do anything about it. I can't be with him because of Pops or because of Coach or because of what people might think."

"Of course you can," she says, like it's just that simple.

My brows rise and I lean forward, wanting her to explain herself.

"The most powerful and insanely beautiful thing you can be is yourself," she says, her voice softer than silk. "When you let yourself unravel, you'll feel more like you than you ever have, G-Bug. See, I've learned you can't hide who you are for too long. Eventually, the real you always shows up."

I let her words kind of sink in. This is deep and makes me feel warm.

"When you love someone, and you're scared to love them, that love doesn't go away. And swallowing that down will create a spiral of darkness for you. I realized that I had to be honest and claim back my happiness to find light again. It's hard to understand, I know, nobody ever gets it, but . . ."

"No, I get it." I might not 100 percent understand the choice she made to leave us, but I *get* what she was going through. I fold my hands in front of me, hoping that could stop me from shaking like I've lost it. But it doesn't work.

I keep quiet and swallow so hard it hurts. I want to hide or camouflage myself in this moment somehow. For years, I mastered the art of hiding what I felt, of disguising it as something else, or conjuring up a way to rid myself of it for a while.

I wonder if she ever wishes people were like caterpillars. Did she ever feel like one herself? The way they take time to peel back layers and skin to be something new, to be that crazy-beautiful thing they really are inside: butterflies. Were there days when she wished she transformed into something braver and brighter—or maybe not even like a transformation, but like a subtle revealing of who she really was all along.

"Are you out at school to your friends?" she asks me.

"Only to Olly and Ayesha. And now Malik."

"That's a great step, Gio. There's no rush."

I need to hear that. Like for real.

"You don't have to be out just yet. You can still be figuring everything out," she says, her voice filled with sympathy. "The biggest lie the world tells you is that you have to have everything figured out. You don't. That's part of the journey of life—figuring out the different layers of you. And when you're ready to share those layers, you deserve to be able to do that. But you don't have to do it till that time comes." She looks at me with these eyes that make me feel like she understands something in me no one else has ever understood before.

"I don't want to be afraid, Mom." It slips out. That word. Mom. And I can't take it back. I don't want to be afraid to be who I am. I don't want to be afraid of what would happen if people found out. And at this moment, I don't even know what Pops would do if I started dating David. I remember him telling me it's one thing to be same-sex attracted, but it's another thing to practice or act on it. Sure, we had a nice little moment the other day, but maybe me dating David will just send him back to his old ways; maybe I'll never get to experience or see the softer side of Pops ever again.

"You can't choose who you are, Gio. Don't let fear stop you from reaching out to grab your happiness." *Like she did when she left?* "Teach fear to fear you."

That sounds nice, and sounds easier said than done. On top of everything else, I'm terrified David will see right through the different layers of me. He won't see this soft, nice, somewhat shy boy, but instead an ugly fucking disaster.

A whole two hours pass as we lose track of time. I listen to stories that she shares of me and Theo growing up and about how when she gave birth to me Pops almost fainted because there was a lot of blood.

Before I forget, I hand her Theo's Christmas wish list.

"He wanted me to give you this. I don't know why, but I told him that I would."

She smiles looking at it, running her fingers across the page to feel the writing.

"Maybe, uh . . . maybe you can talk to him about it someday?" I suggest.

"I would love that. My sweet, sweet Theodore." She clutches the paper to her chest.

We talk a little about how she hopes she can spend time like this with Theo. About how she understands that he doesn't really remember her. That he thinks of Karina as his mom. That she doesn't want to scare him or pressure him, but she hopes he understands that she loves him. I've noticed he's even clingier with Karina than he usually is and with me a little, too. He spends less time in his room playing games and more time down in the living room on the couch beside Karina and Pops. When I asked him, he said he wanted to talk to her someday, but he thought I should go first. He wants me to check her out for him. Let him know she's safe. And that's exactly what I'm doing.

"Can you tell me about him?" she asks. "What is he like?"

"Umm . . . yeah," I say, searching my brain for a moment. "Theo's funny. He's a real prankster, but he's so, so smart. He loves playing video games, watching anime, and eating food. Thanksgiving is his favorite holiday. He eats at least three plates every year. He finishes all the rolls and sweet potato pie before the night is over with."

"He's like his momma," she says. "I love me some sweet potato pie when it's made right."

"I taught him how to ride a bike when he was five and one day, he fell going down a hill and busted his lip. He called out for his mom, but Karina came. For his sixth birthday, we went out to see *Avengers.* He got so obsessed with Iron Man that we had to buy him an Iron Man suit and he wore that thing every day for months. He would wear it to school, to bed, the grocery store. He didn't care. The only reason he ever took it off was because he ended up growing out of it."

"Oh, wow. He sounds like a big ball of fun."

"He is. I don't know what I would do without Theo. He's my world and I love him to death."

"I'm sure you do."

I go on and bring up more stories of Theo as they come to me. And with each story that I tell, we both end up tearing up a little, reliving the memories. That's the wild thing about memories. They're glimpses of the past that still have the power to make you feel like they happened moments ago.

Eventually, catching me off guard, she throws out a big request. "G-Bug. I'm sorry for leaving you behind and not coming back sooner. I was such a young parent and that's not an excuse, but I made a big mistake when I walked out that door. I was ashamed for a long time. First about who I was and then about what I did. It kept me away, even when all I wanted was to be with you two. And I hope you can find it in your heart to forgive me, G-Bug." Tears are pooling in her eyes and cascading down fast.

The world spins slower and slower around me as I pause. Hot tears begin to pool in my eyes once more. I turn back to her and press down all the unsaid things.

"I—I—I do forgive you, but I'm not sure what that really looks like yet," I say to her, my voice climbing higher in pitch, words flying out of my mouth and increasing in speed. "I forgive you for not being around. I forgive you for not telling me that I can reach for the stars and be myself sooner. I forgive you for not telling me I could do anything I set my mind to. I forgive you for finally showing up so many years later to the most important job of your life. And I forgive you for having to make probably the hardest choice you've ever had to make. It shouldn't have been that hard and . . . I'm sorry."

We're both crying messes who can't control ourselves, hot tears erupting over and over again, worse than Vesuvius, worse than Mount Pelée, not letting go of each other. And what I really want to do is grab my birth mom's hand and sprint back through time, reclaiming all the years she's missed, like a little kid collecting lightning bugs in an open field. Going all the way back to the beginning where I can convince her to stay.

She stands up and opens her arms and I meet her there in a big, warm hug, in front of the lady at the counter looking back. She kisses my forehead and I hug her tight, not wanting to let go, crying into her chest.

"I'm so sorry, G-Bug," she whispers as she kisses my forehead.

I want to live my life without the memory of her leaving following me around like a shadow that I don't want to be mine.

I think I just moved a step closer in the right direction.

I hope I did.

It's raining and thundering out and the car ride back to my house is mostly us talking about our passions and hobbies and dreams. She tells me that she loves watching *The Bachelorette* and doing Latin dances, like the flamenco and bachata and merengue, and I tell her about my love for making playlists and of course basketball. That's something we have in common, at least.

"You remember when I taught you how to shoot a basket-ball?" she asks me, briefly taking her eyes off the road. Her hand holds mine the whole time. She doesn't let go. Not this time.

"Yeah," I say. Of course I do. The memory is one I couldn't ever forget, even if I tried. I remember feeling like the greatest of all time just for making one shot on a little hoop in the driveway. That's the thing. Memories can be recycled or forgotten, but feelings cannot.

"I wish I'd been around to see you in your first game," she says in kind of a broken voice.

"Me too," I tell her, and mean it. "But it's okay. Hopefully, I'll have plenty more games for you to be at." Now, more than ever, I'm imagining a career of going pro, playing for an NBA team. But my next step is landing a spot on a college team. I'm only a junior and I've got to impress some recruiters first, but still . . . I'm so much more determined now.

We pass Ms. Diane's store, and it looks all sad there. I mean, everything about it looks the same as it always has. It just looks sad because the lights are off and Ms. Diane isn't in there. Before she got sick, she was always in there.

"Poor Diane," my mom goes. I can tell her eyes are brimming with more tears.

"You should go see her," I tell her.

"I did," she says. "And I even offered to help her out around the store. But you know, Diane's the same as she was before I left."

I smile for some reason even though there's nothing to smile about. "She real stubborn. I see where Malik gets it from."

"That's for sure," Mom says.

"Are you gonna stay with us?" I ask. It's probably a stupid question. It's not like we've got a guest bedroom for her. We live in the Haven, not Hollywood. Besides, Pops might *maybe* be able to have a conversation with her without exploding somehow, but it's a whole other thing to be staying under the same roof again. And Theo wouldn't be able to avoid her.

She just stares at me for a while—almost the whole duration of a red light—before speaking. "No, I couldn't do that, G-Bug," she says. "Monica's got some family around here and we've been staying with them."

"Like in the Haven?" I ask.

"No, on the east side of town," she says. "Her aunt and uncle have a guest bedroom that we've been staying in until we go back."

Until we go back.

Those words feel like punches to the gut. In just a matter of seconds I've gone from planning a future of her watching my games to thinking about her leaving me. Again.

All of a sudden, I'm thinking that maybe Ms. Diane getting sick is the real reason she came back. Maybe it wasn't for me or Theo after all. Maybe we were just an afterthought.

No, I have to tell my brain.

Of course she came back for us.

When we pull up in front of the house, she leans over and hugs me in the seat. It's a rather awkward hug given the way the inside of the car is built and the seat belts we're strapped into, but it's one that I'll take for sure. She unlocks the door and I begin to open it when she grabs my elbow.

"G-Bug," she says softly and slowly, her voice moving like molasses.

"Yes?"

"I love you." Those words fall out of her mouth one syllable at a time. It sounds too smooth. Too perfect. Too good. I don't know . . . but it causes me to lose my breath.

I just blink for a moment and try to say it back just to say it, but I can't even do that. I just nod at her and smile. Hopefully, that doesn't send her away for good. I feel bad that I can't say those words, but I need more time. It's too soon.

Usually, J. Cole has this way of making me feel really good about life. Listening to him rap about his mom in his song called "Apparently" as I lie in bed in the dark is just what I need. I rarely find music that sounds like how I feel. But J. Cole's like that every single time.

I stare out my window, thinking about the raindrops pummeling to the ground hard and fierce. Purple lightning strikes in the distance, and the thunder reminds me of the day my mom left. It's always a thing that takes me back to that day. But suddenly, I'm thinking about something else. When I was younger, I was afraid of storms because of what they meant to me. Then, things changed. I was no longer afraid, but they triggered memories I really didn't want to engage with. But now? Storms are beautiful. My beef was never the storm, the rain, the lightning, the thunder, the sirens. My beef had been with the grief from being abandoned.

That's the thing about grief: it's a sneaky little devil that creeps up on you and catches you off guard. It pops up when you're not prepared and takes shapes that you least expect.

I'm lying in my bed in the dark, headphones plugged in, admiring the beauty of it all. Before I shut my eyes to sleep, I throw up a prayer to God. I thank him for a good day with my birth mom, for some answers. I also pray that she stays. I pray that she really can become more and more of a mom. And I pray that I can say those words that she said to me.

EIGHTEEN

SATURDAY MORNING, MY MOM texts me that Ms. Diane needs help at her store and she'd like me to come. Before I go, Pops makes sure to have a word with me. He sits at the table with a newspaper in hand as usual.

"I'll be at the church most of today. Got nonstop meetings to get to the bottom of who's been stealing from the tithes. If you want to come by and help set up for Sunday's service, it'd be a blessing. But you don't have to."

I'm honestly stunned for a moment. I can't believe what he says to me. Who is this new Pops and what has he done with old Pops? "Really?" I ask him. Last summer, Pops had me work a couple Saturdays a month as part of the setup crew, but I haven't done it in a while, but I'm not planning on asking him about it, either.

"I'll try to help out," I say, and actually mean it for once. We both end up smiling at each other for a while.

He asks where I'm going, so I tell him and Karina.

"Be careful" is all he says before returning to his newspaper. I don't know if this is just the way he's processing everything that's happened with my mom being back, but it's weird. He and Karina were asleep (or pretending to be asleep) when I got home late Thursday night, and yesterday we barely saw each other. The only person in this house I've really told about the conversation is Theo—and even that conversation was careful. I guess we're all adjusting, in our ways. Still, I like that Pops is letting me figure this all out and I like that he isn't being as much of a dick as he has been for so long. It's gonna take me a minute to adjust to this new Pops.

When I finally get to Ms. Diane's store, I see my mom helping pack boxes as Ms. Diane kind of instructs her, Malik, and July on what to put in each box and where to leave them.

My mom sees me and greets me with a hug. "Hey, G-Bug."

"Hey," I tell her. I'm here for Ms. Diane, but I'm also here to spend more time with my mom. There's still so much I want to catch up on.

Some brown-skinned woman comes from the back where the restrooms are. I vaguely recognize her.

Then my mom goes, "Gio, this is Monica."

I hold back my gasp. But the way my eyes bug out says everything I feel inside.

Monica.

It's the woman she left us for. The woman from the photo. She's even more beautiful than the pictures my mom showed me when we were at Kreamy Kones. She's got bright pink lipstick. She's got really pretty curly hair. I probably should have figured she'd be here, but my mind just couldn't go there.

We shake hands. Honestly, I feel some type of way about being face-to-face with her. It's like I'm looking at the reason why I was abandoned. It's like she's the cause of all my anxiety and grief and sadness over the years, but that's unfair to her. I don't know what exactly I'm supposed to feel after meeting her, but whatever it is, I don't feel that.

July and Malik are matching from the head to toe. Red bandannas. Long, plain white T-shirts. Sagging jeans. White Jordans. They're true 7th Street Disciples for sure. They're carrying two, three, four boxes at a time of chips and candy and Little Debbie cakes that Ms. Diane's gonna donate to kids in the neighborhood.

I find the courage from somewhere to ask about why we're putting everything in the store in boxes.

"Somebody bought the building and the new rent is too high," Ms. Diane says. "I couldn't afford to pay the rent for this place, rent for my house, and all my medications."

Damn. I feel sad. No one should have to pick between those options. "Sorry to hear that, Ms. Diane," I say.

"It is what it is" is all she says. "This store was a blessing and a curse over the years. Maybe it'll be a good thing to not have this place anymore."

"There are so many memories in here, though," Malik adds. "I remember coming in here after school and getting a Kool-Aid pickle. Remember that, G?"

"Yeah, I do," I say, and chuckle. "Those were good times."

July's taping up some of the boxes. "I used to think Kool-Aid pickles sounded disgusting, until I tried one. It changed my fucking life."

"Watch your mouth, boy," Ms. Diane tells him.

July laughs and says. "Yes, ma'am."

POW!

POW!

POP!

Everyone ducks or falls onto the ground on instinct, except for Ms. Diane, who quickly wheels behind some shelving.

"What the fuck is that?" July goes. Not holding back.

Mom comes over and brings me close to her. She wraps her arms around me and makes sure we're okay. She examines my body to make sure I haven't gotten shot, then looks over at Monica, who makes a reassuring face. Wherever those shots were, they weren't in here. We're all okay.

Just a little startled.

"I'm tired of these fools out here shooting just to shoot," Ms. Diane shouts.

"Yeah," I say. I make eye contact with Malik, but he gives me a warning look that I don't think anyone else sees.

My mom places a hand on Ms. Diane, who keeps her head in her hands. I don't know how she's feeling, but I can imagine—she's going through one hard thing after another. It's bad enough losing the store, but I know it doesn't help that it means Malik and July are even less likely to straighten out. I'm sure gunshots are nothing but a reminder of what might happen to her sons. And I don't want that to be on her mind. Especially not now with everything going on with her health.

"You okay, Ms. Diane?" I ask her. I'm full of stupid questions today, apparently.

She finally lifts her head from her hands and looks at me with sad eyes. "This store. The memories. My family's future. It's all gone."

"I'm sorry," I say. There's nothing I can say to help, but man, that's terrible.

We remain there in a little circle with Ms. Diane until she asks July to take her home and Malik to stay behind to help. I don't blame her for wanting to get out of here.

There are still a few aisles to pack, but we have enough people left to get it done. No one's in much of a talking mood anyway, so the work goes quickly.

It feels weird to be in the store without Ms. Diane. I make eye contact with Monica a few times as we work, and it's awkward every time. She even tries waving at me, but I try to make it seem like I don't notice.

"Monica, could you help G-Bug grab some cleaning supplies from the back?"

"Sure, I—"

"Nah, that's okay. Malik can come with me," I say.

"Gio—"

"No, it's okay," Monica says, stopping my mom mid-sentence. "Let him go with his friend."

I walk past the two of them and to the back. I'm not trying to be an asshole, but I just don't want to interact with her right now. I'm not ready for that. I don't know if I'll ever be ready for that.

When I'm in the back, I grab for the broom, mop, different cleaning chemicals, and rags.

"You okay, bro?"

"'Lik . . . someone just did a drive-by outside," I say, smacking my lips.

"Nah, nah, nah. Don't even play. You know it's more than just that. Don't lie," Malik says, all up in my grill, grabbing cleaning supplies from a supply closet. "What's really going on?"

"Look, 'Lik, my mom is out there with her . . . whatever . . . the woman she left us to be with and it's just . . . a lot to take in right now."

"Yeah, I wouldn't want to be in your shoes right now."

"Malik, that's not helping . . ."

"Damn. My bad," Malik says. "Gio, just go out there and be with your momma, bro. Just try not to think so much. Trust me, one day, you'll wish you cherished every moment with your momma."

That's easier said than done, but maybe he's right.

Malik and I come back with some cleaning supplies for everyone to use and I try my best not to be such an ass to Monica.

After a few hours of constant work, we manage to pack the last box. It looks so weird to see all the shelves so bare.

Mom asks if I want to grab pancakes with her and Monica at a nearby pancake house that we used to eat at a lot. Remembering my promise to Pops, I look at the time on my phone, but it'll be too late to help out at church anyway. I'll have to make it up to him next weekend. I say yes even though I don't really feel like eating anything.

It takes an untouched Belgian waffle with blueberry syrup for her to ask, "What's wrong, G-Bug?"

Besides thinking about Ms. Diane and what just went down at the store and how shitty I feel about that, I'm thinking about when she's gonna leave. And I kinda don't really feel like opening up with Monica at the table with us. She's nice—like really nice, probably waaaay too nice—but it's not about that. It's about what she reminds me of. I just say, "Nothing," though, to answer her question.

And just like that she doesn't push back or pry. "Okay" is all she says, and gives a look to Monica. "Did you know Monica's fluent in three different languages. She knows English, Spanish, and Dutch. Her parents are from the Dominican Republic. Santo Domingo, actually. That's the capital."

I shrug without making eye contact. Then I stare at my plate. My mind is everywhere but where I want it to be.

My mom finishes her butterscotch pancakes and Monica picks through her eggs.

I don't say anything to either of them, mostly stare down at my plate some more, and occasionally, I'll make eye contact that doesn't stick.

"These eggs taste too . . . *egg-like*," Monica says, which makes my mom laugh.

They look happy together. Happier than I remember her.

I'm quiet for too long. Eventually, it's too awkward for me not to speak. So I try to slow my thoughts and think of something to ask.

"What's Amsterdam like?" I ask. I'm really bad at geography, but I didn't even know Black people lived in Amsterdam. I think the same way about Sweden and Australia.

She and Monica exchange looks again. This time, the looks are filled with excitement, and I don't really know why. "It's beautiful, G-Bug," Mom says. "Words don't do it justice." She pulls out her phone to show me photos.

"These are nice," I say, seeing beautiful snowy trees, huge buildings that look like palaces. It looks fancy as hell. So, this is what Europe is like, huh?

"You should come visit during spring break," she says.

"Yeah," I say. I've only ever seen it in movies when kids have to go somewhere else just to have a relationship with one of their parents, but now that might be my life. I don't want to do that, but it's probably the only option I've got.

"When is your spring break?"

"It's coming up in a few weeks." It's not like I'm keeping track.

"Real soon," she says.

I nod.

"But seriously, you should come. I'll get to show you all around. I can show you the Anne Frank House, the Van Gogh Museum, the Royal Palace, and all the beautiful canals, too."

When I open my mouth, my voice breaks in a bunch of places. I clear my throat and try again. "That could be real cool," I say.

"I think so, too, G-Bug."

"I hear it rains a lot there," I mention. By "I hear" I really mean from a YouTube video.

"Almost every day," Monica answers. I look at her and then look away. It's probably—no, definitely—real tense now. I'm not wanting to be a dick, but this is all still weird and new and I'm trying to figure out how to do basic things.

"Lots of people riding bikes all the time, too," Mom adds.

My brain rewinds her words for a moment. And suddenly

I'm imagining her life all these years with Monica in Amsterdam. Big palaces. A king and a queen. All the bikes. The two of them lying on an Amsterdam-king-sized bed in a suite in some gigantic house. I imagine it to be perfect—or a million times better than life in the Haven, at least. I love the Haven like it's a human, but it still has a shit ton of issues. And suddenly, I get really pissed thinking about how she left Theo and me in this and didn't take us with her. I don't know if I'll ever not be over that part of the whole thing.

"We're considering getting married sometime soon," my mom says.

Wait a minute. What? I perk up a bit. "Are you serious?"

"Mhm, G-Bug. We love each other a lot and we're ready to take that next step."

I shake my head hard and move my fork around on my plate, breaking off pieces of the waffle I'm not even eating. I completely lose my appetite.

"G-Bug?" She reaches over the table for my hand, cold against cold, but I pull away.

"NO!" I shout. "Just! No!" I punch the table, hearing a crunching sound in my hand.

"G-Bug?!" Her voice rises a little higher.

"I can't—I don't know" is all I say. I stare at my hand and wiggle my fingers. It hurts like hell, but nothing seems to be broken.

Monica blinks. Like a lot. Silence washes over the whole restaurant. After a while, I break it with a sigh—no, a groan too deep for words.

"Do you not want us to get married?" my mom asks bluntly with her brows raised and hands out.

I think for a moment. I don't know what to say to that, to be honest, so I'm silent. Silence is always better than speaking before you're ready, and I'm practicing that right now.

"Well?" she presses, leaning in with glossy eyes. "Monica makes me happy and we want this. We want to start a family of our own." She's acting like I should feel so happy for her, but instead I feel nothing—well, not nothing, but definitely not happy. I feel so empty right now, like whatever it is that allows me to feel has been surgically removed.

Then, suddenly, I stand up and blurt out, "You know what? Fuck that. You can't just come back into my life and ask for me to forgive you for abandoning us and then just drop that you're gonna get married again and start a new fucking family. Are we really not enough for you? Are we just such a painful fucking reminder of the past to you? Why don't you want us? Why don't you fucking want us?" I'm screaming now, my eyes brimming. My hands and lips and legs tremble. My head hurts, and my throat is sore as shit.

"G-Bug, I didn't mean—"

"Fuck you, man! That ain't cool!"

I walk out, leaving my mom and Monica behind. I scan my surroundings for the nearest bus stop, then wait there until one comes to pick me up. The bus is packed, and I have to stand the whole ride back. I'm tired and angry at myself. For opening up. For letting her in and getting close. I'm so stupid for believing anything good about her.

NINETEEN

🔹🔹🔹🔹🔹🔹

AT HOME, KARINA AND Pops are in the living room and they're watching some TV show with Theo. When I walk in and they see me crying, they've got a thousand questions. I tell them about everything. About what my mom said to me and about how I reacted.

"I told her not to tell you," Pops goes, shaking his head. He puts a hand on my back and rubs. Then he does the same for Theo, who's crying all of a sudden now, too.

I'm all like, "What the fuck, man? She really don't want us. She almost had me convinced that my life would be different with her in it."

Karina pulls me into her chest, close. "You're okay, honey-bunches," she keeps repeating over and over as I sob and sob and sob, not holding any of my frustration back.

"What's wrong with me?" I ask, wailing. "What's fucking wrong with *us*?"

"Shhhhhh," Karina goes. "Nothing's wrong with you. You're amazing and talented and sweet and—" She goes on, but I don't listen to all of the things she lists off because I'm too wrecked right now, but I appreciate her so much right now, more than ever.

I'm not enough for my own mother. Never enough. Never ever enough.

Pops and Theo come over and join in on the group hug. Pops whispers, "I know, I know," like he would a baby. "It's gon' be all right. It's gon' be all right." Man, I just hope he's right.

Once I finally regain my composure, Karina makes some hot peppermint tea for Theo and me and she puts a lot of honey in it, like we both like it. She takes really good care of us. I'm so damn lucky that we have Karina. And I'm just now realizing that. After all this damn time—all these damn years. I'm lucky that she chose to play the role of *my* mother and Theo's mother, even when I didn't want her to, even when it hurt, even when I was being an asshole to her when she first started coming around. I thought stepparents were supposed to be people I hated. I thought she was coming around as a way of making me forget about my mom. I thought stepparents were like substitute teachers that you'd have for a short period of time until the next one and the next one and the next one, but no, she stayed. Through the good and the bad, she stayed right here and chose it, instead of running away. I'm so lucky that she knows all the right things to say. I'm so lucky that she knows all the right moments when to go to war with me and all the right moments when to let me fight my own battles. But above all, I love that she does everything with love. Like a mother should. So, I run over to her and hug her tight and she hugs me even tighter. It's a nice moment that means everything right now.

Thank you for everything, I want to tell her. But I let my actions speak for me.

I hug her tighter, so she'll hold me back just as hard.

Later on, I find Theo in his bedroom petting on Biscuit between sobs. I walk in and shut the door, plopping on the edge of his bed. His small TV is on—an episode of *The Legend of Korra* plays.

"How are you doing, Theo?" I wanna check up on him. I know he's probably feeling everything I'm feeling inside. I'm still trying to navigate everything, but I want to step up to help him navigate this all, too.

He wipes his face and looks at me. His frown tells me everything I need to know. Sometimes facial expressions are so much deeper than words. I feel bad for him. No kid should have to feel what he's probably feeling. How absolutely fucking wild it is to think that the God who gave us life also gave us the Bible, but not a how-to guide about dealing with crappy mothers.

I give him the tightest and warmest hug that I can. It lasts for what feels like hours because he doesn't want to pull apart from me. He eventually lays his head on his *Adventure Time* pillow and shuts his eyes.

I lean over to kiss him on his forehead. Then I brush his hair with my hand, just being with him for as long as he needs and wants me to be here.

Eventually, Theo and Biscuit are both breathing deeply at the same pace, fast asleep.

Later that night, I'm lying in bed creating another playlist on Spotify that I'm temporarily naming "Hollow." The first song I put into the playlist is one that Olly showed me a while back. It's called "Cherry Wine" by Hozier.

1. "Cherry Wine" by Hozier
2. "Good Goodbye" by Linkin Park, Pusha T, and Stormzy
3. "1-800-273-8255" by Logic, Alessia Cara, and Khalid
4. "How Could You Leave Us" by NF
5. "Crash & Burn" by G-Eazy and Kehlani
6. "Let It Go" by James Bay
7. "Let the Flames Begin" by Paramore
8. "Can't Get Enough" by J. Cole and Trey Songz
9. "Flux" by Ellie Goulding
10. "Poison & Wine" by The Civil Wars

I listen to the playlist on repeat over and over again before I get a text from Ayesha and Olly about FaceTiming. I end up FaceTiming them and letting them know about today. Like the world's most supportive friends, they remind me that they love me and care for me and will be there, no matter what. They stay on the phone with me for as long as I need them to. The only thing that stops me from talking to them all night is the fact that my phone dies. I charge it enough so that it comes back on and when I do . . .

My phone starts ringing—my mom. I can't bring myself to answer it. I just stare at it till the voicemail notification pops up. I hold up my phone to my ear to listen to it.

Hey, G-Bug, I just . . .

I click off. I realize I don't want to hear her voice right now. I don't want to think about her right now. I need some time to myself to process all of this, to calm down.

David texts me and asks if I'm down to play ball on my hoop in the driveway. I remember that I told him we should talk today, so I tell him sure and that I'll meet him there in ten minutes. I grab my *Rick and Morty* hoodie that I haven't worn since Ayesha gave it to me for my birthday a few years ago. I grab my phone with the headphones still attached and shove it in my pocket, then sneak outside to the driveway.

"Sup," I say once I see David.

"Hi." He waves at me. He's wearing black compression pants and his black leather jacket.

"How are you?" I ask, dribbling my ball between my legs, but remaining still.

"Eh, I've had better days," he answers.

"What's going on?" Asking him this feels instinctive for some reason. I really do care how he's feeling. I'm not just one of those people who ask something like this and don't actually care.

"Just got in a fight with my dad. But we're fine now," he says kinda quick, like he just wants to get it out.

"Want to talk about it?"

"I feel like if I talk about it again I might cry, so maybe later?"

"Sounds good," I say, and offer a tight-lipped smile. Then I offer, "I had a rough day, too. I kinda went off on my mom."

"Karina or—"

"Nah. My birth mom."

"Parents, man. What happened?"

"She told me that she was getting married to Monica and that they wanted to start a family. Like how messed up is that?"

David's brows rise. "That's messed up" is all he says at first. Then: "I'm sorry, Gio. I know how much you wanted this to go right with her."

"I know, but same here about the whole 'if I talk about it again I might cry' thing."

"Well, we can cry together, if you want? There aren't very many people in the world I'd offer that to."

"I'll pass on that," I say. "I've done so much crying lately my eyes hurt."

"Fair."

He inhales through his mouth and steps closer. A chill shoots through my body with each step—and I don't think it's entirely because it's below thirty degrees out.

I glance at his mouth.

OMG.

"Wow, are you growing out your mustache?" I ask him. I haven't noticed until now.

He nods. "Yeah, I'm *trying*. You like it?"

"It looks like you drank a glass of Ed Sheeran and Ron Weasley's pubes," I joke.

He laughs. "Gross. But fucking hilarious."

"We playing one-on-one or what?"

"We could . . . or we could go to my place and watch a movie and just chill."

"That sounds nice."

"Which one?"

"The movie and chill," I say.

"Great."

We walk over to his place and climb up the creaky stairs until we're in his room, lying next to each other in his bed, flipping through movies and television shows on Netflix, Hulu, and Disney Plus. Ten minutes go by and we still haven't selected anything. The options are both too many and not enough.

"You know how movies are picked when I'm with Olly and Ayesha?"

"How? If it's what I'm thinking, that's off-limits, dude," he says.

I make a confused face at him. "What do you think we do?"

"Never mind. It was a bad joke that just went right over your head."

"Whatever. Anyway, you pick your favorite category of movie and then you select a number. I'll show you." I grab the remote from him and open up Netflix. "I'm gonna choose thriller and then I'm gonna choose the number nineteen. So I'll scroll until I find the nineteenth movie. It's . . . *The Sixth Sense.*"

"*The Sixth Sense*? Isn't that with Bruce Willis where he—" and then he goes ahead and says the end of the movie.

"You ruined it," I say, staring blankly. "Ass." I can't stay serious for too long, so I crack with a smile. "But yes. That's the plot. Your turn."

David grabs the remote and clicks through. "Action and six in honor of *The Sixth Sense*. Oooh. *Avengers: Endgame!*"

"That's pretty solid," I say.

"But are we committing to a three-hour movie?"

"Do you not want to spend three hours with me?"

"I would spend every hour with you if I could," he says, and just gazes at me in silence as the *Avengers: Endgame* trailer autoplays in the background.

Our eyes avert from each other and we go back to lying next to each other, watching *Avengers* for three hours. At one point in the movie, David reaches over and grabs my hand, lacing his fingers between mine, and squeezes. I don't pull away. It feels good. It feels right. And I feel seen. I feel safe. I can forget about crappy moms. Here. With him.

TWENTY

♦♦♦♦♦♦

COME SUNDAY, I'M HELPING Pops up at the church. I wonder how many people here know about my mom being back in town. I wonder how many people here know about her and Monica. I have to shake my curiosity off fast because I'm here helping the ushers make sure all the pews have Bibles and envelopes for people who want to give money. Deaconess Lisa is wearing an angelic white pantsuit and a matching fedora. She's giving the church announcements, which include a time of prayer at the end for Ms. Diane and her kids. She also announces the light meal following the service. Fried chicken, spaghetti, and rolls. Sounds good, but I don't trust everybody's cooking like that. I'll stick with whatever is in our fridge at home.

When the service starts, Karina and Theo sit up front with my auntie Nisha. I sit behind them with Ayesha and Olly. I'm honestly surprised that Olly still comes to our church. He's probably, like, the only white person in here and his parents go to a church of their own. Olly says he doesn't like it because they always pass out stale crackers for communion and he likes that we give out King's Hawaiian rolls.

The worship band takes the stage and starts to play some

interesting version of "Amazing Grace" that sounds a lot jazzier than I think the writer of the song meant it to be, but it still sounds cool. I look over and see someone walking in the aisle, scanning the crowd. It's David. Make that two white people now.

"David!" I try to get his attention. Olly and Ayesha help me out, too. We flag him over and he nods at us that he sees us. Then he causes everyone in our pew to have to stand for him to join us.

"Hey," he says when he's close to us.

"What are you doing here?" I ask.

"I don't know. I just thought I'd come and check it out," he says.

I smile at him and fix my eyes back on the worship band as they try to get the congregation hyped and into this remixed version of "Amazing Grace" by clapping. I have to teach Olly and David how to clap on beat, which makes me and Ayesha laugh. By the end, they're a little more cultured. I can't wait to see what happens when the band ends the service with some Kirk Franklin.

Pops comes to the pulpit. "Flip in your scriptures to 1 Corinthians 13:4–8. It says, 'Love is patient, love is kind. It does not envy, it does not boast, it is not proud. It does not dishonor others, it is not self-seeking, it is not easily angered, it keeps no records of wrongs. Love does not delight in evil but rejoices with the truth. It always protects, always trusts, always hopes, always perseveres. Love never fails.'"

"Love never fails!" the congregation erupts, repeating over and over again.

"If anyone in here has that one family member that's always

causing trouble," Pops shouts in his preacher voice. "Maybe it's your auntie who's been addicted to crack and she keeps stealing money from your wallet. Maybe it's your son or daughter who's hanging out on the streets late at night now, gangbanging and hustling like that's gon' make them rich? Maybe your momma or your daddy done walked out on you when you were a kid and maybe one day they show back up and flip your life upside down. The Bible is telling us here in this very scripture that love keeps no records of wrongs. Okay?"

"Mhmm. Come on, come on!" some old ladies and saints call back.

My breathing picks up because I think, no, he *definitely* is referring to our family in that. I wonder if everyone else in this building realizes that he's referring to our family. I don't want to look around because it already feels like everyone's eyes are on me and I just want to melt into my clothes.

"The Bible says we are to love them and not keep a record of their wrongs. The Bible doesn't say anything about you having to let them be a part of your life. Sometimes the best thing you can do is let people go!"

"Yes! Yes, Pastor!"

Pops look at me and his eyes stick in place. Suddenly, I get dry mouth and my throat feels tight. I don't even realize my fists are clenching until I feel a set of warm hands on them. Pops continues and says, "Colossians 3:13 says, 'Bear with each other and forgive one another if any of you has a grievance against someone. Forgive as the Lord forgave you.' You know what that means, church?"

"Come on now! Preach that word!" some old ladies and saints call back again.

"It means we have to forgive to set ourselves free! Forgive each other and forgive ourselves."

"Amen! Hallelujah! Preach!" people shout in different voices and rhythms.

Damn, I didn't even know the Bible talked this much about my own family situation. Because suddenly, all I can think about is my mom.

I know it's probably a little too soon to think about cutting all ties, but lately, my life has felt more and more like a long, upside-down emotional roller coaster I don't even want to ride.

My life was entangled with grief and the feelings of abandonment before she returned, but when she did, there was a brief moment of light until that light burst right in my face.

But, man, Pops is preaching truth—maybe a little too much truth and it all maybe is too directed at me, but something about it makes me see everything in a whole new way. He used words like *forgiveness*, *love*, and *freedom*. Those are things that I want, and I know I'll have to sit with this message for a little bit longer so that I can sort through all my thoughts. David grabs for my hand. I try to shake my head at him and retract my hand. We're in church and can't do that here, right?

David's lips tighten and he sinks a little into his seat, leaning back. I know what I did just hurt him, and I feel shitty.

"To summarize the Lord, he says that He is our refuge and strength, a helper who is always found in times of trouble,"

Pops shouts in his pastor voice, a towel balled up in his hand to wipe away the sweat leaking into his eyes. "Always found in times of trouble, I say, church!"

Some of the crowd erupts in "mhmms" and "amens," and the praise band plays a little something after every point they deem to be good. I used to always hate coming to church for the simple fact of seeing old people pretend like they're fainting and the way the pews smell like some little kid peed on every last one of them, but I can ignore all that right now, because everything Pops is saying in a sermon is about me . . . about us . . . about our family. It makes me feel like I'm being split at the seams and stuffed with peace. Peace realizing that I don't have to have her in my life. If she wants to go, she can go and stay gone.

"Y'all must not be hearing me this morning!" Pops says up there on the stage, standing in front of a giant portrait of Black Jesus. "Turn with me to the book of John and the tenth chapter."

I watch as the congregation feverishly flip through the pages in their Bibles to find the place in scripture we'll be looking at for the next hour.

Ayesha leans over to whisper in my ear. "How were things for you last night after we FaceTimed?"

"Fine," I whisper to her. "I was just hanging out with David."

She doesn't say anything, but when I look at her she winks extra dramatically.

"Ayesha!" I whisper a little too loudly. "Not like that. We're in church."

"I'm just playin' around with you," she says. "What you gon' do, though?"

"I don't know. We can talk about it after church," I tell her.

Apparently, Pops or whoever is in charge of the heating in this place decided to go all in because it's hot as hell and my blazer and button-up are both sticking to my back. Ayesha keeps having to unstick her little dress from her thighs. I hate how there aren't any windows that open. They're all just stained-glass windows of figures in the Bible.

I look around the crowd, scanning who's all here. I make out Malik and Ms. Diane and Tatiana in one of the first rows. Across the aisle from us sit Tristan, Nylah, her daddy, Big Blue, and that new girl he's with. Plenty of Black kids from school who live here in the Haven. I even see some 7th Street Disciples standing, no, posted up in the back like they're too good to sit down. My cousins Ishmael and Kehlani, my auntie Nisha's kids, are the ushers and wear white gloves and stand in the aisle with gold trays for people to donate money and tithe.

I look back at Big Blue, who's raising his hands up in worship. He graduated from Ben Davis a few years ago with July. He used to be a 7th Street Disciples Leader before he asked to get jumped out. I'm glad he got out of that, even if it was the hard way. I only wish July and Malik did the same already.

Pops leads the congregation in prayer, which always makes me feel like I'm a little kid again back in grade school. "Our Father who art in Heaven, hallowed be thy name," he says.

We all repeat, "Our Father who art in Heaven, hallowed be thy name."

"Your kingdom come. Your will be done," he continues on, smacking his lips as each sentence comes to an end.

We all repeat, "Your kingdom come. Your will be done." Some people even mimic the way he smacks his lips.

"On earth as it is in heaven," he keeps on going.

The congregation shouts even louder on this part of the prayer—everyone sounding so in sync and monotonous, this feels more like a cult than a way of worshipping. There's no life in anyone's words, but I join in anyway. So do David, Ayesha, and Olly.

The band plays a couple Kirk Franklin songs to end church and then we're dismissed. Karina greets us with a "Hi, Ayesha and Olly. Hello, David, how are you?"

They wave at her. "Hi, Karina," David says. "I'm doing great."

"That's good to hear. I never got to tell you how much I enjoyed your dessert."

"I'll be sure to let my mom know that," David says.

"Anyway, do you want me to wait on you, Gio?" Karina asks me. She's about to begin walking home with Theo.

"I'm good," I say. "I'm gonna hang out with Ayesha and Olly and David for a little bit."

"All right," Karina answers. "I'll see you at the house. I need to get something in the Crock-Pot for dinner. Maybe a roast. Sound good?"

"Sounds really good," I say back. "With lots of potatoes?"

"I'll make sure to put more potatoes than I normally do. I know how much you like them." Soon enough, Karina's grabbing for Theo's hand and they're out of sight.

"Ayesha, Ayesha, so glad to meetcha," a voice raps nearby walking toward us. We both look back. It's Malik. That Bunny guy that's with Tatiana is next to him.

"What's up, 'Lik?" Ayesha says, and they hug. They used to have a thing together, but now they have another thing together.

"We still good for tonight?" he asks her, and licks his full, bright pink lips. I've never seen him this dressed up for church before. He has on a full tux with the cummerbund and everything. He's not dressed like the other 7th Street Disciples in here who're just wearing plain white T-shirts, red bandannas, and jeans.

"Yeah," she answers, fluttering her eyelashes.

"Oh, and by the way, this is Bunny," Malik goes, pointing to the tall guy next to him.

"We met before. What's good, Bunny?" Ayesha says to him, shaking his hand.

"Sup," I tell him, meeting him again.

"A'ight, we aboutta go and roll up," Malik says unashamedly. By roll up, I know he means weed. They walk between us to get out the door.

"That boy something else," Ayesha says. "But fine as hell, ain't he?"

I don't answer that. Instead, I just glance at David and smile. I'm honestly glad he came.

"Was this your first Black church experience?" Olly asks David.

"Yeah. It's different than what I'm used to, of course, but I loved it," he says. "Everything is so alive and electric." Even though I didn't hold his hand during the service, I could tell by the look on his face that he was having a good time.

"Yeah," I say. "I'm glad you liked it. I've not been in a few Sundays, so I'm glad things were cool today."

"Me too," Ayesha adds.

"Gio, a friend of mine from my old school is doing a show tonight. Would you want to join me?"

"I'm down," I say with a side smile. "What kind of show?"

"Let's just say . . . they're an actor," David answers. That doesn't really clarify anything. Now other questions bubble up in my brain.

"An actor?"

"They're doing a reimagining of *Macbeth* at Indiana University," he explains

"Oh cool," I say. I'm not a huge Shakespeare or theater guy, but I'll do this for David. On the plus side, IU could be a school I end up at after high school. It would be nice to see the campus with David.

"Can we come, too?" Olly asks. I love Olly and Ayesha, but I think part of me actually wants it to be just David and me.

"Sure, if that's cool with you, Gio," David answers.

"I'm actually going to see a movie with Malik tonight and then going to Enzo's for dinner, so I'm out," Ayesha says. "But have fun without me, though."

Olly tilts his head, waiting for an answer from me.

I give in. "Sure, Olly, I don't care if you tag along. As long as you promise not to talk about Grace the whole way there."

"But Grace is awesome!"

"Olly . . ."

"Fine, fine," He lifts a hand, his version of waving the white flag.

"Thank you," I tell him.

"Anyone want to play *Mario Kart* until then?" Olly asks. He's always trying to get somebody to play that game.

"I'm in," David responds kinda quick.

"I'm gonna walk over to my parents' store and see if they need any help," Ayesha says.

"I'm gonna go with, Ayesha," I say. "Sorry, Olly."

"No worries," he says. "David and I will just compete for dominance. Okay—no homo. That sounded weird. I definitely didn't mean it in that way. Definitely not gay, David."

"No homo," David says. And for some reason it's funny that he says it.

David offers to drive Olly, and after he agrees, they drive away to Olly's place, leaving me and Ayesha to walk to the Chamberlain Grocery Store by ourselves. It's nice. I don't get a whole lot of time with just me and her. I mean, I think the last time we spent a lot of time alone together was when we were dating. Those weren't our best days, but they were days nonetheless that I think about a lot.

"So you and Malik, huh?" I bring it up before she does.

"Yeah," Ayesha says, her dimple showing. "What about it?"

"I think y'all are cute together," I say. "Maybe I was pissed the last time you got together, but Malik is good people and you are good people, too."

"Thanks, Gio," she says, and kicks at a rock on the sidewalk.

"Enough about me and Malik, though. I wanna know about how you're doing. When we hung up after FaceTiming, something didn't sit right with me. I knew you were taking things hard. I know you."

"Mhm" is all I can say to that. She's right. Like *really* right.

"I . . . just . . . but she promised me," I say. I can't even say actual sentences all of a sudden. "I wanted to give things a chance."

"You did give it a chance," Ayesha says, speaking truth. "And it's okay if things don't work out. You have family all around you. You had family when she was here, and you'll have family if she leaves again."

Damn. I need to hear this. It's such a good reminder.

Ayesha keeps going, though. "But I hope things work out."

"Me too," I say. "I just can't believe her."

"Keep your shit together and be strong," Ayesha says. "I got you."

"Man. Thanks, Yesh," I say.

A quick beat of silence passes and then she shouts, "You should ask him out!"

I play dumb. "What are you talking about?"

"David, fool. You should ask him to be your boo or something."

"What? Nah," I say.

"And why not?"

"I don't know. I can't bring him into my mess."

"What mess?"

"The mess of my life," I answer. "There's no way I could be

a good boyfriend to anybody. I thought the only thing I would ever have to hide was the fact that I liked dudes. But my own grief and family issues feel like something so dark and gross that I have to find ways to hide that, too."

"Quit that, Gio. Everyone is going through shit. Look around you." She starts pointing at different people who are walking along the sidewalk, minding their own business. She creates these fake stories for them as we walk to her family's store. "Like that old lady over there is probably a widow who hates children playing in her garden. That guy over there is probably so lonely he watches the same episode of *Friends* every single day. And that girl right there? She's probably feeding her kids bologna sandwiches for dinner tonight for the seventh time this week because she can't afford anything else."

Something about what she's saying does ring true. I think about David and his sister, Malik and what's happening to Ms. Diane. "I guess you're right."

"I'm not saying your feelings aren't valid, because they are, Gio," she says. "I'm just saying that you're in a very large canyon of people who are going through hard shit, just like you. You're not alone in that."

I blink and nod. "Thanks."

"Let's play a game," Ayesha insists.

"Okay. What game?"

"I'm gonna give you a topic and you have to give me three words that come to mind."

"Sure, fine, I guess."

"Zendaya," she says. "Like the actress."

I think for a moment. "Beautiful, talented, magical? I don't know."

"Pumpkin pie," Ayesha says next.

"White, people, shit." This causes her to bust out laughing and that makes me laugh. She's got a laugh that does that for anyone.

"Paramore."

"Greatest, band, ever," I say quick. "Too easy."

"David."

"Fun, real, perfect, selfless, loyal, honest, determined, loving . . ." I have to stop myself from going overboard.

"See, look at that. You ain't even have to think about it. You got a special place for that white boy in here." She flicks my chest where my heart is and keeps going. "I can't make you do anything, but all I'mma say is we waste our lives by always taking the easy way out or maybe by taking the path that feels safest. But there's a jackpot waiting for you if you just take a risk—one risk. For love."

"Damn, Ayesha," I say. "You're too good."

"I know." She grins from ear to ear and flips her hair.

Finally, we arrive in front of the store. There are discount signs in the windows and an open sign hanging on the door.

We walk in and the sound system above sings some old R & B song. Mr. Chamberlain likes his R & B oldies. He sees us as soon as we pass near the registers. "Hey, Giovanni. Hey, Mini-me."

"Hey, Daddy," she goes.

I wave at him. "Good to see you, Mr. Chamberlain."

"How's your old man doing these days, Giovanni?"

I take a moment and stay safe by saying, "He's good."

Ayesha tells her dad that she can't work her shift today for some reason she completely pulls out of her ass, but her dad doesn't care and allows her to take the day off. She's so spoiled, I swear. She could get away with anything if it were up to him.

I walk through the aisles to find the perfect snacks I'll need to give me the necessary brainpower required to successfully do AP Government and chemistry homework later tonight. I end up getting Golden Oreos, Cool Ranch Doritos, and a shit ton of candy.

"Y'all hear about Ms. Diane's store?" Mr. Chamberlain says as we get ready to check out.

"Yeah, it's sad," I say. "I just feel so bad for her."

Mr. Chamberlain rings me up. "Eight dollars and forty-two cent."

"That's it?" I ask. "I got a lot of stuff, sir."

"Yeah, after your family discount, kid," he says, and winks at me.

I pass him a ten-dollar bill. "Nah. Keep the change, Mr. Chamberlain."

He grasps it tightly and smiles. "Thanks, Giovanni. You've always been a good kid. You know that, right?"

"Thanks, sir."

"Stay out of trouble and be safe out here, Gio," he says.

"I will."

It's a bit warm outside for it to be February in Indiana, but there's still a nice steady breeze that blows that reminds me of the crispness of winter. I don't even need a jacket or a coat, because I'm still in my blazer.

Some silence tides in and birds chirp above our heads, the sun beaming down on us between some clouds. I avoid all the cracks and rocks and needles and cigarette butts on the sidewalk, looking down, my thoughts flying in a bunch of different directions again.

"For real, though, talk to David," Ayesha says, and stops walking completely. She narrows her eyes at me. "I'm pretty sure he won't care what hard stuff you're going through. I'm sure he would want to be *in* it with you."

"He knows what I'm going through. He *is* in it. I just don't know in what way."

"Well, the only way to find that out is to bring it up. You're not going to figure it out on your own."

"I will talk to him," I say after a little bit for thinking. "At some point."

"Some. Point. Soon." She claps her words out.

Eventually, we get to our block, where our houses sit only a few homes apart. Ayesha's house is before mine, so she gets home first. Before she walks in, she glances back at me quickly, then says, "Let me know what he says when you talk to him."

I just wave her off. That's something for later. As I walk to my house, I pull out my phone and clear my notifications of new followers from Twitter and Instagram and Bible verses from Pops, and then stare at the red button of missed calls and voicemails.

I click on the voicemail to listen to it. I tell myself not to hang it up after the first couple seconds like last time. Her voice plays, but some of the words I can't make out. There's a lot of static or rushing wind or bad signal wherever she calls from.

G-Bug . . . I don't even know what to really say after what we talked about. I feel really bad for bringing that up to you that soon. I should've waited longer. I just didn't think there was a right time . . . I'm not sure what I can say besides I'm—we're—sorry, and that we were just excited to let you know about a big step we want to take. You and Theo are my children and even if I have other ones with Monica, that won't change. I hate the way things were left off at the pancake house. I don't want things to be tense between us anymore, G-Bug. I love you. Give me a call back when you can.

I can hear her click off. I wipe my eyes—and I didn't realize I was tearing up.

My brain does that thing where I replay her words back. I don't even need to replay the voicemail because it's all stained into my thoughts. I think about her having kids with Monica. I wonder if their future kids will be able to grow up with both of their parents, unlike me. I wonder if they won't have to deal with being abandoned by their mom. And I think about how fucking unfair that is to me and how she's planning all of this and not even considering how I feel. But then I think about how she never really considered how I feel, because she wouldn't have left in the first place if she did. Grown-ups really need to get their shit together and stop lying to young people. Time doesn't heal wounds like they try to get us to believe. It only makes things fucking worse.

TWENTY-ONE

A FEW SCHOOL DAYS roll past and I don't give any attention to my mom's voicemail. After school on Thursday, David gives me a ride home. We've hung out every day this week so far after practice—we've watched NBA games, started watching *Stranger Things* on Netflix together, studied together, tossed M&M's in each other's mouths, and played one-on-one in my driveway—and I still haven't told him about how much I appreciate getting to know him better and having him as an anchor that keeps me grounded.

Soon enough, we end up in his room with the TV off, but we're listening to a playlist that he came up with. Right now, "New Rules" by Dua Lipa is playing.

"Such a good playlist," I say to him.

"Thanks," he says, his teeth showing. "It's a playlist that I made when I first met you."

"Really?"

"I swear," he says. "A lot of upbeat ones in it."

"Dang, that's dope," I tell him. "I didn't make one when I met you, though."

He laughs. "That's okay. I'll just make one for myself and imagine that it was made by you."

Now I'm laughing at him. "Whatever," I say, play-punching him in the arm. We're both lying in his bed, but in opposite directions. His head is by my feet and my head is by his feet. He's holding a tiny canvas and a tiny paintbrush and he's painting something—I'm not sure what.

I stare at his ceiling for a moment and then lift up a little to watch him do his thing with the canvas and brush. This is how he lives his life. One painting after another. To capture the moments. To feel the past. To savor memories.

When he finishes the portrait, he shows it to me and instantly I lose my breath. I blink at myself—how perfectly he painted my skin, how he captured even the small wrinkles around my mouth and the fullness of my lips. "That's me."

"It's you."

"It's . . . perfect," I say. "It looks so real, like someone took a picture of me on an iPhone."

"Thanks," he says.

"What are those white dots in my pupils, though?"

"They're stars," he says. "When I look in your eyes, I see constellations."

My heart beats faster in my chest. "Whoa. It's seriously amazing, David."

He smiles at me really wide. I don't think I've ever met anyone who smiles as much as he does. He'll die an old man with wrinkles, not from age, but from how often he smiled in life.

I open my arms to hug him. He sits up awkwardly and we hug awkwardly, but it's a nice awkward hug where he stays in my arms and doesn't move, and I hold him tight like he's a source of life and I want to live forever.

"David, remember that time you said I was brave?" I ask him, interrupting our moment.

He nods.

"*You* make me brave."

He leans over and I lean over and our lips latch together like missing puzzle pieces and I forget the world for a moment.

Someone knocks on his door.

"Come in," David says. A head pops in and I see long red hair that drapes low and then I see a face. It's his mom. She looks so much like David.

"Sorry if I'm interrupting, boys, but I made some puppy chow." She offers us a giant bowl.

"We're good, Mom, thanks."

"Speak for yourself, David," I tell him jokingly. I reach into the bowl and grab a handful. "Thanks!"

"No problem. I'll leave it on the desk here for you boys. I'll be back later tonight, David. I've got some errands to run, so you can fix whatever you'd like for dinner."

"You can come over to my house for dinner," I offer. I'm sure Karina would like that. I don't know about Pops, though. But it's too late to take back the offer.

"Really? I'll do that, then," David says.

"Sounds great," David's mom says. "Let me know if you need anything, munchkin." When she leaves his room and closes the door, I look at him and give him a hard time about the nickname she has for him.

"Munchkin, huh?"

"Shut up!" He punches me.

"I don't have room to talk. Karina calls me honeybunches," I tell him.

"Like the cereal?"

"I know, right? I'm used to it now."

There's a dinging sound. It's my phone. A text from Malik. I never get texts from him these days, so I open this one kinda quick.

Malik

Details for Ayesha's Birthday Bash—Big Blue's house on the corner of Ninth and Madison. 7 p.m. tomorrow. Bring a friend. RSVP by texting me back.

Me

I'm there. So is David.

"Malik just texted me. Confirming the details for Ayesha's birthday party."

"Oh, that's cool," David says. "I like birthday parties."

"I don't, but I love Ayesha, so I'm going," I say. "I told him you're in, too."

"For sure," David says. "Just let me know when. And I'm there. I hope there's dancing."

Another buzz comes from my phone. I think it's a text back

from Malik about David and me RSVP'ing. But it's not. It's an email notification.

I'm nervous.

I don't want to click on it.

But I do it anyway, with shaky hands.

It's an email from my mom.

I read it out loud to David.

To: GioTheGr8@gmail.com
From: missjackie01@global.net
Subject: Sorry to bother you . . .

G-Bug,

It's me again. Sorry to email you. I know you might want space right now. I don't know if you've had the chance to listen to my voicemail from last week. But I just was writing to you to tell you how truly sorry I really am for just throwing all that on you. It wasn't the right time. But I wanted to let you know that Monica and I will be in town for a few more days before we fly back home to Amsterdam. I'd like it if the last time that we were face-to-face wasn't a fight, if that's okay with you? Just message me back or call me. I'd love to talk and see you again before we go.

Thanks, G-Bug. Love you.
Mom

"You want to respond to her?" David asks me.

"I don't think so," I say to him. "She wants to leave. She can. My life was okay before she came back and I'll figure out how to be okay without her, like I did before." I don't know where this comes from, but it spills out like it's been overflowing within me.

"Proud of you," David tells me, and I feel warm and tingly inside.

He puts a hand on my shoulder and leaves it there, like he's reminding me that he's here and he's on my side to support me in whatever. If there's indeed a bright side in any of the shit I've been going through lately, it's how close I've gotten with David. And if there's anything that I learned from my mom, it's to pursue what makes me happy.

"You know what, man?"

"What?"

"Fuck Captain America. Fuck Iron Man and his rich people problems. I'm Team David. You're the hero of my life. I'm so thankful for you."

"I'm thankful for *you*, Gio. This world can be so dark and cold and cruel and lonely. I'm so glad that we can face it all together. No matter what comes our way next, I'll be at your side."

The words roll off his tongue so smoothly I want to melt. He kisses me and we shut up. It's so unimaginable each time, but my eyes shut, and I enjoy every second of it.

I sit back against the headboard of his king-sized bed in this king-sized room, and I open up my chemistry textbook. Chemistry, probably the worst school subject to ever be invented. Luckily, Mr. Silva is cool, and I like him, and that makes his class so much more manageable.

David leans against the wall about halfway down his bed and he bites down on a pencil as he reads his chemistry textbook out loud to me. We're supposed to be reading up on Dalton's law for some presentation we have to do, but I really wish I could pay someone else to do it.

The more I glance at David, the more I see how he's cratered by perfections. He reaches over and places a hand on my upper thigh. And now there's something happening in my pants that I have to use my textbook to cover up.

"What's the ionic compound formula for magnesium phosphate? And holy shit. That was probably the nerdiest thing I've ever fucking said in my life."

David makes his thinking face. "Isn't it $Mg_3(PO_4)_2$?"

"Yeah, I think that's right," I say, scribbling that onto a sticky note and putting that inside my textbook. "We'll need to know that for our presentation."

A beat.

David clears his throat and rolls over on his side. "Question now for you."

I turn a little bit in his bed to face him better. "Yes?"

"Have you ever . . . uh . . . ?" He stops and does this thing with his eyebrows, like he's trying to wag them. "Have you ever done *it*?"

I blink. "No. Never. Have you?" I ask, some amount of embarrassment present. There's so much pressure to have had sex by now, but I've never done it. At least, not all the way.

"My ex-boyfriend and I did it once, but that was like two years ago. He was bad at it. And hell, maybe I was bad at it, too. We never talked about it."

"So, you're experienced, huh?" My heartbeat thickens. Chest heaves.

"Somewhat experienced," he says with a grin.

He lifts up from the bed a little bit and puts his chemistry textbook on his desk. I toss mine to the side, too.

He looks down at my crotch area and says, "Someone's excited."

The room just got a hundred degrees hotter, and suddenly, I'm getting this feeling that maybe we're about to learn some chemistry of each other, not Dalton's law.

I kiss him softly on the lips. It's the kind of kiss that inspires the sun to stay pinned in the sky and never set. The kind that inspires the stars to shoot across the whole sky.

He stops and grins, his eyes so serious. I know what he means. No words are necessary. But he says it anyway: "I really want you."

I nod at him. And he pivots on the bed. I slide down the headboard and he gets on top of me and kisses me softly at first until we're both smiling at each other. His mouth traces down my neck, my chest, my stomach, my legs as he kisses lightly, sending chills shooting up my spine.

I let out some moans from how good it feels. He looks up at me. "Feel nice?"

"Mhm." I nod at him and shut my eyes.

He starts wrestling with my pants until he gets them

unbuttoned and off of me, leg by leg, laughing at how my socks slip off, too. His hands slide beneath my boxers and those come off, too. I begin trying to take off layers from him as well—shirt, pants, boxers, everything. Until we're bare bodies colliding, skin touching, kissing and kissing time away.

We roll over and I'm on top of him, hands tugging at his red curls, his hands almost clawing at my chest as we grin at each other. So much grinning is happening. Is this normal during sex?

I feel David's chest and notice a tattoo near his lower stomach. It says: *tomorrow and tomorrow and tomorrow*. It's Shakespeare, I know that. I kiss my way across the words. And suddenly our mouths are in play, all over.

The only way to keep track is to notice that songs are passing by. Otherwise, it's like we're in control of time, marking it with movements instead of minutes.

"Do you want to go further?" David asks.

"I want to," I tell him.

David slides me off of him and onto my side. He reaches beneath his bed and comes back with a tiny square package. He bites it open and I realize that it's a condom.

"Do you want me to wear it or do you want to wear it?" he asks. And I'm caught off guard, my chest heaving and heaving. I guess that's the thing about two boys having sex. You have to decide which one of you will wear the condom. Who's on the top and who's on the bottom. From the porn I've watched for practice in the past, I always imagined I would do both, but I don't know which one I want to be right now more with David.

I think for a moment. Then I say, "I'll wear it, if you want."

He smiles and puts it on for me, which excites me almost a little too much. David flips over onto his stomach and I try to find the right place to put myself as we press together and ignite into something that feels so beautiful and so perfect, like there's a surprise party happening in every cell in my body. I feel like in a way I'm breaking free, like I'm witnessing all the layers to my own purity being ripped away in all the best ways.

When we finish, we both lie side by side staring at the ceiling, so out of breath, still holding each other's hands.

"That was so good," he says. "Like . . . so good."

"Yeah, it was," I say, swallowing some oxygen.

A beat. Deep breaths.

"Did it hurt?" I ask. I want to know for next time. Maybe we switch. Oh God. I hope there's a next time.

"A little bit at first, but after a while it starts to feel good. Like really, really good." By the way he smiles so big, I believe him.

Some silence comes as we catch our breath and slip back into our boxers and pants.

We spend the next hour or so actually forcing ourselves to do work so that we're able to finish our chemistry presentation fully, and it helps that we take tiny breaks to kiss or just chat when we need to. Like extra motivation to keep going and going and going. It's the kind of fuel I could live on.

TWENTY-TWO

FRIDAY NIGHT IS AYESHA'S birthday party and Big Blue's house smells like weed and alcohol and is filled with almost every single "popular" guy from Ben Davis, grinding up on some girl—so close they need to be taking it to the bedroom or something. Condoms, birth control, and all.

I'm scanning this place as I take small steps forward, every cell in my body resisting. David follows me in, too.

Shit. This house is packed wall to wall. I don't even wanna know what it's like upstairs.

David's holding my hand the whole time we're pushing through sweaty bodies to get to wherever Malik, Olly, and Ayesha are—and I don't care who sees really. I want to be free. I want to feel free. I deserve to be free every day, always. And I'm tired of feeling like a prisoner in my own body every damn day. I guess sometimes we meet people who remind us of all the reasons why we exist. For me, that's been David. He's been a light in the darkness.

Part of me also regrets wearing my brand-new Jordans. They'll for sure be scuffed before the night is over with, which means I'm going to have to take an hour in my week just to clean them.

I finally can see Ayesha and Olly. Ayesha's dancing and I'm watching her curls bounce over her shoulders, the bass from "Congratulations" by Post Malone rattling the floor. Malik's even got a DJ who's behind a table, yelling in a microphone for everybody to put their hands up in the air and say, "Hey," followed by "Hoe!" I'm caught off guard when everybody up in this house erupts in their own versions of it. Honestly, between the nausea from the smell of recently lit weed, the sweat wiping on my skin from other bodies, and the loud-ass music, the only thing I might be drinking tonight is water to prevent me puking every-damn-where.

We finally get to a break in the crowd when we see Malik talking to a group of girls.

"Ayesha!" I yell out over the loud-ass music. "Ayesha!" I repeat, and she finally turns around.

"Oh, hey, Gio! Hey, David!" Ayesha shouts, hugging me. Malik comes over and joins us.

"Sup," I say. "Happy birthday."

Olly and I shake up.

"Malik, this party is so damn lit," Ayesha says. "It's way more lit than Big Blue's spring break bash last year—and people were talking about that for months."

"You know how I roll, baby girl." Malik chuckles. "I got drinks over here for y'all." Malik walks us over to a table where a crowd lingers. The table is covered in red Solo cups and glasses of some golden liquid. I don't trust any of them.

He hands one to each of us.

"What is it?" Ayesha asks.

"It's punch. Just try it," Malik goes. "All of y'all. Act like y'all came to party. Grab a drink and get loose."

I hesitate, and David and I stare at each other for a minute. Meanwhile, Olly's throwing his cup back, no fucks given.

Then, before I can even break eye contact, David starts drinking it, downing it like he's been drinking his whole life. It worries me how fast he drinks it, but it doesn't even faze him any. It's almost inspiring.

I take a small sip. It burns going down. "What the hell is this?" It tastes like straight-up hard liquor. "Where's the punch?"

"The punch is the burn," Malik says. "It's mostly vodka and a little peach juice."

I sit down my cup and grab a cup of water.

"Enjoy the party, fellas. I'm gonna take the birthday girl upstairs for a while," Malik says to us, and I can smell the alcohol on his breath. Ayesha and Malik gallop away from us and we watch them stumble up the stairs.

"Wanna dance?" David asks me. One of our earliest conversations was about how much he loves to dance—and how I can't do it to save my life.

I look at Olly and point at him. "What about Olly? He won't have anyone."

"No, go ahead, man," Olly says. "Don't worry about me."

"You sure?" I ask him, hoping he'll save me.

He nods. "I'm sure."

He reaches for my hand with a smile and pulls me into the mob of people as the song changes to "Act Up" by City Girls.

The regular lights go out and a colorful strobe light appears from the ceiling.

I put my hands around David's waist, watching and feeling his hips move side to side. Some people crane their necks around and stare or make disgusted faces, but I don't care. Fuck them. Some people look once, but then look away. I need to stop looking around and look at David.

My hands around him feel warm and safe. For a guy, he's still got curves, and I've never appreciated them as much as I do right now. I'm damn near getting a boner, and I have to take a step back in my thoughts, putting my hands up higher.

"All my fellas, if you'd so kindly move out to the perimeter of the room so the ladies can have this next one to themselves," the DJ says. "This is Ayesha's request. Let's get in formation, ladies."

Suddenly, "Single Ladies" by Beyoncé blasts through the speakers. I should've guessed Ayesha would request a song like this when she's not even single. She comes back down just to dance to this song.

I put my hands in my pockets, racking my brain for something to say to David. "Enjoying yourself?"

He scratches his head. "Uh . . . umm . . . ye—you know, I'm not even going to lie. When I think of dancing, this isn't entirely what I have in mind. There's a lot of grinding happening."

"There's a lot of grinding at Black parties," I say. I haven't gone to too many lately—or any, really, but when we were freshmen, we'd go all the time.

"Hmm. I didn't know. I'm having fun, though," he adds.

"Good," I say, and grab a drink from the table. I try to sip on it slowly, but it's just too strong for even sips.

"Nice moves out there, you two," Olly says.

"Thanks," David says for both of us.

"Are *you* enjoying yourself, Olly?" I ask him. "You've been standing in the same spot since you got here."

"I'm A-OK," Olly answers, signaling with his hands, too. "I wish Grace could come."

The way he says it is kind of sad, so I don't think right now is a good time to give him a hard time about how I don't believe she's even real. But I just give him a little nod.

"Wobble" comes on. It's a song that probably plays at every Black gathering—birthday parties, celebrations of life, weddings, and family reunions. I grab for David's arm and then Olly's to drag them to the dance area. I teach David the motions of how to do the dance—Olly's already a pro from all the events he's gone to with me and Ayesha over the years—and after the first minute or two, he finally can do it even if he's slightly off beat.

At some point, David grabs my arm and sneaks me upstairs. We pass occupied rooms where people are making out or more until we find one that's empty. David shuts the door behind us. I don't know whose room this is, but they must really love WWE with all the posters of wrestlers—some I recognize, others I don't.

I sit on the edge of the bed and David comes over and straddles me, kissing me quick on the lips. I'm kissing him back twice as hard, running my hand through his red hair that I like a lot. He unbuttons and unzips my pants, pulling me out. He lifts up my shirt to kiss his way down. Right when he gets to my belly button, the door flies open.

"Holy shit! Holy shit! Holy shit!" Olly says and immediately covers his eyes.

David jumps back and I rush to zip my pants back up.

"Olly, what are you doing here?" I ask. Both David and Olly are bright red.

"I was just coming—oh shit, bad word to use. I mean, umm, I wanted you to know they're about to sing to Ayesha for her birthday."

"You could've knocked," I say back.

"Umm, noted. Holy shit! I just saw my best friend's dick. That image will forever haunt me."

"Shut up," I tell him, pushing past him.

The three of us file down the stairs awkwardly where everyone's already started singing "Happy Birthday" to Ayesha. She closes her eyes to make a wish before blowing out her candles in one try. I wonder what she wishes for.

A couple days after Ayesha's party, I take Theo out for a bro date. We go see a movie, eat chicken strips and Blizzards at Dairy Queen, and then stroll through the aisles of a GameStop. The game selections are few, and I'm almost certain they'll be going out of business soon enough. But it's Theo's favorite store, so I hope they live on for his sake.

Theo and I both needed this bro date more than we originally thought. Things have been so weird lately, I haven't seen him laugh as much as he has today in a while. It's nice, and I can't wait to have more moments like this.

On the walk back to the house from the bus stop, Theo says, "Are you gonna see Mom again?"

"I . . . I don't know, bro," I say, kind of stuttering as the words roll out. "Why?"

"Because I still don't want to," he says with such sad eyes and trembling lips. "I keep having nightmares about her."

I know those nightmares. And I don't wish them on anyone, especially not Theo.

"You won't have to if you don't want, Theo," I tell him.

He offers a smile that's different than the smile he's had all day. This one's accompanied by some sort of relief. "Thanks, Gio. I like Karina better."

I take a deep breath and glance at him. "Me too, li'l bro. Me too."

If I've learned anything from our mom, it's that going forward, I've got to be more careful about who I open up with, who I spill my heart to, and who I give second chances to. But I don't know how to explain this to Theo, though.

As we walk into the house, Theo runs ahead to play the new game I bought him from GameStop, but I pause as my phone vibrates in my jacket pocket. It's a text from Ayesha that Ms. Diane's died. My heart pounds, my stomach drops, and my throat tightens.

Fuck, man.

My eyes fill with tears.

My stomach twists tighter and tighter.

I punch the side of the house, screaming, "Fuck! Fuck!"

I knew this day would come around, but I didn't know it would come this soon. I just saw her the other day and passed what used to be her store. Somebody was fixing it up. Maybe the people who are moving into it next. I don't know.

I try to call Malik. I know for a fact that he can't be taking it well, but he doesn't answer. I consider leaving a voicemail, but I don't. I'm sure he's getting a shit ton right now.

I don't move from the doorstep. I can't move.

I open up Twitter, then Instagram, and sure enough, I see posts from a bunch of people about Ms. Diane. Several posts range from *RIP* to *gone too soon* and *fly high, angel*. Each post I come across makes me instantly lose all the air in my lungs. I try and call Ayesha to see if she's with Malik, but she doesn't answer, either.

Me

Hey, give me a call back when you can. I can't believe this.

A few minutes later, she replies with just a single word.

Ayesha

Okay.

I finally am able to walk inside. I talk to Pops and Karina about the news. They're sad, too, but they aren't as big of a mess as I am. They take turns saying comforting things and hugging me. It's still weird getting that from Pops, but it's nice, especially right now.

Eventually, I get a FaceTime from Ayesha and she puts Malik on the phone for me. He doesn't say much, even when I ask him questions, but I think I get it. I can't imagine how lost for words he must be. I used to imagine my birth mom was dead because that was a lot easier than thinking about her being gone in a different way—thinking about her abandoning me and Theo—but I don't think I'll ever fully know what Malik and July and Tatiana are experiencing right now.

"When's the funeral going to be, 'Lik?" I ask him.

Finally, he's able to say something. "Ain't one," he says. "We ain't got money for a whole funeral."

"Really?"

He nods.

"We're just gonna plan a small community vigil by her store on Saturday," Ayesha explains. I can see that she's rubbing Malik's back and that they're both at Ms. Diane's.

"What about her body, though?"

"They gon' cremate her," Malik answers. His voice cracks and his eyes are bloodshot.

"Damn, that's crazy, 'Lik," I say. "I'm just so sorry, man." Ms. Diane is gone and now Malik, July, and Tatiana are on their own.

Damn, man, this is really messing me up.

I'm nervous all morning the following Saturday that my mom will end up at the vigil out in front of what used to be Ms. Diane's store. She's not there when I arrive.

The sun's setting against all the buildings and houses in our hood, and day fades into night. People bring lit candles and bunches of flowers and are wearing T-shirts with Ms. Diane's face on them. Ayesha's up front with Malik. She doesn't let go of him. But she lets him cry and even walks with him to put a flower in a giant vase that's sitting in front of the store.

Theo holds my left hand and David stands to my right. Karina and Pops stand behind us, beside Olly. Everyone's quiet and everything feels sad. Within minutes, it feels like everybody and their momma from the Haven arrives at the vigil.

July stands up on a metal trash can with a megaphone and clears his throat. "Thanks for coming out tonight," he says. "Our family appreciates y'all. Tatiana, Malik, and I have felt all the love from you guys."

I look around and see Tatiana sitting on a bench with a stroller in front of her. I see other people who I've never even seen before have tears in their eyes. People move up front and squeeze between bodies just to put cards and letters and money on the ground next to the flowers and vase.

"Our momma's gone but her spirit is alive and with us right now," July shouts.

People clap and cheer for that. Some people even say things, like "That's right, that's right." Chills shoot through my body. I haven't seen our hood come together like this for anything, except for that one time when we protested police brutality around Indianapolis.

July keeps going and the metal trash can shakes underneath his weight, but he's unfazed by it. "Our momma really loved the Haven. Even in these last weeks, even after we closed the store, she still saw all the joy and beauty around here. She loved her kids and she loved everybody else's kids like her own. Ayesha," he says, pointing at her. His eyes meet mine and I know he's gonna say my name. "Giovanni. Theo. Nylah. Bunny. Devante. Quinta. Tony. She loved all y'all like y'all were her own."

I nod. He's right. I didn't always check up on Ms. Diane when I grew up. But she definitely had a hand in raising me. I remember her having me over for dinner when I was little even after my mom—her best friend—left. I remember her telling me I would have a second home for as long as she lived. I remember her giving me my first spanking for breaking something in her house. I remember she was always there for me. I remember even when I didn't visit, she would show so much love to me whenever I would come around. Damn, I'm gonna miss her so much. I'm so thankful for women like her and Karina in my life. I just wish I could have a do-over. That I could tell Ms. Diane thank you. That I could go back in time and not be an asshole to Karina growing up. Karina's here now, but one day, maybe she won't be?

Tears cascade down my face. Luckily, David's here. He puts his arm around my shoulders like a real one. Karina occasionally grabs my bicep and tells me that it's okay.

"Love you, Momma! Live on!" July says, and points up at the sky.

More applause and cheers. Somebody even starts a chant of what July just said. "Live on! Live on! Live on! Live on!" And then people change to chanting her name.

At some point, Pops shares something from the Bible and I push through the crowd to Malik. We might not be all that close anymore, but he's still a friend of mine, and at one point in our lives, his mom would have us take baths together. I can tell he's not gonna stop crying for a long time. But I hug him. And he hugs me back. I hug him, reassuring him that I'm here for him over and over. And that he's okay. That I'm okay. And that Ms. Diane is okay, too, in whatever layer of sky she's in. That we all will be okay.

TWENTY-THREE

IT'S THE LAST DAY of school before spring break, but all that runs through my mind are thoughts about tonight's game against North Central. It's the last game of the season, too. Thankfully, I pass all my midterms, even Mrs. Oberst's midterm essay about *To Kill a Mockingbird*. I was worried about that one, not gonna lie. Mostly because I didn't study, but also because I wrote about life in West Haven and how being a Black kid in the hood means being afraid; it means swallowing down that fear so that you stay alive. But I got a 95 on it. I guess God really does work things out for my good.

It's been a few weeks since I've talked to my birth mom and I've been mostly okay, but at one point between chemistry class and AP Government, I almost have to step outside because I can't stop thinking and imagining what my mom's new family would be like.

How happy she'll be without me.

How happy I've got to try to be without her.

At lunch, I let my chicken sandwich get cold by not eating it. I take the straw I use for my strawberry milk and poke at the bun.

Ayesha waves a hand in my face. "Hello. You're Gio-ing again," she says.

"I'm Gio-ing?" I ask. Since when did I become a verb like that? But I think I get what she's saying.

"You look like you're in deep thought," she says.

"Yeah, you do, Gio," Olly adds, taking a giant bite of his ham and cheese.

"Whatchu thinkin' about?" Malik asks me.

Malik's sitting at our table now. He's stopped sitting with some of the other 7th Street Disciples who go to our school, but I know it's only because he's dating Ayesha and she's kind of making him do it. Either way, it's nice to have him at the table.

I swallow. "I'm not thinking about anything," I lie. Truth is I'm thinking about what I always do, but it's so goddamn depressing and I don't entirely want to sound pathetic in front of my best friends and my boyfriend. I can't think of another lie quick enough, so I just end with "But thanks for looking out, guys."

Olly changes the subject, thankfully. Now he's attempting to entertain the table with some new hot take, like usual. This time he's talking about Disney movies. When we were kids, Ayesha, Malik, and I all picked our favorite Disney movie of all time and we would take turns watching them every weekend. Ayesha picked *Monsters, Inc.* Malik picked *The Incredibles.* And of course, I picked *Toy Story.*

"*Coco* is definitely the greatest Disney movie ever created," Olly says.

"What? Whack!" Malik says, shaking his head. "*Coco* was the shit, but are you gonna forget about *The Lion King* like that? Simba, Timon, and Pumbaa was tight."

I want to be mad at Olly, but the thing is, I actually agree. I like both *Coco* and *The Lion King*, but I'd probably take *Coco* over *The Lion King*. "*Finding Nemo* was the shit, too," I say opening-up.

"Yeah, but my girl Mulan is *that* bitch," Ayesha says, and chuckles. "Don't sleep on her. Animated or live action. Both are straight fire."

David clears his throat and we're all looking at him for his opinion. But he swallows and then says, "I actually have only ever seen one Disney movie in my whole life, and that was only because I took my little cousin to see *Frozen 2* when it first came out."

We all look offended. And he gets so flushed. "We gotta watch some," I say.

"I'd love that," he says. "Once we finish *Stranger Things*." We're on the latest season and are almost done, but I want to finish even more now so we can start some Disney movies.

"The *Cars* movies were so much better than the *Toy Story* ones," Olly says between mouthfuls of Doritos. "There was waaaay more action in them. And Mater is comedic gold."

"Yeah. Hard disagree on that one, Olly," I push back.

"Sir, this is a Wendy's drive-through," Ayesha says, and rolls her neck. I laugh so hard because I love that meme. And it's so nice to laugh right now.

David looks at Ayesha like he's confused and so does Olly. Instantly, I know they don't get it.

"Wendy's?" David says, a puzzled look on his face, brows raised.

"Yeah, it's a joke," Ayesha explains herself. "Somebody says something weird or wrong and then you make fun of them by saying, 'Sir, this is a Wendy's drive-through.' Twitter thinks it's hilarious."

"That joke is almost as bad as Wendy's french fries," Olly says seriously, turning around his snapback to the forward position. He's been wearing it backward a lot lately.

"They have the best, actually," Ayesha says. I don't know if I agree with her now.

I make a face. "Nah, Five Guys for sure has the best. David?"

"Chick-fil-A . . . just kidding, I don't support restaurants that hate me," David says. "I'll say In-N-Out."

The three of us look at Malik. "What do you think, boo?" Ayesha asks him.

He makes this face like he's pondering it. "Hmm. I don't agree with nunna y'all. McDonald's, bruh. If you get them boys fresh, they hit different."

Olly kind of pouts that none of us agree with his trash take. "Fine. Look, the next time we all hang out, we'll drive around and get a bunch of fries from all those places and do one of those blind taste tests. You'll see then."

"Ha. Whatever, bro," Malik says.

"So, Gio," Olly says, "is David . . . you know . . . the one?"

My eyes get big and I've got cotton mouth. David and I exchange glances like he's waiting for me to say something, but I don't know what to say back to that. I mean, there's no such thing as "the one," right? Soulmates aren't real. That was proven by my parents. They thought they were soulmates, but they didn't work out. I need to start a petition to change the word soulmates to soulmaybes. You've got a much better chance at finding Bigfoot, the Loch Ness monster, or some other mythological creature. You're much more likely to find someone that you like enough to love. I like David enough to love. He makes me brave. All this time, I thought Jesus was the only good person, the only person who actually practiced what he preached, but David? David is a sermon that doesn't need words. One that sings a joyful noise to my bones better than any choir. He's helped me kick down all the fences grief had put up that worked to keep the fear in and the happiness out. Fuck butterflies. Every time I'm around David, my chest heaves so deep and lets out a warmth with his name on it.

I settle for just saying, "Yeah, I think so."

David grabs for my hand underneath the table and a smile eases on my face.

"So y'all official, official or what?" Ayesha asks, pressing.

David answers for us both, not taking his eyes off of me. "Yeah. Yeah, we are."

"Yaaaaaassss!" Ayesha celebrates, Milly Rocking in her seat.

"You ever hurt Gio, I will pop you," Malik says, staring intensely at David.

"'Lik, chill!" Ayesha shouts, and grabs his bicep.

"Nah. Gio's my guy," Malik says back.

"I promise I won't," David responds, still smiling at me.

"Are you gonna be social media official, though?" Ayesha

asks. "I just wanna know so I can be the first to like, comment, and share!"

"I don't think we're ready to do that yet. There are too many people I want to tell before they find out over Facebook or Insta. And I don't need Coach finding out anytime soon."

David nods. "I think I want to lay low for a little while, too. We got some weird and scary looks at your party."

"Really? From whom? Who was it?" Ayesha gets really defensive, taking out her earrings like she's about to go fight a bitch on my behalf.

"Yeah, tell me who so I can put them in line," Malik says. "Was it Brandon and Regina? Darnell? Or was it Bunny and Jakori? Nobody better fuck with y'all and that's on my momma. I'm a Seventh Street Disciple for life, but I'm still gon' make sure y'all ain't fucked with."

"I don't know. Thanks for caring, guys, but it's okay," I say.

"It's not okay, Gio," Ayesha says.

"Right!" Olly adds.

"No, seriously, it's okay. Just give us some more time," I say.

"Okay," Ayesha says, rolling her eyes all the way to Heaven, putting her earrings back in.

And now Malik's all like, "But if somebody start messing with y'all, you come and find me. You hear?"

I don't have the heart to tell him that I don't want him to kill someone for me, but I really do appreciate how protective he is of me. This is the Malik who always had my back as a kid. I'm so glad that hasn't changed now.

TWENTY-FOUR

🜄🜄🜄🜄🜄🜄

LATER ON, I'M GETTING changed at my gym locker for the game against North Central. So far, it's just me and David in the locker room. To be fair, we're early. We're always early. We're still playing it safe around the team because we don't want to start a house fire and burn our entire operation down. I don't think any of the other guys on the team, besides Malik, were invited to Ayesha's party. So, I think we're good for now.

"I made you something."

"You did?" he asks. "What did you make?"

"A playlist. Wanna listen to it?"

"For sure," he says, and smiles big.

"Like, right now?"

"Why not?"

I pull out my phone and load up the Spotify app. I quickly text it to him but click the shuffle button once I select the playlist named: **For David**.

I'm excited about this playlist. I chose eleven songs that most remind me of David or of how I feel when I'm around him:

1. "Until You Are Here" by Tyrone Wells
2. "Finery" by Penny & Sparrow
3. "First Time He Kissed a Boy" by Kadie Elder
4. "Can't Feel My Face" by The Weeknd
5. "365" by Zedd and Katy Perry
6. "Send Me the Moon" by Sara Bareilles
7. "Falling" by Harry Styles
8. "Rose-Colored Boy" by Paramore
9. "Autumn Tree" by Milo Greene
10. "LOVE" by Kendrick Lamar (ft. Zacari)
11. "Happy Together" by The Turtles

We only get through about three songs before our other teammates come in to get changed and ready for the game.

When it's time, Coach huddles us up to do our usual chant call and response before the game. Then, as a team, we walk out into the tunnel slowly, walking in pairs. I stick by David, keeping him close to my side. Brushing up against him a little sends chills up my spine. The rest of the team walks onto the court and we stop in the tunnel for a brief moment.

He gives me a quick peck on the lips and my eyes flip open like blinds. This was the extra motivation I needed to go into this game as confident as possible.

The five starters on the court for us are Malik, Jason, Savtaj, David, and me. Erick, Nick, and the rest of the team waits on the bench for Coach Campbell to give them some playing time.

I scan the crowd as I wait for the tip-off. At first, I can't make out anyone in the crowd, but then I see Ayesha and Olly sitting in the first row behind the bench. Next to them, I see Karina and Pops and Theo.

The referee blows his whistle and Savtaj wins the tip-off for us, so we start with the ball first.

I'm guarded by North Central's #23—a scrawny Latino kid with spiky hair who's a little bit taller than me. He's got a lot of nerve to have MJ's number. He is trying to keep me from seeing the ball by blocking my view with his head. He's a great defender, but he's still no match for me, I tell myself, powering myself up like I'm leveling up in a video game.

I step to the side to get #23 off of me. And I'm pretty successful.

David's dribbling the ball and he's trying to get to the net to lay it up. He's dribbling through his legs and behind the back. So much fancy ball handling, like he's Pistol Pete or Kyrie or some shit. He looks smooth doing it, though.

He passes it to Jason, who's waiting at the free-throw line. I run out to the three-point line and get open.

Someone passes me the ball. I catch and fire. *SWOOSH!* It goes in. Some people cheer and some people boo. But both are my motivation right now.

The announcer announces in a booming voice, "ZANDER . . . FOR THREE!"

Malik's our vocal leader so he shouts at us to get back on defense on the other end. "No easy buckets!" he calls out. "No easy buckets!"

At halftime, Coach Campbell puts in some benchwarmers in

place of me and Savtaj. I don't really mind it, though. The score's 44–39 and we lead.

I've got twelve points so far and counting. I really am on fire and I'm playing well and words can't describe how fucking happy I am that my shots are actually going in.

I drink some water to catch my breath, my heart thudding and thudding from the energy on the court. *Thud-thud-thud. Thump-thump-thump.*

It's always nice to be sitting on the bench, watching David completely mesmerize the crowd with his ball handling and shooting ability. There's a stereotype that white boys who play ball are good shooters, but David takes it to a whole other level, I swear. The boy got mad range, too. Hell, I'm sure he could hit a triple from the parking lot.

Coach puts me back in when there's about five minutes left on the clock. Crunch time, he calls it. I'm all charged up and ready to go. I feel the adrenaline pumping through my veins. There's nothing I want more right now than finishing what we started and getting this dub.

North Central has upped their defense game and block a bunch of the shots we try to take, but luckily, we're good at getting those rebounds. Savtaj has double digit rebounds and that helps us get a shit ton of second-chance points.

David sets a screen for me the next time I get the ball and I make a three. I'm out of breath already, but I'm still running on adrenaline, like I'm high or something.

On the next possession, #11, some real buff white kid with short military-like hair on their team banks a three and roars in my face like a lion. He's taunting and trash-talking me and I'm not even guarding him. David is.

"Let me switch out!" I tell David.

We make a smooth switch so I can guard #11 and prove that I'm not the one for him to act like that with.

I get low in my defensive stance the next time #11 has the ball. He pretends like he's looking for an open lane before driving straight to the rim. I meet him underneath the basket and block his shot from going in. It's all so very epic. The crowd gets so damn loud because of me, cheering and chanting my name. It makes me feel warm inside.

There's barely a minute left of this game and the score's 68–52 and so far, they've missed their last five free throws, which is incredible, really. I've never seen anything like it in a high school game. It's almost worse than that time the Houston Rockets missed twenty-seven straight threes against Golden State.

North Central's offense has completely collapsed, and they can't really guard us that well on defense. David holds on to the ball for the final possession to run out the shot clock, just dribbling back and forth, not letting any of the other team's guys to try and steal it.

The crowd counts down as fast as they can. People are already cheering.

The buzzer goes off, signaling our dub.

We celebrate together in our team huddle, taking turns high fiving each other and slapping each other on the butt.

"Hell yeah! That's what I'm talking about," Malik cheers and chugs a bottle of water.

Savtaj pours his cup of Gatorade on top of David's head and he reacts like he just got electrocuted, which makes everybody laugh.

David and I hug tight and he gets Gatorade on me.

"You killed it out there," I tell him. "Ten steals in a game. That's a new team record."

"Thanks, Gio," David says. "You killed it, too. Twenty-two points. Legendary."

People—our teammates, fans, students, parents—all huddle around us. But David and I try to break through the crowd to get away from all the attention. When we're outside the gym and in the hallway, he grabs for my hand and pulls me into a nook that's usually reserved for when people try to have sex at school.

"Can I . . . ?" He stops in place and flexes his jaw. He's trying not to smile, but it's not working because his dimple waves hello. "Can I kiss you?"

I pull him out of the nook and into the open. I want to prove something to him. My hands gently touch the back of his neck and he presses his mouth against mine at once, softly and then firm. He moves his arm around my waist and pulls me closer and we're full-on making out in the hallway for about thirty seconds. I want to savor this moment, this slice of time. Its stillness and passion and chests heaving.

Outside, the streetlights and parking lot lights shine bright on the gravel parking lot. I feel like I'm on the surface of the moon. Tonight's been a lot of fun so far, and getting to do it all with David, of course, makes everything so much better. I walk out, holding David's hand. Our grip is sweaty and warm, but I like the way his hand feels laced with mine. I don't care who sees us. I'm done caring. I like David. And I like what we have, and I want to keep that for as long as I can.

"G-Bug?" I hear a voice say behind me. I freeze in place and spin my head around.

I thought she'd already left town. I mean, I didn't see her at Ms. Diane's vigil and I didn't hear anything else from her since her last email. But she's standing in front of me. Again. I would ask where has she been—or at least, what has she been doing that she couldn't come to Ms. Diane's vigil. But part of me doesn't really care. I don't want to talk to her. There's nothing left for me to say.

She folds her hands in front of her. "I'm gonna get out of your hair, but I just wanted to see you one last time before we went back to Amsterdam."

"You could've just left," I snap. David doesn't let go of my hand, but I squeeze his. I feel the brush of his fingers, comforting me.

"I couldn't do that without . . . I couldn't live with myself if I got back to Amsterdam and felt like you hated me."

I'm silent. I don't think I hate her, but I definitely don't think I love her, either.

"You should go before Theo sees you," I tell her. "It won't be good for him."

"But I—"

"Please," I tell her. "Go!" I say this even though my voice shakes.

"But, G-Bug," she pleads. I notice that Monica's not with her. She takes a step forward and reaches out her hand, but I take a step back and David joins me. My birth mom makes a face like she's confused and hurt, and tears begin to border her eyes. I shake my head no hard. She lets out a deep sigh and walks away into the dark, and I watch her disappear like the nightmares I used to have about her.

David pulls me into his chest for a moment. But we break away from each other when Ayesha, Olly, Karina, Theo, and Pops join us outside to celebrate our win. Pops seems to be okay when I'm around David, but I think that's because he just doesn't know everything that's going on between us, or about how David's kind of my boyfriend now. I'm sure Karina's already tipped him off, but I know I'll have to talk to him anyway.

I try to force a smile on my face and not mention anything about how I just saw my mom and how I told her to leave and how that felt strangely good, like saying goodbye to her was like saying goodbye to all of my childhood wounds—there's something freeing about that. And I don't want to mention how I think that might be the last time I'll ever see her again.

"Proud of you, son," Pops says to me. And I never thought he knew how much I craved to hear those words from him, but they fill me up.

"Thanks, Pops," I say.

"You're a better baller than I thought," he says.

"What's that supposed to mean?" I joke.

"Lots of parents tell their kids that they're good at something when they really aren't. But you're actually really smooth on the court, son."

"Thanks for saying that," I say. "I'm glad you think so."

Karina and Theo take turns hugging me, too, and congratulating me on scoring twenty-two. Theo even promises that he'll make me my favorite vanilla cake and he'll light twenty-two candles on it.

And suddenly, standing in this parking lot, I realize how happy I am for this family—my family.

Ayesha.

Malik.

Olly.

David.

Theo.

Karina.

Pops.

They're my family. Your family can be the people you're born into or the people you choose or some combination of both, but we all step into love. We're all on this crash course of life figuring out the people who we're meant to let go and the ones who are worth every risk. And these seven here with me? They're worth every risk. Each of them has helped me see that just because we've been dealt a certain hand doesn't mean we can't still figure out a way to have the destiny we want. And for me? I want my destiny to be rooted in pursuing happiness above anything. Surely, life will throw its shit at me every damn day until I die, but what's important is that these are seven people I can trust to be in my corner throughout it all.

I'm so thankful that they've opened my eyes to see that just because I was abandoned by my mother doesn't mean that's the thing that defines me forever. I spent most of my life feeling stuck and wondering how I'll one day escape the feelings of grief and abandonment caused by my mom, imagining the future where everything just works itself out into some sort of happy ending where we pick up where we left off. But that's not what went down. I know how to reach her if I ever suddenly have a change of heart, but for now, I think I'm okay.

At least, I'm determined to be okay and to keep living my life, and someday, I'll have a family of my own—maybe a little boy named Josiah and a little girl named Millie—and I can love on them the ways my mom couldn't love on me or Theo. Until then, I'll be here, finding joy in all the little moments with my family and friends who won't leave me behind. If Ms. Diane could still find joy even in her final days of living, then so can I.

David said it best. This world can be dark and lonely. The future is uncertain, but looking at each person around me, I know that I've found my light. Light that'll carry me forward through whatever life brings. I know happy endings aren't real and yet here I am, standing in this parking lot and wondering if maybe I'm wrong. Maybe this is my happy beginning.

Acknowledgments

First and foremost, thank you to my Lord and Savior, Jesus Christ, for getting me through all the ups and downs, sleepless nights, moments of anxiety, and all the tears shed while writing this book. I couldn't have done it without Him.

Special thanks to . . .
My parents for bringing me into this world and showing me how to use my voice. Mom and Dad, I love you so much and am so thankful for all the ways you fight for me.

My grandmother Charlene, I still remember visiting you in that hospice room where you asked me all about this book. Thank you for believing in me until the end. Your absence never goes unnoticed. I'll never forget our memories, Granny. I miss you so, so much and can't wait to see you again. In the meantime, R.I.P. I hope Heaven's treating you well!

Lauren Abramo, my delightful and brilliant literary agent and friend. Thank you for championing this story and championing *me*. I'm so, so glad that I get to be teamed up with you. I owe you my firstborn for real.

David Levithan, my phenomenal and wise editor and friend. Thank you for taking a chance on this book and acquiring it in the middle of a global pandemic. You have made this book so much stronger in ways that I didn't even know were possible. I'm so humbled and honored that I get to work with you. Cheers for our future together.

Kacen Callender & Pam Gruber, thank you for your countless notes and all the ways you've been cheering for Gio from the sidelines. You two are my heroes.

The team at Dystel, Goderich, & Bourret. Thanks for cheering me on behind the scenes as much as you all have over the years. I feel your love for sure.

Baily Crawford, thank you for designing such a killer cover. I'm so obsessed with it. It's vulnerable, vibrant, and powerful. I'm so incredibly lucky, I swear.

My fantastic and fierce publicist Alex Kelleher-Nagorski, you are an absolute rock star! I'm so glad that I followed you over from LBYR to Scholastic. You've been such a great encouragement to me in the journey of publishing this book. Thank you for all that you do for me behind the scenes, big and small.

Everyone over at Scholastic, especially Rachel Feld, Shannon Pender, Lizette Serrano, Emily Heddleson, Melissa Schirmer, and the whole sales team.

Hayley Williams & Paramore, thank you for your music. It has saved my life in more ways than you'll ever know.

Chris, Emily, and Jonah Portillo, I'm so thankful that you allowed me to live with you all and be a part of your awesome family. You guys are my family for life. I love you three so, so much.

Iesha Alspaugh, thanks for kind of letting me steal your name for a character in this book. You've been a great friend to me over the years and I can't wait for all the years we have ahead.

Nick Smith, for being the literal best and reading the original draft of this book back when it was a flaming pile of garbage. Thanks for your kind words and constructive criticism—you helped take this book from *meh* to something I'm extremely proud of.

In no particular order: Reginald Hayes, Molly Hayes, Deyon Brumby, Alexis Brumby, Christopher Glotzbach, Brittany Glotzbach, Bekah Whelchel, Zach Whelchel, Zach Shimer, Carly New, Mitch Schuessler, Anna Park, Brandon Clemens, Jenna Clemens, Courtney Bishop, and Zane Bishop, and so many others—thanks for all the love, encouragement, and wisdom as I stressed out about this book.

My guys—Logan Arnold, Paul Butler, Peyton Trowbridge, Spencer Vredingburgh, Connor Barr, Nathan Ganger, and Brennan Schansberg. You guys know what you did. Thank you, thank you.

My Carriage House roomies, Matt Kimball and Adam Garner, thanks for letting me lock myself in the room to write. You two mean a great deal to me. Thank you, thank you, thank you.

The Revolution fam, y'all are the best. Thank you for all the constant encouragements and support. I couldn't have finished this book without your affirmation and friendship.

My author buddies who make this job a little less lonely: Nic Stone, Scott Reintgen, Dave Connis, Eric Smith, Adam Silvera, Adi Alsaid, Randy Ribay, Mark Oshiro, Emily X. R. Pan, Alex Gino, Simon Curtis, Dhonielle Clayton, Angie Thomas, L. L. McKinney, and Adrianne Russell. (Sorry if I forgot anyone on this list. It's not intentional, I swear.)

My family and loved ones who have cheered me on from the sidelines since I started out in this whole author thing. I'm so grateful for each of you, especially my two sisters, Diamond and Taya. I love you both more than words can contain. You two make me brave.

And to my readers, especially my QPOC readers. Thank you for picking up this book. I hope you enjoyed reading *Things We Couldn't Say*. I'm so thankful for you. You are seen and loved!

About the Author

Jay Coles is a graduate of Vincennes University and Ball State University. When he's not writing diverse books, he's advocating for them, teaching middle-school students, and composing for various music publishers. His debut novel *Tyler Johnson Was Here* is based on true events in his life and inspired by police brutality in America. He resides in Indianapolis, Indiana, and invites you to visit his website at jaycoleswrites.com.